Fields of *Blessing*

AMY BLASSINGAME

A NOVEL
BASED ON THE BOOK OF RUTH

Reflections and Deeper Study Included

BIGHORN PUBLISHING

Fields of Blessing
Published by Bighorn Publishing
35 La Canada Way
Hot Springs Village, AR 71909

Scriptures NKJV
All Scripture taken from the New King James Version®. Copyright ©1982 by Thomas Nelson, Inc. Used by permission.

ISBN 978-0-9722808-9-1

Published in the United States by Bighorn Publishing
Printed in the United States of America
2013—First Edition

Author Contact/Artist Contact: fieldsofblessing@gmail.com

This book is a work of fiction based on The Book of Ruth.

Dedication

To my Lord and King

May I live a life acceptable in Your sight, my Lord.

To my Loved Ones

Thank you for your prayers, help and encouragement
through the writing of *Fields of Blessing.*
Bob Blassingame
Dr. Fred & Wilma Boling
Mark Boling
Emily Grace Blassingame
Bonnie Slack
Judy Hevener

The Lord bless you and keep you;
The Lord make His face shine upon you,
And be gracious to you;
The Lord lift up His countenance upon you,
And give you peace.
Numbers 6:24-26
(New King James Version)

Novel

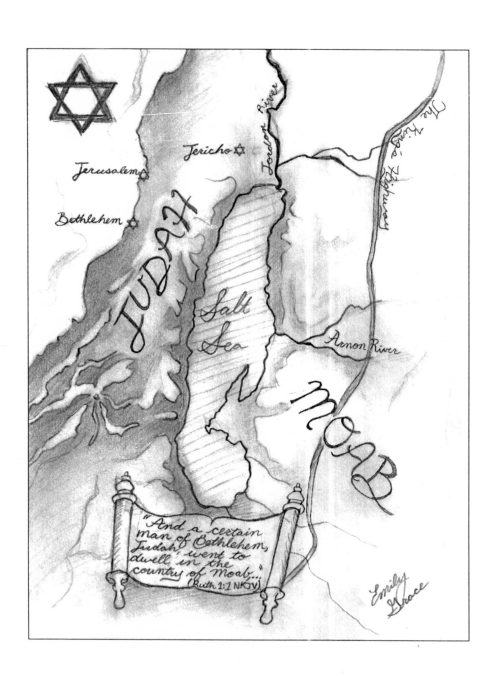

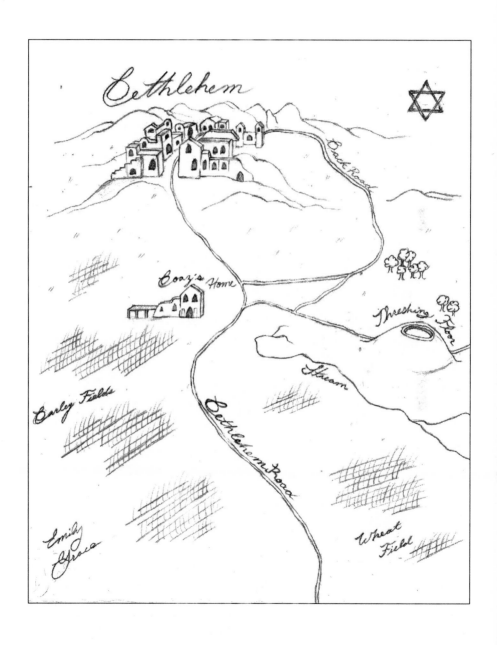

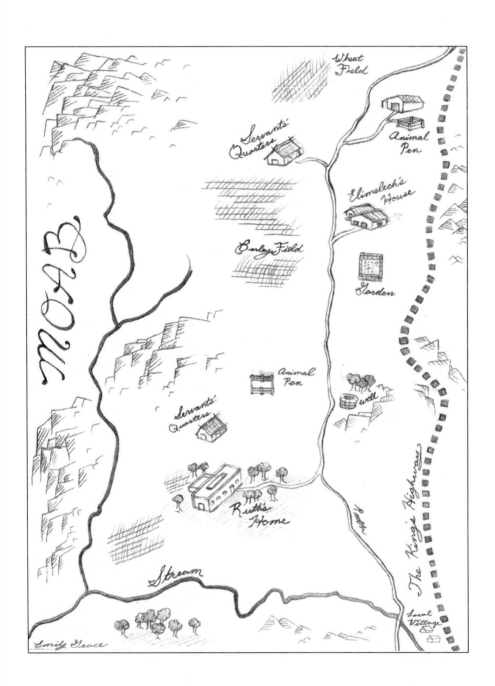

Prologue

Now it came to pass, in the days when the judges ruled, that there was a famine in the land. And a certain man of Bethlehem, Judah, went to dwell in the country of Moab . . . (Ruth 1:1, New King James Version).

Anxiously awaiting his arrival in the land of Moab was a young Moabite maiden named Ruth. His arrival would forever alter the life of the young maiden—changing the course of history for all mankind.

Chapter 1

THE ARRIVAL

Rays from first light crept through the open window as Ruth frantically kicked the linen sheets free and sat up, gasping. Filled with dread, she scanned her room as a wave of nausea washed through her. How her mother expected her to tolerate *that* priest with his foul breath and harsh demeanor was beyond her ability to understand.

"There must be a god of compassion," she said, flashing her deep hazel eyes about the room.

Relieved to find herself alone, she scornfully eyed the exquisite robes fashioned from fine, white linen, lying crumpled on the floor. She tiptoed to retrieve them, grasping the soft fabric as if it were barbed wool.

"Ruth!" her mother shouted. Her shrill voice sliced through the solitude of Ruth's bedchamber, sending a cold chill down her spine. Flinching, she grabbed the robes and scurried to stuff them into the chest sitting at the foot of her bed. Scrambling over the top, she landed askew on the cushions as her mother entered.

"Are you talking to yourself *again?*" Dahlia asked, crossing her slender arms. "Must I remind you it is unbecoming a young maiden to hold conversation with herself?"

Dahlia jerked her head toward the chest. Her long dark locks followed and then fell neatly in place. Ruth cringed, observing her mother's look of disdain as she lifted the lid and eyed the robes. "Ungrateful," Dahlia scoffed, slamming it shut.

The hollow thud reverberated and startled Ruth. "Please do not be angry, Mother," she said, looking away.

Dahlia's ornate, linen robes swished roughly along the stone floor as she paced the length of Ruth's spacious chambers. Turning, her sandal caught the leg of an ivory washstand, sending its priceless Egyptian basin crashing to the floor. Servants appeared in the doorway, but were dismissed with a flip of the hand.

"You look lovely this morning, Mother." With her fair skin and slender, curvaceous figure, Dahlia had been admired by many a Moabite, but Ruth's father had won her heart.

Stopping mid-pace, Dahlia turned to face her. Her hazel eyes flickered, her lips pursed.

"Do not attempt to distract me with compliments," Dahlia said, wagging her finger. "Why do you try my patience so? Why does your father not listen to me in these matters?" She began pacing again. "The priest is a man of great wealth, just like your father. He would have been a fine husband and your life would have continued in the fashion you are accustomed."

"Please understand, Mother. I do not love him. He *scares* me!"

"Scares you? That is the most ridiculous statement I have ever heard!"

"He worships—"

"The same god we worship."

Ruth shifted nervously, brushing wavy auburn locks away from her delicate face. Inching toward the chair at the head of her bed, she reached for the garments draped neatly across the back.

"Do not touch them! You exhaust me." Dahlia sighed and held out her arms, awaiting her traditional morning embrace. Ruth eyed her with suspicion and then yielded without protest. What else could she do? Her mother was beyond reason.

"I would think it an impossibility you were of *my* flesh and blood—had I not borne you," Dahlia said, releasing her. She clapped her hands and several servants entered. "You are up and about early this morning . . . considering."

One of the servant's gaze met Ruth's. *"Run away!"* the servant had whispered the evening before, while weaving strands of tiny pearls through wavy tresses of Ruth's silken hair.

Ruth grimaced. "Please do not ask me to talk about last night," she said as the servants removed her nightgown.

"Agreed," Dahlia said. "But only because your father demanded I leave the subject alone for now. Tell me, why are you up and about so early?"

Ruth lifted her arms as the servants lowered her robe and tunic over her head. "Well," Ruth hesitated. Should she be forthright? Probably not . . .

"Enough! What *are* you up to?"

"Why must I tell you everything, Mother? I am fourteen years old. When will I be allowed to do as I wish with my day?"

"When you marry—*not* before."

Ruth winced, recalling the priest ogling her body with lust-filled anticipation. His wild eyes and sour smelling breath still turned her stomach. Were it not for her father's mercy, the priest would have forcibly taken her innocence—and with it her soul. "I am going for a walk to Father's field."

"Which field, my dear daughter? He has several."

"The field Elimelech will supervise."

"I know all the townsmen in this area. His name is unfamiliar."

"He is not from here. He is sojourning here from Bethlehem, Judah."

"An Israelite! Goad did not bother to tell me. He knows how our townspeople feel about those—"

"Mother!" Ruth said, grabbing her sandals and moving toward the open doorway.

Dahlia stepped in front of her. "Why would you want to spend time with those foreigners?"

"I am only curious."

Dahlia snapped her fingers and pointed toward a small table. One of the servants bowed, grabbed the brush and head covering and began arranging Ruth's hair.

"So this Israelite you speak of—which field will he be supervising?"

"Father's prized field."

"The field whose supervisor recently died? Ah, yes, I remember him well." Her eyes softened. "Why Goad would hire an Israelite is beyond me." Dahlia scowled at the servants and motioned for them to leave. Bowing, they hurried from the room.

"He needed someone reliable to oversee the barley harvest."

"Well, I do not want you getting your pretty head filled with their way of life and most assuredly not their God."

"Understood. Now, may I please go to the field?"

"After you have stopped by the kitchen. The servants will prepare your provisions for the day."

"Yes, Mother."

"Be home by the evening meal. *And* do not go near The King's Highway. Remember what your father said."

"I remember." She slipped on her sandals and scooted past her mother as she hurried to the kitchen.

✡ ✡ ✡

Safely outside her home, Ruth recalled the events of the previous evening as she swallowed the last bite of apple and tossed the core aside. Had her father not intervened, she would have been defiled by that vile priest and wallowing in a bed of sorrow—hoping death would take her. Shuddering, she recalled her father's attempt to reason with her mother.

"She needs more time, Dahlia," he had said. "She is not ready for marriage, especially to that priest *you* chose for her."

Her father had come to Ruth late in the night and wrapped his strong, comforting arms around her. "Do not cry, sweet Daughter," he said.

"I will not shed another tear, nor will you," Ruth said as she wiped the tears from her father's face. "Thank you for saving me from that horrible man!"

"We will not talk of marriage. You need a diversion and I have one for you."

"What is it?"

"There is a new land supervisor coming to Moab from Bethlehem, Judah, and he is bringing his family with him."

"Foreigners?"

"Indeed." Her father laughed. "I knew that would interest you. They should arrive within a few days. Perhaps they will take your mind off that priest."

"Tell me about their journey."

"They will arrive in Moab via The King's Highway."

"The Highway!"

"Of course. It is the only viable route."

"Are you worried for them?"

"I am. The Highway is a challenge with its mountainous terrain, deep canyons and winding valleys. There are also unscrupulous men who hide and wait for those vulnerable enough to pillage. That is why you are not allowed to walk The Highway alone."

"Do you think they will arrive safely?"

"I am sure Elimelech will take every precaution necessary to protect his family."

✡   ✡   ✡

Filled with anticipation, Ruth skipped along the path leading to her father's prized field. The land spread in every direction, open and lush with vegetation. Mountains towered in the distance like lofty gray clouds. The sun shone brightly. She adjusted her head covering. "A maiden's skin must remain fair with no hint of a freckle," her mother had lectured.

She eyed wild flowers lining either side of the path. Stopping for a moment to admire them, she stooped and tore a handful free. Shaking moistened earth from the roots, she closed her eyes and savored their sweet, alluring scent. Each petal was intricate in design and rhythmic in pattern. How could something so beautiful come into being on its own? Was she the only one who wondered about such things?

She continued along the path until her father's field came into view. It stretched before her, vast and white unto harvest. The fragrance of ripening grain filled her senses. She sighed, realizing her mother was right. The townspeople would not look kindly upon an Israelite taking up residence on their fertile plains. But her father, thankfully, was unmoved by such prejudice.

"I would never dismiss an overseer based on the origin of his birth," he had said to her the night before.

Competent supervisors were scarce, so her father had sent messengers along The Highway inquiring as to a replacement. Word came back of the famine in the land of Israel and a well-known, respected Israelite who was willing to sojourn into the land of Moab. Her father had requested Elimelech arrive as soon as possible, as the barley was near harvest.

Upon reaching the garden lying just south of the house, Ruth left the path and entered, walking along the low stone wall. The grapevines were beginning to bud and the pomegranate trees' vibrant red, tube-shaped flowers released their sweet aroma in the gentle breeze. She strolled the boundary of the garden, inspecting the various shrubs and trees.

Exiting, she approached the small, neat stone structure that would house the new tenants. Tall palms encased the back and sides with branches extending over portions of the thatched roof. Peering in the window, she scanned the open living area and then looked toward the door leading into the room where the family would sleep.

This dwelling had been her father's when he first married her mother. They did not remain there long. It had not been fine enough, or so her mother had insisted. When the new land supervisor occupied the house, her mother had the two additional rooms at the back sealed off. "No tenant should have the luxury of more than two rooms!" Dahlia had insisted. Ruth shook her head in bewilderment. How her father endured her mother's airs defied understanding.

Upon leaving the house, Ruth continued down the path until it began a gentle slope downhill toward the servants' quarters.

She waved at two older servants standing just outside the door. "Good morning, Gardish! Haron!"

"Good morning, Ruth," Gardish responded in a deep, gruff voice. "Why are you out and about so early this morning?"

"I am taking a stroll to The Highway."

Haron frowned and his thick, unruly brows arched downward. "Does your father know?"

"Do not worry," Ruth said, giggling. "I will not set foot on The Highway."

Gardish made his way to where Ruth stood and then pointed his gnarled finger toward the animal pens, which lay across the path. "Your father had several new goats delivered this morning, and a young donkey by the name of Bess. We are in the process of making a few repairs before the new tenants arrive."

"I hope Bess proves more cooperative than the last donkey we had."

"That would not be too difficult!" Gardish said, smirking. "Stubborn old animal . . ." he added, walking away.

Ruth waved at Haron and then continued down the path until she arrived at The Highway.

Standing at the edge of the road, Ruth recalled her father's words,

"Elimelech's journey to Moab will take approximately two weeks by foot, possibly longer," he had said, "considering his family will accompany him. They will begin their journey in Bethlehem and travel northeastward through Jerusalem on to Jericho. The Jericho Road will take them directly east and past the top of the Salt Sea. After crossing the Jordan River they will turn south and begin their journey down The Highway, traveling adjacent to the Sea. When they cross the Arnon River, they will be in the land of Moab."

Excitement welled within her as she looked down the road expectantly. There must be more to life than fancy robes and endless days of leisure. She tired of it.

She recalled her father's warning, as a dense grove of trees captured her attention. "No young maiden should walk The Highway alone," he had said.

She eyed the grove auspiciously. Her decision made, she backed away from the road and retreated to the safety of the grove. Upon choosing a tall palm, she sat down and scooted her back against its trunk.

The sun shone directly overhead as she wiped moisture from her red cheeks and pulled long locks of damp hair away from her neck. She closed her eyes for a moment and then opened them. Had she heard voices? Fixing her stare on The Highway, she followed the road until it curved out of view. Soon she saw a tall, older, heavyset man appear from the bend. He led a donkey with a woman riding on its back. Jumping to her feet, Ruth waved eagerly and then dropped her hand. She must be patient.

Surely this was Elimelech! His chest was broad, his walk confident. His clothing was similar to that of her people in some ways and noticeably different in others. The head covering he wore fell to his shoulders and was secured with a brightly colored, woven cord. A small pouch was tied to his forehead and rested just above his hairline. She studied it, wondering what it contained.

Chapter 1 – THE ARRIVAL

Above his left elbow was a similar pouch secured by a strap, which twined about his forearm, disappearing in the grip of his hand. He wore a tunic over his robes, which fell to the top of his ankles. A tassel hung at each corner of his tunic and danced back and forth with the steady movement of his large sandaled feet.

Ruth walked purposefully toward the road. The older woman looked in her direction, without acknowledgement. Dark brown tresses sprinkled with strands of gray had escaped here and there from beneath her head covering. A long robe protected her fair skin from the unrelenting sun.

Just as Ruth was wondering where their children were, two young men rounded the bend. Her excited waves went unnoticed. She quickened her pace until she was standing at the road's edge.

It was apparent the first young man was the older of the two. He was tall and slender with broad shoulders. Jet-black hair and brows complimented his dark eyes and ruddy complexion. Robes, similar to his father's, were secured at his waist with a coarsely woven sash. He was walking in front of a large, heavily laden cart drawn by oxen.

Turning back, he spoke to the second young man walking a short distance behind and leading another donkey. She wondered how old they were . . . perhaps sixteen, but no more than eighteen.

By this time, the older man was even with Ruth. He stopped, staring intently at her, but did not speak. Blushing, Ruth looked down at her feet for a moment and then lifted her head. "Are you Elimelech?" she asked, addressing the older man.

"I am," he responded.

She smiled. "Greetings in the name of my father, Goad," she said, moving her shy gaze to meet each member of the family.

"And you are Goad's daughter, Ruth?" Elimelech asked.

"I am! You already know of me?"

"Yes. We have heard all about you."

"I am relieved to see your family has arrived safely."

"Thank you, Ruth. We are grateful to Adonai, Whose grace has blessed us, Whose eyes have watched over us, and Who has directed our steps into the land of Moab in order to support us."

His greeting stung. Her eyes watered. Adonai? Was that the name of their God? The words he spoke—what did they mean? They sounded oddly familiar, as though whispered in the recesses of her soul. Had she heard them before? A spark of hope and joy ignited within.

The older woman's gaze settled on Ruth. They studied each other intently. Her face had gentle wrinkles, the kind that come from smiling.

Elimelech cleared his throat. "Please allow me to introduce my family," he said as he motioned in the direction of the woman. "This is my wife, Naomi."

Naomi and Ruth nodded.

"This is my eldest son, Mahlon," he said as his hand moved toward the young man with the oxen, "and my youngest son, Chilion."

Ruth pondered their names, burning them into her memory and wondering the meaning of each. Naomi, Mahlon, Chilion, she repeated silently, until Elimelech drew her attention.

"I am sorry," Ruth said. "I am sure your journey has been difficult. Let me take you to your home and then I will get Father."

"Sounds wonderful." Elimelech smiled and then motioned for his family to follow.

They exited The Highway, continuing on the path toward Goad's field in silence. As they walked, Ruth looked back to study the older of the two sons. Elimelech said his name was Mahlon. She made note of his chiseled face and long feet. His hair held an occasional curl, like his mother's. His eyes and brows were dark and strong like his father's. Ruth flushed. Embarrassed, she looked away.

She walked a short distance and then peered back again. Mahlon's gaze met hers and he grinned. Her eyes widened and she frowned. Did he *know* she was studying him?

Chapter *1* – THE ARRIVAL

"So your name is Ruth?" Mahlon asked.

She nodded, letting her eyes meet his. His grin slowly grew until his lips parted into a captivating, uninhibited smile. She sighed and clasped her hands awkwardly. *Ruth! What is wrong with you?*

Mahlon laughed. She eyed him. His smile grew broad. She stood tall.

She glanced at his younger brother, Chilion, determining further study of him would have to wait.

As they neared the field, they ascended the hill by the servants' quarters and then continued along the flat plain. Arriving at the house, she watched Elimelech as he scanned the expanse of barley and then took a long, deep breath. "Thank you, Adonai," he said, raising his hand toward the sky.

Elimelech turned his attention to the small stone structure as he lifted Naomi from the donkey. She was shorter than Ruth imagined with perfect posture and slender feet. Grasping the cord, which held her head covering in place, she tugged it free, releasing long wavy locks of brown and gray. While weaving her fingers through her hair, she walked into the main living area, looked at her husband and nodded.

They turned to their sons as the family gathered together. Elimelech held out his hand toward Ruth. With raised brows, she stepped back. What was this unexpected custom and why would they bother to include her, a Moabite? Timidly offering her hand, Elimelech tugged her into their circle.

The four bowed their heads and closed their eyes. Ruth thoughtfully considered them as Elimelech prayed, "Adonai, our God and King, we thank you for the provision You have given us in bringing us into the land of the Moabites in order to sustain us. We covenant with You, LORD our God, to walk in all Your ways, to keep Your commandments, to hold fast to You, and to serve You with all our heart and soul. We thank you, El Shaddai, for Ruth and her father Goad, who has been gracious to allow us to reap what we have not sown. We pray Your grace toward him and his family."

The words of Elimelech's prayer pierced through the recesses of Ruth's soul, evoking a sadness and longing she had never felt before. Mahlon opened his eyes, inspecting every detail of her face. She did not look away. The corners of his mouth curved up slightly, his eyes soft and unmoving. She held her breath.

Naomi crossed the length of the room, running her fingers against the stone walls. She was obviously pleased. Ruth sighed. Perhaps they would stay beyond the barley harvest. She hoped so. An image of intricately designed flower petals came to mind as she contemplated Elimelech's prayer to his God.

"Father will be sending food to sustain you for several weeks while you settle into your new home," she said to Elimelech.

"Tell Goad we are thankful for his kindness."

"I will." She fidgeted, searching for an excuse to extend her stay. Finding none, she bit her lip and then clasped her hands behind her back. Stepping just outside the door, she sighed and pointed south. "Our home is located down the plain and just beyond the well. If you need anything, please let us know."

Mahlon stepped into the doorway and then looked at his father. "Should we ask Ruth to inquire if there is someone who could help Mother settle into our new home?"

"Of course." Elimelech chuckled.

"Yes! I am sorry I did not consider it sooner. I will ask my parents for you." Ruth took several steps backward and then waved goodbye. Her heart raced as the four of them crowded in the doorway.

She smiled, stealing one last look at Mahlon. Turning, she lifted her robes and began running down the path toward home.

Chapter 2

RUTH'S HOME

Gray streaked clouds gathered overhead and the air felt damp as Ruth hurried down the path. The wild flowers that drew her attention earlier in the day went unnoticed. Wringing her hands, she contemplated her dilemma. Had Mahlon wanted *her* to help Naomi? There was something about the way he asked his father that caused her to wonder. Had Elimelech seen it too? But they did not know her mother!

Stopping abruptly, Ruth paced back and forth between the narrow boundaries of the path. Her mother's high-pitched droning was almost audible as she imagined her sarcastic laugh and the barrage of opposition to follow.

"*No!* I will not hear of it," Ruth said, mimicking her mother. "No daughter of mine will serve in a tenant's home!" She wagged her finger. "*Foreigners* mind you! *Ab-surd!*"

"Futile!" She rolled her eyes and began pacing again. "I will never convince Mother!"

Stopping midstride, she left the path and made her way through the open plain. Arriving at the stream, she knelt, appraising her reflection as it rippled over the surface. My how she looked like her mother with her fair skin, full lips . . . and sour expression! She winced and then forced a smile.

She kicked off her sandals and dipped her feet into the cool water, enjoying the feel of the current as it meandered through her toes. As she cupped her hand and drank, her thoughts wandered to Elimelech and his God. There was something about his conversation with Him that caused a longing in her heart. She wanted to learn more about Him. But first she must convince her mother to allow her time with the foreigners.

Suddenly the answer came! Slapping the water in triumph, she jumped to her feet. Her mother would never consider her request, but her father surely would! She must find a way to ask him without her mother's knowledge. Feeling a pang of guilt, she lowered her head. Her plan was sneaky and quite definitely unbecoming a maiden.

Please do not be angry with me, God of Elimelech.

Dark clouds began to billow overhead. The air smelled of dust and rain as lightning flashed in the distance. Ruth slipped on her sandals and hurried to the path while recalling her father's childhood.

He had grown up as a servant, but his master noticed his uncanny ability for harvesting and trading goods along The King's Highway. He listened to her father's advice and compensated him well for his council. Her father was a wise man. He took the compensation and invested in trade along The Highway. Over time, he acquired fields of his own, eventually becoming a wealthy man.

She felt sure he would consider her request.

Please say yes, Father! You are my only hope.

Ruth ran until her home came into view. Leaving the path, she stooped behind a small myrtle tree. The exquisite, sweet smelling aroma of the leaves filled her senses. Peering through the branches, she examined the opulent structure. Few in the land of Moab shared their privilege.

Her mother oversaw every detail of their dwelling's creation. With its long, stone walls and oversized courtyard, it was stunning to the eye, but cold in spirit.

At one time, her parent's bedchamber was adjacent to hers. Recently, however, her father had fashioned it into a room of worship, moving their chambers to the rear of the house. She hated *that* room. Was it wrong to hate? Perhaps. But she hated it just the same.

A drop of rain trickled down her brow. Wiping it away, she continued to study each stone. They lay perfectly one atop another. The lush foliage surrounding the house was filled with a myriad of colors.

Scanning the vast garden at the back of the house, Ruth saw her father leaning against a large palm. Even from where she stood, his presence held an air of authority. He was tall and muscled. In truth—he was as handsome as her mother was beautiful. He often told Ruth she was an exact image of her mother. Remembering her sour reflection in the stream, she grimaced, hoping it was not true in every way. Ruth loved her mother, but did not want to be like her. She certainly did not want to worship *her* mother's god!

A streak of lightning flashed along the sky like a spider's web. Taking a deep breath, she mustered the courage to face her father and then raced down the path.

Goad looked in her direction and waved. She held her finger against her lips.

"Shhh!"

He shook his head and held out his arms—waiting.

She ran into his embrace, knocking him backward and causing his broad shoulders to tip precariously to one side. She smiled. Her father always had the fragrance of the sun and earth upon him.

"Ah, Ruth, my sweet daughter," he said in a hushed voice. "What makes you so happy, the arrival of Elimelech and his family?"

Grasping his arm, she tugged him behind the palm.

"Yes," she whispered, looking into his deep, golden-brown eyes. "How did you know they would arrive today?"

"I received word from my tradesman a few days ago that Elimelech and his family were seen on The Highway. I estimated they would likely arrive today."

"Why did you not tell me?"

"And ruin the adventure?" He tilted his head and smiled. "You know me better than that. Tell me, what did you think of them?"

"I think they are wonderful! Did you know Elimelech has two sons?"

"Yes, I was aware of that. And I believe his wife's name is Naomi?"

"It is. And, well, Father . . . she is quite a bit older than Mother."

Goad narrowed his eyes. "Is that so?" He grinned. "So she was tired from the long journey?"

"Indeed. Her oldest son, Mahlon, seems to think she may need some assistance to settle into their new home."

"I see," he said, raising his voice in friendly banter.

Could he read her mind? She clasped her hands and twiddled her thumbs. This conversation was not going as planned. "Elimelech wanted me to ask if there is someone who could help her settle in."

"Is that so?" he asked, grinning. "And I suppose you are just the one to help her. Is that what this is leading to, my daughter?"

"It is. Oh, please, Father!"

"Well, I happen to agree." Taking a lock of hair lying askew, he tucked it behind her ear. "Spending time away from your mother will do you both good, especially since she insists on protecting you from learning to cook or clean. I will visit with your mother and we will see what can be done."

"It will not be an easy task, Father." Ruth bit her lip. "Mother is—"

"Overly protective? Opinionated? Unwilling to budge?"

"She is." Ruth lowered her head, feeling another wave of guilt.

"Not to worry, Daughter." He patted her cheek.

Ruth tried to smile but could not. Why had she thought her father could persuade her mother of such an absurd idea?

Raindrops began spattering around them. Grasping hands, they ran to the house, entering in silence. Ruth retreated to the corner of the main living area, settling into her father's favorite chair. She fidgeted as he disappeared into the room of worship.

Ruth avoided the room. The sight of her mother bowing and chanting before a stone idol of the Moabite god, Chemosh, was disturbing. Ruth was afraid of him. She wrinkled her nose. *This is one time I hope he speaks, declaring approval!*

"Dahlia," Goad called. "How was your day without Ruth?"

Her mother's response, sounding at first sweet and melodious, changed abruptly. "Absolutely not!" she hissed.

Ruth slunk down into the chair.

Their voices continued to echo about the room—her father's, soft and low—her mother's, shrill and unyielding.

Ruth heard movement and sprang to her feet as her mother entered. Her father stood directly behind her.

"I do not understand you, nor do I think I ever will!" Dahlia said. Her lips were thin and pinched, her eyes glaring.

"Dahlia," Goad warned. Tucking his arm around her waist, he pulled her gently against his chest.

Ruth dropped her head. Even her own father could not convince her mother!

"Look at me, Daughter," Dahlia commanded.

Shaking her head in resignation, Ruth surrendered.

Her mother's inscrutable reproach mingled with the thunder as it rumbled overhead and shattered her resolve.

Goad captured her attention with a calculated movement of his hand. She tipped her head inquisitively. A mischievous grin crept across his face.

"Do you understand?"

"Understand what, Mother?"

"No more than one week."

"I can help Naomi? Oh, Mother, thank you!"

Dahlia raised her hand. "Do not thank me! This was not my idea."

"But why can I only stay one week. I—"

"Ruth!" Goad frowned.

Dahlia crossed her arms. "You see, Goad! What did I tell you? One week it is and no more. By then we should be able to find a local servant girl to take your place."

"Thank you, Mother."

"It is settled then," Goad said, walking to Ruth. He placed his hands on her shoulders. "Go and change your robes and prepare for the evening meal. Your mother has had enough excitement for one day."

"Yes, Father," she said as she retreated to her room.

Stepping into her bedchamber, Ruth peered back at her mother and then shut the door.

Chapter 3

THE FIRST DAY

Ruth sat on the edge of her bed swinging her feet impatiently. Hours had passed since the sun had set, but sleep still eluded her. Standing, she peered out the window. The moon shone bright and full, casting its yellow glow across the courtyard. The foliage glistened as drops of rain clung to the leaves.

Turning, she pondered the garments resting on her moonlit chair. She wanted to appear common on her first day with Naomi, but found nothing suitable among her vast array of robes. Approaching the chair, she lifted the tunic and rubbed the soft, fine linen between her fingers. It would have to do for now.

As she removed her nightgown, the moon's glow cast a silhouette of her frame on the wall. Her mouth dropped. Was she pretty? She had never really considered it before now, but the shadow on the wall certainly was. Suddenly shy, she hurried into her undergarments and then pulled the robe and tunic over her head. Retrieving a linen sash, she tied it at her waist and then lay down on her bed and dozed.

She hoped to slip away from the house unnoticed. Although her mother gave her permission to help Naomi, Ruth knew she might change her mind. The storm had continued well into the night, providing her mother ample excuse to foil Ruth's day.

The melodious chirping of a Crested Lark roused Ruth from a light slumber. She rushed to the window. Hues of orange and yellow traced along the horizon as a hazy light moved over the earth. The morning breeze smelled clean and fresh as it flowed through her long locks.

Weaving her fingers through her hair, she arranged it about her head and then inserted a wooden comb. Tiptoeing across the room, she lifted the latch and peered around the frame.

"Mother!"

Dahlia lifted her head, staring at Ruth. Her eyes were red and swollen.

"Where is Father?"

"He already left for the day," Dahlia said, sniffling.

Ruth cautiously approached the chair and knelt at her mother's feet. Placing her hands on her lap, she examined her pink, puffy nose and tear-streaked face. "What is wrong?"

Ruth felt Dahlia's delicate fingers as she moved them over her cheek. She closed her eyes. How long had it been since she felt accepted by her mother? Her touch brought fond memories of childhood—her mother swinging her about, laughing joyfully. She missed the way her mother used to be.

"Ruth, did I seal your destiny by allowing your father to choose your name?"

"Father chose my name?"

"Yes. I wanted to name you Alessa, *Noble One*, but your father insisted on Ruth."

"What does my name mean?"

"It means *friend, companion.*"

"Then it fits me, Mother. Do you not see it?" Ruth took her mother's hand and held it against her face.

"Perhaps, but *Ruth* is much too common a name for a girl of your standing!" Dahlia pulled her hand away. Her countenance hardened. "I want you home every evening in time to worship with me."

"Why?" she asked, recoiling at the thought of Chemosh. Why did her mother worship him? He seemed a cruel god.

"Have you forgotten that you are a Moabite?"

"Does worshipping Chemosh determine if I am a Moabite or not?"

"You best hold your tongue," Dahlia said, her voice low and hushed.

Ruth followed her mother's terror-filled eyes. They were fixed on the room of worship. "Are you afraid of him too, Mother? Has he hurt you?"

"You are to obey me without question. Is that clear?" Dahlia snapped.

Her mother's face contorted. Ruth trembled and the hairs on her arms rose on end. Chemosh held her mother's soul in a vice. Did he want Ruth's soul, too? Unnerved, she retreated to the open doorway.

"Please do not be afraid. I will be home in time to worship with you."

As the color drained from Dahlia's face, her skin turned pasty white.

A wave of panic coursed through Ruth's body and her heart pounded erratically. Run! Her soul screamed. But should she stay and help her mother? *RUN!*

Turning, she ran from the house as her mother's terror-filled warning lingered. Pressing her hands against her ears, she attempted to stop the torment, but it was futile. She ran faster, tripping along the muddy ground. As her legs gave way, she dropped to her knees—her lungs burning.

Observing her mud-spattered tunic, she covered her eyes and moaned. What was she to do now? Remembering Elimelech's prayer, she lifted her face skyward and cried out, "Adonai, can You save me from Chemosh? Are You more powerful than he? He wants my soul!"

Suddenly she heard a deep, calming voice, *"If you search for Me with your whole heart—"*

She moved her head this way and that, scanning the area. Was someone hiding nearby, watching her? Or perhaps she imagined the words? Holding her breath, she listened, but heard nothing more.

Standing, she turned full circle, surveying the landscape, repeating the words, *"If you search for Me with your whole heart—"*

Every attempt made to understand their meaning was met with silence. Was Chemosh mocking her? What would he do, knowing she cried out to the God of Elimelech? She would not succumb to his trickery! Strengthening her resolve, she pushed all thought of him away.

Examining her tunic, she frowned. She could not go to Elimelech's in such a state and returning home to change was too risky. Removing the tunic, she studied the mud spatters and then gave it a firm shake, but it had little effect. Looking toward home, she sighed, pondering her dilemma. Lifting the hem, she studied the underside. Why had she not thought of it before? Turning the tunic wrong side out, she shook it again. It looked almost as good as new! Her mother was such a perfectionist, one could hardly tell the difference in the seams!

Thank you, Mother!

She pulled the tunic over her robe, retied the sash and walked determinedly down the path toward the field. Nearing the well, she spotted the familiar form of her father sitting nearby. Relieved, she approached.

"Good morning, Daughter. Is something wrong?" he asked, looking at her tunic as he handed her a freshly filled skin of well water.

Perhaps a little of the mud had shown through. "No. I am fine." She forced a smile and then drank. "And why did you not wait for me at the house?" she asked, attempting to change the subject.

"I knew a motherly lecture was coming and thought it best if you and your mother shared that special time alone."

Ruth grimaced and then wrapped her arms around his neck. Had he seen the distress in her eyes? She hoped not.

Goad pulled her hands free and then held her at arm's length, inspecting her face. "Your mother is concerned about you, Ruth."

"Do not worry, I promised Mother I would be home every evening in time to worship her god."

"You mean *'our god,'* do you not, Ruth?"

His eyes were sad. It pained her. Disappointing her father was more than she could bear after the morning she endured. Attempting to avoid further discussion of Chemosh, she tucked her arm inside his and tugged him in the direction of Elimelech's home. They walked the rest of the way in silence.

Arriving at the house, Goad approached the door and rapped lightly. The door flung open and Elimelech reached for his hand. "Goad, it is good to see you this morning," he said.

"Thank you." Goad smiled. "Is Naomi getting settled into your new home?"

"Yes. We were thankful to find it large enough to accommodate the four of us, and Naomi is grateful for the provisions delivered. We appreciate your kindness."

Naomi stepped forward, extending her hand. "I made extra food in anticipation of your arrival this morning."

"You are a woman to be admired, traveling from Bethlehem all the way to Moab, and on The King's Highway, no less!"

"I had Elimelech and our sons to look after me." Naomi motioned for her sons to approach.

Mahlon and Chilion shook his hand. "Two sons to help with the harvest," he said, slapping their shoulders. "You are indeed fortunate, Elimelech."

Elimelech nodded, taking Naomi's hand while gesturing for the others to join them. Mahlon extended his hand to Goad and he accepted, joining the circle. As the family bowed their heads, Goad tilted his gaze in Ruth's direction.

"Adonai," Elimelech prayed, "thank you for Goad's kindness toward us, by allowing us to come and supervise his field. Thank you for watching over us and directing our steps. Forgive us where we have failed and have mercy on us as we seek to serve You. Thank you for the food You have provided for us this day. Amen."

Elimelech's prayer perplexed Ruth. He said their God watched over them and directed their steps. *Directed* their steps? How could that be? And what *powerful* God would show mercy! Chemosh had no mercy; he only condemned.

Goad kept his eyes focused on Ruth as they gathered around the table. Recognizing his inquisitive stare, she smiled. He nodded and then with a full grin, turned his attention to Elimelech.

Ruth savored the light-hearted conversation among the men as Naomi placed several platters of food on the table. She was thankful to share the morning meal with them. The aroma of freshly baked bread and fish filled the room. It tasted as wonderful as it smelled. Mahlon explained how he caught the fish in the stream nearby. Ruth found his excitement quite entertaining. He was obviously pleased with himself. She giggled, watching her father. Goad looked intently from Ruth to Mahlon. Her face flushed and she looked away.

After breakfast, Goad and Elimelech went outside to discuss the arrangements they had made concerning the field and livestock. Mahlon and Chilion followed behind, keeping a respectful distance.

At last, Ruth was alone with Naomi. "I can come and help you, Naomi. My parents both agreed I could come for one week . . . at least."

"At least?"

"I hope to convince my mother to allow me to stay longer."

Naomi raised her brows. "I am thankful your mother is allowing you to come for one week. Are you sure you want to come every day? It must be a long walk to and from your house and the work here will be tiring."

"I can do it, Naomi! I help out on occasion at home, when Mother allows me. She seems to have the peculiar idea that I should simply sit and look pretty."

Naomi laughed and Ruth sighed, relieved.

Reaching for Ruth's hands, Naomi examined them. "I am sure your mother will not be pleased with me *if* you stay more than a week."

As gently as Ruth could muster the courage to do so, she pulled her hands free. Walking to the window, she scoured the field in search of her father, finding him with Elimelech and his sons, waist deep in barley. She watched, filled with longing. "Naomi, I want to learn more about your way of life."

Naomi approached, resting her hand on Ruth's shoulder. "Let us begin our chores and I will share as we work."

The touch of Naomi's hand brought comfort and Ruth was excited to spend time alone with her. Naomi picked up two milking pails and they walked down the hill to the goats' pen. Entering the pen, Naomi pulled a small stool next to a goat and sat, placing one of the pails under its belly. Ruth knelt beside her and wrinkled her nose. The goats' strong odors turned her stomach.

Naomi smiled, looking amused as she grasped the udders in her hands and then pulled one downward. Ruth was still attempting to hold her breath when a stream of warm milk suddenly squirted from the udder and flowed to the bottom of the pail. Ruth giggled, delighting at the sight. She would learn to tolerate the smell!

"Did you know, Ruth, that we are related?"

"Related? How can that be? I am a Moabite and you are an Israelite."

"Well, there was a man—whose name at the time was Abram."

"What do you mean by *at the time*?"

"That is another story, but for now we will call him Abram."

"I understand. Please continue."

"Abram lived many generations ago. Elimelech and I descended from him. Abram had a brother named Haran. You are a direct descendant of Haran."

Ruth stared at Naomi and then frowned. "Are you saying Abram was my uncle?"

"Yes," Naomi said, laughing. "Abram's brother, Haran, had a son named Lot.

"I have heard the name before." *But where?*

"Haran died, leaving Lot fatherless. Abram loved his nephew and took him into his own family."

"So if Lot was Abram's nephew, why then am I not an Israelite?"

"You are not considered an Israelite because at the time God spoke to Abram he was not an Israelite. He was—"

"God *spoke* to Abram?" Ruth interrupted. Her heart quickened, remembering the words she heard on the path that morning.

"Yes, God spoke to Abram. Elimelech also heard God speak to him in a dream, but I will tell you about that another day."

"I understand," Ruth said. "Please forgive my interruptions. Mother says it is unbecoming a maiden to interrupt her elders. It is another social grace I would do well to remember."

Naomi's mouth puckered, her eyes crinkling around the corners the way her father's did when he wanted to laugh, but should not. Clearing her throat, Naomi continued, "God spoke to Abram one day, telling him to get out of his country and away from his kinsmen and travel to a land God would show him. He obeyed, taking Sarai, his wife, and Lot with him."

"Why did God tell him to leave his kinsmen?"

"Because God had a very special plan for Abram, telling him that one day, he would be a great nation with many descendants. You must understand, however, that Sarai was old at the time of God's promise and had never borne children."

"Never borne children!" Ruth laughed, incredulous. "How could God make a great nation of a man whose wife was past the ability to even bear a child?"

"Exactly!" Naomi said. "Sarai responded the same way you did when Abram told her of God's plan. She did not believe, but Abram trusted God and obeyed, traveling into the land of Canaan. When he arrived in Canaan, God told him he was standing on the Promised Land and that one day, it would belong to his descendants. He asked Abram to look toward heaven and count the stars. There were so many stars that Abram could not count them all, to which God responded, 'So shall the number of your descendants be'. Trusting, Abram built an alter to Adonai on the very spot where God gave the promise."

"Sarai was with child and bore a son then?"

"No, not yet. There was a great famine in the Promised Land, Canaan, so Abram left the land of promise."

Ruth thought of Naomi and her family. "Abram left the land God promised his descendants because of a famine. That is what happened to your family, too. Do you think Adonai allowed the famine in Bethlehem, forcing you and your family to leave?"

Naomi stopped milking and turned toward Ruth.

"Perhaps." Her voice was filled with sorrow. "I do not pretend to understand all the ways of Adonai, but I trust Him, just as Abram did."

Trust? Ruth did not trust Chemosh! Adonai was not like Chemosh, or Naomi would not trust Him, of that she was certain.

"If Abram left the land God promised, where did he go?"

"He and Sarai sojourned into the land of Egypt, taking Lot with them. However, eventually the famine lifted and they returned to the Promised Land and dwelt there. During those years, Lot grew to be a man, with flocks, herds and tents of his own. But the land could no longer support both of them and their herdsmen began to quarrel."

"What did Abram do?"

"He knew it was time for them to separate, but he did not want any strife between him and his nephew. He asked Lot to choose the land he wanted to live on. Lot looked at the fertile plains beyond the Jordan River and left Abram to travel there."

"And Abram stayed in the Promised Land?"

"Yes, and Lot dwelt in the cities of the plain, even as far as Sodom."

Ruth winced. Sodom! There was some uncomfortable memory

lurking in the recesses of her mind, but the details eluded her.

"Did Lot settle in one location?"

"Yes. Over time Lot's descendants settled on the very land we are standing on."

"This very land!" Ruth repeated, amazed. "And how old was Sarai when she gave birth?"

"Ninety years old."

Ruth gasped as Naomi handed her the pail. "Ninety years old?"

Naomi nodded as she pointed to the other goats. "I will share more about Sarai on another day. For now, please milk the rest of the goats. When you are finished, bring the pails to the house." She stood stiffly, stretching her back before turning to leave.

Ruth worried for Naomi as she moved slowly up the hill. The journey to Moab would have been difficult for an older woman like Naomi. She admired her determination.

Focusing her attention on the next goat, she placed the pail beneath its belly. Grasping an udder in each hand she began pulling in rhythmic motion, mimicking Naomi's movements. The goat cocked its head back as if in protest.

"I am sorry, goat," she said, giggling. She continued her efforts at pulling and releasing until a stream of milk sang its way effortlessly into the pail. "Yes!" she said, proudly. "You see goat, I can get milk out of you just as Naomi did. And I can learn to cook and clean, too, if given the chance."

Slowly, she lost herself in thought, filled with questions. So what happened to Lot after he left Abram? She peered at the goat as if she would answer. And why was she not an Israelite? She still did not understand. Vaguely remembering something about Lot's wife and a place called Sodom, she grimaced. She best ask Naomi about Lot, not her parents. All she had was a fleeting memory and it was not a pleasant one, either.

Her thoughts wandered back to the moment before Elimelech prayed, when Mahlon reached his hand toward her father. There was something in Mahlon's gesture that touched her deeply. He was different than any Moabite boy she had ever known, but she was unsure why she found him attractive. Perhaps it was his dark curly hair. Or was it his eyes? His steady gaze seemed to pierce her defenses, reading her thoughts—irritating and captivating her at the same time. And then there was his mouth. There was something about the way it curved up slightly at the corners, just before he smiled. She was drawn to him. Had her father seen it? That made two subjects she would be wise to avoid, Lot *and* Mahlon!

Ruth continued milking until she had drawn every drop possible from the goats. Standing, she picked up the pails and hurried up the hill. As the milk sloshed over the sides, she slowed her pace until at last she reached the house.

Entering, she beamed as Naomi turned to face her.

"Ruth!" Naomi said, her mouth dropping.

Elimelech hurried to Ruth, taking the pails and placing them on the table. "Your first attempt at milking goats has been *very* productive," he said as the room erupted in laughter. The family gathered around, inspecting the pails.

"I do not believe those poor goats have ever been milked more thoroughly," Mahlon said as he pushed a curl of hair away from Ruth's eye. Stubbornly, the curl fell back in place.

The four of them continued looking at Ruth until she finally smiled, blowing the curl to the side.

Elimelech shook his head and grinned. "Chilion will walk you home today. There is a story Naomi began that Chilion will continue."

"Thank you, Naomi!"

"You are welcome, Ruth," she said, motioning for her to come and then hugging her. "Thank you for helping me today."

"Gladly!" Ruth said. "I will see you tomorrow."

Exiting the house, she stood on the path waiting for Chilion.

Chapter 4

THE WALK HOME

Ruth glanced at Chilion as they walked in silence. Did he expect her to speak first? She kicked a small rock off the path and then crossed her arms. Elimelech said he would finish the story Naomi started. At this rate they would arrive at her home before he said one word!

Perhaps he was silent because he did not like her. And who could blame him? He was uprooted from his homeland and brought into a land of foreigners.

He looked at her sideways with his dark brown eyes and then wrinkled his long, narrow nose.

Ruth sighed and smiled. He did not appear to be angry. She busied herself assessing his features. He was handsome in an odd sort of way. He was tall, but spindly and his hair was straight and unruly. It was pulled at the nape of his neck in a haphazard way with a rough bit of twine. Even his robes seemed a bit bedraggled. He was obviously not trying to impress her!

He leaned his head back and laughed.

Wide-eyed she frowned. "Do you find me amusing?"

"No harm meant!" He raised his hands in surrender.

"None taken then." She grinned, eyeing his thick brows. Hopefully he would grow into them!

"Do you want to ask me any questions?"

"Yes. I am curious as to how old you are?"

"I am eighteen."

"Really, eighteen? I thought you were younger."

"How old are you?"

"Fourteen."

"Fourteen?" He gasped. "You look *much* older!"

Ruth took aim at his shoulder, swinging. He slid out of reach. "I can handle boys like you!" She missed having an older brother but supposed if she did, their conversation would be similar. "How old is Mahlon?"

"Twenty."

"Twenty and unmarried?"

"Who told you that?"

Ruth blushed. "I assumed he was not married."

"You assumed correctly," he said, looking amused. "Mahlon could be married, as could I, but we are not, as you can see."

"You win! I am no match for your wit. Can you *attempt* to be serious?"

"An arduous request, but yes. Actually, any thought of marriage on Mahlon's or my part was interrupted by the famine. I was wondering how old Moabite girls are when they marry?"

Avoiding the subject of her own culture had been her hope, but if she wanted information, she would have to reciprocate.

"Most Moabite marriages are arranged by the father and girls often marry as young as twelve." Ruth winced.

Chilion looked at her evenly and then continued, "Girls in my culture can also marry as early as twelve, although it is uncommon. So if you are already the ripe old age of fourteen, then why are you not married?"

"Fourteen is too young for me!"

"Ouch! Did I hit a nerve? It appears you are not interested in arranged marriages or marriage in general, for that matter."

Ruth eyed him with a friendly smirk. "And what about you? Will your father choose your wife?"

"More important for my father is not that he choose our wives, but that we marry from among our people."

"You are required to marry an Israelite?"

"We are. Marriage, however, will have to wait until we return to the Promised Land. But I am sure there are other subjects that interest you more. Mother told me to make constructive use of my walk to your home." His countenance grew serious. "She said you were interested in the stories of Abram and Lot."

"Yes, when Naomi and I last spoke, she said Abram and Lot went separate ways. Did they ever see each other again?"

"Oh, yes!" Chilion nodded, "Lot eventually went to live in the land of Sodom and Gomorrah. It happened that while Lot was there, some kings from other nations went to war with the inhabitants of Sodom, capturing the city and taking the people and all their belongings with them. Among the captured were Lot, his family *and* all he possessed."

"Lot was a wealthy man at the time?"

"Without a doubt, he was. He had vast flocks, herds and tents of his own."

"Did Abram find out what happened to his nephew?"

"Actually, yes. Someone was able to escape, telling Abram that Lot was taken captive."

"Abram still cared about Lot?" Ruth asked, still wondering why God had not allowed her family to be one of His chosen people.

"Of course. He loved Lot. When Abram heard of Lot's trouble, he took over three hundred men and trained servants with him and went in pursuit of Lot's captors. He attacked them and rescued Lot, his family and possessions—along with all the people of Sodom."

"Abram must have been wise and fearless to accomplish such an impressive victory."

"No." Chilion shook his head in disagreement. "He was victorious because God gave him the victory, not because of his *own* wisdom or bravery. Abram *knew* that."

Ruth grasped Chilion's arm, stopping him. "How do you know God gave him the victory?"

"Because the priest of God Most High—"

"*Priest!*" Ruth interrupted, her eyes wide with disdain. "My mother tried to marry me to a priest. He was an evil man."

"*Really?*" He raised his thick, unruly brows.

She looked away. "I do not want to talk about it."

"You brought it up, not me. When did this happen?"

Ruth sighed, wiping beads of perspiration nervously from her forehead, "Two nights ago. My father saved me from him. That is all I will say about the subject."

"Is that so?"

"Yes." With her chin held high, she continued down the path. "The priest you mentioned, he was not like a priest of Chemosh?"

"No. There is no priest like him on earth. He pronounced a blessing over Abram:

And he blessed him and said:
"Blessed be Abram of God Most High,
Possessor of heaven and earth;
And blessed be God Most High,
Who has delivered your enemies into your hand." (Genesis 14:19-20).

"God Most High delivered Abram's enemies into his hand? How many gods do you serve?"

Chilion tilted his head and frowned. "One. Why do you ask?"

"Because I heard Elimelech refer to the God of your people as Adonai, LORD and El Shaddai. Naomi called him God. Just now, you said God Most High and Possessor. All those names for one God?"

"Yes, all those names and many more. We serve The One True God,

Father and Creator. He is one God with many names that describe Him.

"I want to know all His names."

She thought of Chemosh. He had only one name but many disturbing attributes like fierce, inescapable, consuming and even destroyer. She shuddered.

"Is something bothering you?"

"Not at all. I just got lost in thought." Perhaps one day she would tell Chilion about Chemosh, but now was not the time. "So why did Adonai choose to make Abram a great nation?"

"That is an interesting question." He paused, rubbing his chin. "I suppose He searched Abram's heart and found him acceptable."

"What would Adonai have found there that pleased Him?"

"What would please Adonai? Hmm, I guess it would be trust!" He shook his head and then continued. "Yes, He was pleased that Abram put his trust in Him."

Apprehension crept through Ruth and she measured her words carefully. "How could Abram trust God when what He promised was impossible for Abram to achieve at his age?"

"Are you referring to the baby God promised him and Sarai?"

"Yes."

"The baby was only the beginning, Ruth. There is much more to his story."

"I do not think I would believe God if He told me I would have a baby in my old age."

"Yes, Ruth, but Abram did believe God, and God credited it to him as righteousness."

"What do you mean when you say—*credited it to him as righteousness?*"

"It means that Abram trusted God. Imagine being in Abram's place. He was seventy-five years old when the LORD first gave the promise that he would have a son. God did not fulfill the promise until Abram was one hundred years old."

"*After* God promised him a son, He made him wait *twenty-five* years until Sarai actually had the baby?"

"Yes. Sarai was sixty-five years old and well past her childbearing years when God first gave the promise. She would not bear her son, Isaac, until she was ninety years old."

Ruth shook her head, "Ninety years old! God waited until all hope was gone to fulfill His Word."

"But Abram never lost hope. He trusted God. There is nothing greater I can do in this life than to believe—to trust—God."

"God was pleased with Abram because he trusted?"

"Yes, Ruth, and it is the same for me. When I trust God, He is pleased with me."

Lowering her head, she pondered all Chilion shared with her. So to please Chilion's God, Adonai, she would need to trust Him. But would the LORD allow a Moabite to trust Him? Would The One True God accept her even though she was not born from the children of Israel? Ruth could not bring herself to ask, fearing Chilion would say what she could not bear to hear.

Was she destined to be separated from Chilion's God? If so, why? The hope that filled her heart was now replaced with deep sorrow. No longer able to endure the thought of God's rejection, she retreated. Silence stretched between them as they walked.

Chilion gently touched her shoulder as he pointed and said, "It appears that Mother will need to continue the story of Lot. Is that your home?"

She nodded. "Yes. Thank you, Chilion. I will see you tomorrow."

"I am sorry, Ruth, but you cannot come tomorrow."

"Why? Have I offended your family in some way?"

"No! Of course not, Ruth! Tomorrow is Shabbat."

"What is Shabbat?"

"There are six days when we may work, but the seventh is a day of rest. It is our day of worship. On that day we are not to do any work, not even to walk to and from your home."

"I see. So I cannot walk to your house tomorrow because it is Shabbat, but I can come the day following?"

"Yes, of course! We will see you in two days." Chilion nodded and then turned to leave. "Goodbye, Ruth."

"Goodbye. Tell your parents I will see them soon."

Ruth stood watching Chilion as he walked away. He took several steps and then turned back to wave. She waved in response. They continued their unrehearsed ritual until he rounded the bend and was out of sight.

✿   ✿   ✿

Dahlia stood in the doorway watching her. The fear Ruth struggled to overcome earlier in the day, rushed through her body. Hesitating, she approached, attempting to discern her mother's mood. Dahlia smiled. Ruth studied the corners of her mouth, relaxing.

"Was that boy you were walking with one of the foreigners?"

"Yes. It was their youngest son, Chilion."

"He certainly is not concerned with his appearance. His robes appeared rather wrinkled."

Ruth giggled. "I would have to agree, Mother."

"You are home in time to worship." Dahlia hugged her. "Daughter! What is that horrible smell?"

"Goats, Mother. Perhaps I should bathe."

"No! You cannot get out of worshipping with me that easily!"

Ruth sighed as sorrow and trepidation consumed her. Her mother was right. There was no escaping what awaited her in the room of worship. She was mired in the circumstances of her birth. Had she been born to Abram, she would be an Israelite, and Adonai would be her God. As it was, she was born to Abram's brother. She was so close to the blessing she could almost touch it, but not possess it. *Why? Am I cursed?*

Bowing her head, she followed her mother into the house.

Chapter 5

THE ROOM

Dahlia gripped Ruth's hand as they walked down the narrow, dark hallway leading to the room of worship. The air grew stale and cold as they neared the room. Suddenly Ruth froze—eyeing the lamps evenly placed at the base of the walls. They flickered, casting an eerily fluid silhouette of Chemosh across the ceiling. She moved her eyes over the gray, shadowy form until her eyes rested on the stone idol. It stood next to a bowl of smoldering incense on a finely carved, ivory table. She thought of her father. She seldom saw him in this area of their home. Whether he worshiped Chemosh or simply tolerated her mother's worship of him, she did not know.

Dahlia entered the room, motioning for Ruth to join her.

Ruth hesitated. "Mother?" she asked in a hushed voice.

"Yes, Daughter."

"Why does Chemosh have a sun as his crown and a sword in his hand?"

"He is known as the great destroyer and his powers are strong like the rays of the sun."

"This morning, you were afraid. Why?"

Dahlia exhaled in a deep, gruff tone. Yanking Ruth by the arm, she pulled her down the hallway and outside the house. Ruth tripped and stumbled along behind her until they were beyond the courtyard. With one final jerk, Dahlia spun Ruth around.

"Why would you ask me about *fear* in front of Chemosh?" she growled, her eyes narrow and glaring.

"I am sorry, Mother." She rubbed her arm where Dahlia's nails bore into her skin. "I was not thinking."

"You *must* be careful what you say in his presence!" Dahlia yelled as spittle spewed from her mouth.

"Please stop!" Ruth shouted as she clamped her hands over her ears. "I hate that room!"

Dahlia pried them away. "Ruth, hold your tongue!"

"Mother, I loved our house when there was no room of worship and you were not afraid! Do you not remember?"

"I am more afraid for you than for myself."

"Why?"

"Because Chemosh *must* be respected!" Dahlia sighed, laying her arm around Ruth's shoulder. "You are young, but will grow to understand, just as I have."

"Did you hear him speak to you about me, or visit you in a dream?"

"That is an odd question."

"I ask because Adonai, the God of Elimelech, has spoken to His people in dreams and visions."

"Do not compare Chemosh to their God!"

"I am sorry, Mother."

"The only people who need fear Chemosh are those who refuse to bend to his will. Any who do not serve him should fear for their lives."

"I have not served him, Mother. Is that why you are afraid for me?"

"It is my fault." Dahlia lifted Ruth's chin. "I have allowed you to do as you please *far* too long. Chemosh will not tolerate your ignorance. He *is* your god. Do not make the mistake of resisting him."

Chapter 5 – THE ROOM

Turning, Dahlia made her way through the courtyard. Ruth followed in obedience. As they entered the house, Dahlia grasped Ruth's hand and guided her into the vapid, lamp-lit room. The pungent smell of smoldering incense burned her eyes. They took slow, deliberate steps until they were standing before the statue of Chemosh. He looked powerless to Ruth as she knelt beside her mother. Dahlia leaned forward until her hands were outstretched in front of her body, touching the ground. Ruth mimicked her movements. Her mother lay motionless as stillness settled in around them. As Ruth listened to her mother's steady, shallow breathing her thoughts wandered to the prayers of Elimelech. Twice she heard him speak to Adonai. The words he prayed were powerful and sharper than the sword brandished by the statue that loomed before her. Each word Elimelech uttered to his God pierced her soul, leaving hope in its wake.

Bowing before Chemosh she felt like a slave, but her resolve grew stronger. She longed to learn more of the Israelites' God, but would need more time than the five days that would remain after their observance of Shabbat.

Suddenly, a solution occurred to her. Her mother often complained that Ruth needed a servant to attend her. *No* had always been Ruth's response. Why would she want to be doted on and followed around? Now, she reconsidered. Perhaps a servant would appease her mother and secure her more time with the foreigners. Asking her mother's permission might be futile, but she must try.

Dahlia began to chant. The dissonant sounds were haunting and sent a cold chill down Ruth's back. She wanted to run from the room but felt compelled to stay. She dare not upset her mother; doing so might prevent her from returning to the foreigners.

An hour or more passed before Dahlia looked at Ruth.

"Thank you, Ruth, for joining me today." Ruth nodded as they rose together. "This will change your life as it has mine. Chemosh has spared our family because of my devotion to him."

Dahlia strolled beside one wall and Ruth the other as they extinguished each flame until the room was dark. The room seemed a fitting homage to the statue of Chemosh. His crown was a sun, but he was void of light. As they left the room, Ruth hoped her mother would tire of sharing this ritual with her. Perhaps Ruth should pray to Adonai, asking Him to free her from the Moabite god. Would He hear her prayer? After all, she was not one of His chosen people.

Ruth followed her mother out of the house and into the garden. They made their way to the back where various herbs flourished. Dahlia knelt beside a clump of dill, inspecting the delicate, feathery leaves. Their fresh, aromatic smell drifted upward. Kneeling beside her mother, Ruth touched the long, slender stems and savored the fragrance of the tiny, yellow flowers.

"It is time for tea," Dahlia said as she stood and clapped her hands. A servant appeared in the doorway and then scurried through the garden.

"Hot tea with dill. Prepare it immediately," Dahlia commanded.

The servant stooped near Ruth, snipping several stems from the plants, and then hurried back to the house.

Standing, Ruth studied her mother's countenance and then lowered her head.

Adonai, if You will consider my prayer, please sway my mother's heart.

Taking her mother's hand, Ruth raised her gaze. "I know Chemosh has your devotion, Mother, but I wonder about Father. Does he feel the same for Chemosh as you?"

Dahlia frowned. "He chooses to join me on occasion," she said, her voice constricted with irritation, "but is unwilling to worship daily, as I feel he should. I have long ago given up trying to convince him. Goad knows he has acquired great wealth, but assumes it came from his own efforts. I know better. My worship of Chemosh has protected your father *and* our family from further destruction, whether your father believes it or not!"

Further destruction? Could Mother be referring to–

"Ruth! Are you listening to me?"

"Um, yes, Mother, of course."

"Worshiping Chemosh will change your life for the better."

"Do you really think so?"

"Yes! You will never be the same after giving him your heart and soul."

"True." Ruth shook her head in agreement. For once her mother was right! Giving her soul to Chemosh would change her, but not in the way her mother hoped. Chemosh was a god of evil and she wanted nothing to do with him.

"I am sorry, Mother, if my asking about Father upset you."

"On the contrary. You made me very happy by joining me today. Now, tell me about the new tenants."

Her heart raced with anticipation. "Not much to tell, Mother." Steadying her voice, she continued, "However, there is more work than I can do by myself."

"What work did you do today?"

"I milked goats."

"*Milked* goats! That explains the horrid smell you brought home with you! Let me see your hands. I do not want you getting calluses."

"Not to worry, Mother." Ruth managed a light-hearted tone as she held out her palms.

Dahlia moved her fingers over Ruth's soft skin. "Hmm. They seem fine."

"It is obvious you have never milked a goat." Ruth giggled, pulling her hands away. "I do not believe I would get calluses from milking a goat, even if I milked ten in a day."

Dahlia sighed. "Perhaps not."

"There are other things I want to learn from Naomi, like how to make bread and cook fish."

"Why do you want to learn such menial tasks?"

"I tire of endless days filled with leisure. I want to go to Father's field and watch the harvesters gather the grain. I want to pick berries and pomegranates."

"I *try* to understand you, Ruth," Dahlia said, shaking her head in exasperation, "but the value gained from picking berries *or* milking a goat for that matter, escapes me. Above all, I worry about the influence those Israelites may have on you."

"I have been thinking about that Mother, and have come up with a solution."

"Solution? What do you mean?"

"A servant to attend me. You have *always* wanted me to have one and I agree, it is time."

"Hmm. And what caused this sudden change of attitude?"

"I know you are concerned with my spending time with the new tenants—" Ruth paused, weighing her response.

"That is true."

"There is no need for concern, *if* a servant accompanies me to the field each day."

"Why would having a servant lessen my reservations about *that* family and your spending time with them?"

"She will look after me, making sure I do not get calluses and—"

"Daughter!" Dahlia laughed. "Does this idea of yours have anything to do with your desire to go to your father's field for more than one week?"

"Oh, yes, Mother, I admit it. Would having a servant make you feel more comfortable with my continuing to go to Elimelech's?"

"Well actually, Ruth, it would. The servant would be there to keep an eye on you and talk sense into you if you get any strange ideas in that pretty head of yours."

"I was not expecting you to agree, Mother! I am speechless."

Dahlia crossed her arms, looking satisfied. "Well, I would protest, Ruth, but I know your father will be in agreement with you. He always is! I am glad you asked me first so I can say yes before your father." Dahlia rubbed her hands together and smiled. "I cannot wait to see the look on Goad's face when I tell him the news. He may faint away from shock!"

"I agree, Mother, he will be surprised."

"Do you have someone in mind?"

"No one in particular, although she should be near my age, with a pleasant disposition. I have been lonely growing up an only daughter."

"Hmm, a servant near your own age? Yes, we need to find someone as soon as possible. The servant can do the majority of the work *and* watch over you. She must be a Moabite from a respectable family. I will discuss it with your father and let you know what we decide."

"Can I inquire in the village also, Mother? I want to take a walk there tomorrow."

"So you are not going to help Naomi tomorrow?"

"No, tomorrow is something they call Shabbat and for them it is a day of rest."

"Then yes, go into the village and inquire if you wish, but know that your father and I will make the final decision."

Dahlia cradled Ruth's hands in hers, raising them to her lips. "You do know I love you, Ruth?"

"Yes, Mother, of course I do."

Dahlia smiled, then lifting her head high, strode toward the house.

Ruth observed her mother's long, straight hair as it swished from side to side. Holding her hand over her mouth, she muffled a laugh. Her mother agreed to her request! Had a miracle just happened? Ruth looked across the plain in the direction of her father's field. What would Naomi and her family do on Shabbat? She was certain they would not leave their home.

Would Adonai be upset with Ruth for walking into the village on

53

His day of rest? She waited and listened, hoping for an answer—but there was only silence.

Chapter 6

THE SERVANT GIRL

A crisp breeze wafted through the window as Ruth snuggled beneath the warm linens. Grasping the cover's edge, she pulled them beneath her eyes and gazed into the night. A sea of twinkling lights lay suspended on a canvas of blue and gray. Filled with wonder, she recalled Adonai's promise to Abram.

'Look toward heaven, and count the stars if you are able, for so shall the number of your descendants be.'

She struggled to comprehend Abram's trust. How could he believe Adonai when he and Sarai were physically beyond the ability to bear children?

Imagining her own grandmother at ninety and with child—her belly protruding, Ruth laughed.

"Ruth?" Goad called in a raspy voice.

"Yes, Father. Sorry to awaken you. I just had a preposterous thought."

"Will you share it with us?"

The light-hearted sound of his voice caused her to smile. "I was imagining what it would be like to bear a child at the age of ninety."

He chuckled. "Let us hope your mother and I will not have to wait that long for grandchildren. Now go to sleep, sweet Daughter."

Ruth sighed, knowing her father loved her completely. He would do anything within his power to provide for her and keep her safe.

Her thoughts wandered to Adonai as she remembered her prayer earlier in the day. Had He granted her request? What else could explain her mother's change of heart? But would He ever accept her and love her as His own?

A prayer fluttered through her mind, but the words faded in and out as she struggled to overcome sleep. Sitting up, she closed her eyes as she had seen Elimelech's family do, and whispered a prayer. "Adonai, if You are The One True God, You created *all* mankind. Would You create me, but not allow me to know and love You?"

Opening her eyes, she studied the heavens and then continued, "I long to be one of Abram's descendants, but it is too late for me. Perhaps, You could love me anyway," she paused, realizing the absurdity of her request. "You could adopt me as Your own," she reasoned as the words caught in her throat.

It was futile, as futile as attempting to convince her mother to accept an Israelite. Tears ran down her cheeks, dripping off her chin and onto her nightgown.

Do You see me, Adonai? Do You not care that I am searching for truth–for meaning in my life? Somehow I know You are not like Chemosh, but how do I know? Is that what trust is? If I try hard enough–can I convince You to love me?

The words she heard on the path to Elimelech's field echoed through her, *'If you search for Me with your whole heart–'*

"I *am* searching!" she whispered, beating her fists into the bed.

'–you will find Me,' the voice resonated.

Rising to her knees, she looked into the heavens. "I will search for You, Adonai. And if You are The One True God, I will find You–if You will only let me."

She nestled into bed, drifting off to sleep, wondering if the words she had heard were created by her own heart's longing.

✡   ✡   ✡

Sunlight streamed through the window, rousing Ruth from sleep. Jumping from bed, she pulled off her nightgown and slipped into her robes. Running her hands over the front of her plain tunic, she attempted to smooth the wrinkles spreading in every direction. At first glance, her mother would know these roughly woven robes were not hers. Ruth wanted to appear common, so she had snuck into the servants' quarters the previous day with one of her own robes in hand and negotiated a trade. One of the petite older women was more than willing to oblige. Ruth recalled with satisfaction the look on the woman's face as she removed her garments in a frenzy, anxious to try on Ruth's fine linen robes. Ruth had watched in amazement as the woman twirled around like a young girl, the room erupting with resounding laughter.

Ruth peered out the window as she arranged her long silky tresses and then secured them about her head with a sash. She hoped to be out of the house before her parents, but slept later than planned. Failing in that regard, she settled for slipping from the house unnoticed.

Ruth recalled her mother's words as she crept to the door, 'Go into the village and inquire if you wish, but know that your father and I will make the final decision.'

She lifted the latch and peeked around the frame. "Father!" she cried, flinging the door open. "This is getting to be a ritual with you and Mother," she said, approaching the chair where he sat waiting.

He tilted his head with a boyish grin, focusing his eyes on her rumpled tunic. "What ritual?"

Ruth threw her hands in the air and shook her head as she knelt beside him. "I need not respond to that question," she said, crossing her arms. "Did Mother tell you about the new servant girl?"

"Brilliant idea, Ruth. Your mother tells me you are growing more like me every day."

She sighed. "I do not *really* want a servant. But a companion would be nice, would you not agree, Father?"

"Companion? I am happy to hear it. I want to walk with you into the village today and tell you about a young Moabite maiden who may be just the right servant for you."

Ruth tried to smile, but she was not happy. She wanted to pick her own companion.

Reaching for Ruth's hands, he pulled her to her feet. "Not to worry, my dear. She comes from a very respectable family, as your mother requested. I am confident you will find this girl to be a wonderful friend."

"You know me well, Father," she said in a hushed voice, looking toward the room of worship. "I do not want a servant. I want a friend who is willing to help me with my chores at Elimelech's."

"I thought as much," Goad said as he motioned for Ruth to precede him out the door. They continued through the courtyard and began their trek to the local village. "The maiden is about your age," he said, pausing to study her. "She is the daughter of one of our tenants and I am hoping you will find it in your heart to have compassion for her and her family."

"Compassion? What do you mean?" Ruth asked as she stooped beside the path and pulled a bright purple wildflower from the ground.

"Her family has fallen on hard times. Her father was one of my most reliable supervisors, but fell very ill about six months ago and has been unable to work at full capacity."

Ruth sniffed the fragrant flower pedals. "You did not turn him away, did you?"

"Of course not!"

"I am sorry, Father."

Goad took Ruth's hand in his. "No offense taken," he said nodding as they continued toward the village. "Her father remains in my employ, but his duties are greatly reduced. I am able to compensate him, but not to the extent I would like to. Choosing his daughter would allow me to do more for his family, without the local townsmen assuming I was showing them undue favor."

"So do you think he would mind if his daughter became one of our servants?"

"No, my child, I do not think he will mind. I also believe she will be happy to serve you when she realizes you will not treat her cruelly. Her name is Orpah."

"Why will we find Orpah in the village this morning and not with her family?"

"She is currently a servant in Harrash's household—"

"Harrash!" Ruth interrupted, incredulous. "He is known to be cruel to his servants—beating them mercilessly." Ruth shook her head in disbelief. "He is even rumored to be involved in *human* sacrifices!"

"I have heard the rumors also," her father said, his voice softening. "An opportunity has presented itself and we may be able to rescue Orpah from Harrash. The final decision, however, is yours to make."

Ruth fell silent, contemplating her father's words as she moved the soft, purple pedals between her fingers and then tossed them aside, frowning. What if she did not like Orpah? Or even worse, what if she was a mean girl? Shaking her head determinedly she concluded that none of her excuses were valid. No matter what Orpah was like, she would choose her. It was the right thing to do. Satisfied with the outcome of her inner debate, Ruth looked at her father, her eyes revealing her thoughts.

"Am I to assume, my daughter, that you have made your decision?"

Ruth nodded. "I promise that I will love Orpah as my own sister—whether she likes it or not!"

Goad laughed, stopping to turn Ruth toward him.

"You are a rare treasure indeed." He kissed her forehead. "If I am destined to have only one child, I am thankful it is you!"

"Even though I am not a boy?"

"Yes, my sweet daughter, even though you are not a boy."

"And even though you have no son to inherit the fields?"

Goad's countenance fell. Knowing she grieved him, she looked away. Her parents' only son died ten years previous, the result of a tragic accident. Ruth was very young at the time. So young, in fact, she had difficulty recalling her brother's face. Her mother refused to speak of him since the day he passed.

She felt her father's strong, calloused hand as he lifted her chin.

"I will give all that I have to you, Ruth," he said softly. "And to the husband you choose."

"And what if I never marry?" she asked, regretting her words for a second time.

Goad winced and Ruth's heart fell.

"We will worry about that when you are old enough to make such a decision and feel at peace with it in your heart."

Ruth saw the village in the distance as Goad tapped her shoulder and pointed at a young maiden walking in their direction.

"Is that Orpah?"

"I believe so."

Ruth assessed her features. She appeared to be about Ruth's height. Her robes were colorful for a servant girl, but perhaps her father was able to provide fine clothing before he fell ill. Ruth continued to watch the girl impatiently, hoping to draw her attention. She did not oblige, but kept her eyes fixed on the ground.

Ruth started to speak, but from the corner of her eye, saw her father raise his finger to his lips, tapping it lightly. Shrugging, she acknowledged him.

The maiden continued on until she was even with them. Ruth shot her father a glance, imploring him to speak.

Goad seemed to wait patiently until she took one full step past them.

"Orpah?" he asked.

She stopped. Turning to face him, she lifted her gaze from the ground, meeting his questioning eyes. Could this be Orpah? Her complexion was fair and smooth without a hint of a freckle or blemish. Her dark eyes were striking, her lashes long—almost touching the tops of her brows.

"Orpah?" he asked a second time.

"Yes. I am Orpah," she stated in a flat, monotone voice. "I am sorry; I do not know who you are."

"I am Goad."

Her countenance held no hint of recognition.

Goad smiled, seeming undaunted. "Your father is one of my supervisors."

Ruth saw a flicker of recognition in Orpah's dark eyes. She nodded and managed a weak smile before dropping her gaze. Ruth wondered if it was embarrassment or shame that caused her to look away. Had Ruth ever seen more sorrowful eyes in a maiden her own age? She could not recall.

"Yes, I do remember your name," Orpah said, "but not your face."

"It is not surprising. It has been several years since we have seen each other. I dare say we have both changed. You are much taller and more grown up than I remember."

Orpah glanced shyly in Ruth's direction.

"I want you to meet my daughter, Ruth."

Orpah studied her, but did not speak.

"Are you going to be serving in Harrash's home today?" Goad asked, breaking the silence.

Orpah closed her eyes and grimaced as she nodded.

"Do not go to Harrash's house today. I want you to go home."

Her eyes flew open. "But I must!"

"Why?" Ruth asked.

"My father will be very upset with me if I do not!"

"I understand your concern, Orpah," Goad said in a calm, low voice. "But I want you to trust me. I am going to speak to your father at the field and after I have spoken to him, he will explain everything to you."

Her mouth dropped. She looked as though on the verge of speaking, but uttered not a word as she moved her eyes from Goad to Ruth and back again.

"Do you understand?" Goad asked.

Nodding her head, Orpah faced Ruth. Ruth watched in amazement as Orpah's mouth curved upward into a broad smile. "Go home, Orpah!" Ruth said, laughing.

Orpah turned, took several steps and then raced up the path like a deer freed from a snare. Ruth laughed as Orpah twisted her head back on occasion, flashing the same broad smile, until she was out of sight.

"Ruth," Goad said, placing his hand on her shoulder, "I want you to trust me and go home."

"But Father!" Ruth crossed her arms in protest.

Goad narrowed his eyes.

Wrapping her arms around his waist, she clung to him for a moment and then stepped away. Realizing the matter was settled; she lowered her head and began walking toward home. She walked a short distance and then turned back, observing him as he left the main road and headed up the path in the direction of Harrash's home.

✡   ✡   ✡

Ruth strolled home, kicking pebbles as she went. On occasion, she looked back, hoping her father would appear on the path behind her, but he did not.

As her home came into view, she observed one of the male servants standing beneath a fig tree in the courtyard.

"Have you seen Mother?" she asked, hurrying toward him.

The servant plucked several of the ripe figs from the branches and then popped one into his mouth.

"In the garden," he said, chewing.

"Best save some of those for Mother," she warned.

A sly grin spread across his face. "Yes, Ruth."

She ran through the house and into the garden, finding her mother reclining on a blanket beneath a shady palm.

"Mother!" she panted.

"What is wrong, Ruth?"

"I am afraid for Father!"

"Why? Has something happened?"

"He is going to see that cruel man."

"You mean Harrash?"

"Yes!"

"Do not be afraid, Ruth," Dahlia said as the worry lines faded from her face. "Your father can handle a man like Harrash."

"You knew Father was going to see him?"

"I knew he planned to see him if he could find Orpah before she arrived at Harrash's home. I am assuming you met Orpah?"

"Yes, Mother, we met her. Well, sort of."

"*Sort of?* Please explain your meaning."

"She did not say much."

"Was she unhappy?"

"I believe so. She is a beautiful girl, but I have never seen sadder eyes. Well, they were sad until Father told her to go home."

"Then she was happy?"

"Oh, yes, Mother! Orpah smiled the biggest smile! Then she spun around and bolted for home. I do not think I should ever be able to run as fast as she did!"

"I would have run home, too. Harrash is a cruel master."

Dahlia patted the blanket and Ruth lay down next to her.

"Why would her father allow her to serve such a brutal man?"

"Of necessity, I am sure. It was likely a difficult decision for him to make."

Ruth closed her eyes, enjoying the fresh garden fragrances.

"Flowers have it easy," Ruth said.

"You have it easy, too! That is all that matters to me."

"Do you not care for Elimelech's family? Or Orpah's?"

"I care for you and your father. I care not for foreigners. As for Orpah, if Goad can help you by helping her then I am content."

Ruth shook her head, baffled. "Father cares for Orpah."

"Yes, yes!" Dahlia said, rolling her eyes. "Your father seems forever willing to help others and look where it has gotten us this time!"

"What do you mean?"

"Now you want to spend more time with those Israelites! It spells nothing but trouble to me, but I tire of the subject," Dahlia said, sounding withdrawn as she stood and began walking toward the house.

Closing her eyes, Ruth was thankful to be alone with her thoughts. She breathed deeply, again relishing the sweet aromas drifting across the garden.

Flowers have no worries, do they, Adonai? They simply look pretty for a season and then are gone. Why is life not like that for us? Do You set the limits of evil? Do You love my father? If You are all powerful, please protect him.

✡   ✡   ✡

The late-afternoon sun warmed Ruth's skin. She licked her parched lips, and wiped beads of perspiration from her brow as she drank water from a skin. How long could it take her father to visit with that horrible man? He should have come home long before now. Standing, she paced in circles around a sycamore tree, scraping the bark with a small limb.

"Ruth!" Dahlia yelled, clapping her hands.

Ruth clutched her chest. "Mother! You almost scared the life out of me! Is Father home yet?"

"No! No! No! For the last time, he is not home. Come in this house immediately! You are getting too much sun."

"I am fine, Mother. I keep shifting my blanket to follow the shade."

"See that you do! I do not want your skin red or blistered. And the next time you see me, do not ask if your father is home! You will see him when he gets here! Father this and Father that," Dahlia huffed as she turned and stormed into the house.

Ruth lay back down on the blanket and closed her eyes as a deep foreboding grew in her heart. Opening her eyes on occasion, she determined the location of the sun and moved her blanket. Panic began to fill her heart as the sun crept beneath the horizon.

Ruth watched as her mother appeared in the doorway, her eyes glaring. "Ruth! Come in this house immediately! Your meal will get cold!"

"I cannot eat. If I tried, I could not keep it down."

"Then get ready for bed. I tire of your worry. I will wake you when your father arrives."

Ruth rose obediently, stooping to retrieve the blanket.

"Leave it!" Her mother's voice bellowed. "That is why we have servants."

Weary from the burden of worry, Ruth did not protest. Dropping the blanket, she walked past her mother and into her bedchamber. Closing the door behind her, she climbed into bed, not bothering to change into her nightgown. Laying her head on the pillow, she struggled to stay awake.

"Please come home safely, Father," she mumbled as sleep overcame her.

Chapter 7

HARVEST CLOTHING

Ruth's body flinched and her eyes flew open. "Father!" she screamed. Tossing the covers aside, she attempted to leap from bed, realizing too late the linens were wrapped around her ankles. Falling forward, she landed with a thud.

At the sound of shuffling feet, her eyes darted toward the door. She stared wide-eyed as the servants poked their heads around the frame, looking amused.

Sitting up, she folded her arms across her chest. "Where is my father?" she quipped, red-faced.

One by one, the servants parted until Goad stood alone in the doorway. With an inquisitive look, he grinned.

"What in the world is wrong, Ruth?" he asked, approaching and kneeling beside her.

She buried her face into his chest. "Oh, Father, you are—alive!"

"Of course I am alive. Why would you think otherwise?"

Ruth eyed the servants as they crowded back into the doorway. Pouting, she wiped a tear away and then yanked the linens free. "You did not come home yesterday, like you promised! I was afraid Harrash had killed you."

Goad's body shook and the corners of his mouth turned suddenly upward, but not a sound came forth.

Ruth glared at him, the muscles in her jaw clinching. "Can you not see I am angry with you?"

Goad bit his lip and sighed. "I can see you are upset, but for the life of me I do not understand why."

"You were supposed to wake me when you arrived home. Mother promised you would!"

"I tried, my dear. I nudged your shoulders until you sat up and threw your arms around me with such force that we fell backward. Do you not remember?"

"No. I do not remember anything."

"I thought perhaps you would not."

The servants giggled. Goad jerked his head in their direction, arching his brows in warning. They fell silent.

"What did I do?"

"You seemed determined to pry my lips open. When I relented, you performed a thorough inspection of my mouth, turning my head this way and that. At last, you sighed and said, 'No teeth missing'. After patting my cheek, you lay back down. I tried talking to you, but you were fast asleep."

"I assume some of the servants were in the room when this took place?" The servants bobbed their heads. She grimaced. "I guess I provided some much needed entertainment?"

The servants laughed as they left the room to resume their duties. Goad stood, pulling Ruth to her feet.

"Why were you so late getting home?"

"After I went to see Harrash, I visited Orpah's father and from there went to Elimelech's."

"You went to see Elimelech?"

"Yes. When I arrived, he insisted I join them for their evening meal. By the time we finished eating and discussing Orpah, it was late."

"I want to hear all the details."

"I knew you would." He pointed at a new robe and tunic draped on the chair. "Your mother had the servants design harvest clothing for you last night while you were sleeping."

"They must have been up most of the night finishing them." Ruth hurried to the chair and studied the fabric. "They look plain enough!"

"Indeed," Goad said as he left, shutting the door behind him.

Ruth closed the shutter and then removed the servant's garments she had worn the previous day. Dipping a cloth into a basin of cool water, she washed her body and arranged her hair. Retrieving a small vase, she poured some lavender-scented oil in her hand and massaged it into her face and arms.

As Ruth pulled the new robe and tunic over her head, she noticed the soft, light feel of the material. They were perfect for working in the sun. She wrapped a plain-woven sash around her waist and tied her sandals.

Emerging from her room, she looked for her father, but he was not in the house. Walking into the courtyard, she saw her mother.

"Hmm," Dahlia said as she walked around her, examining her new garments. "I am not fond of the dull color, but the fabric is acceptable."

"Thank you, Mother. These will do just fine."

"Did you leave those horrid, rumpled robes in your room?"

"Yes, I thought the servant might want them back."

"I almost gave her a lashing she would not soon forget?"

"Mother! You would not!"

"She has been warned never to give in to your silly schemes again!"

"Please do not be angry with her. She obeyed my wishes without regard."

"Do not let it happen again or you will be responsible for the discipline she receives!" Dahlia handed Ruth a pouch filled with dates and freshly cooked bread. "Now go, your father is waiting," she said, pointing down the path.

Scanning the path, she observed her father standing some distance away. She ran until she was almost even with him and then slowed her pace.

"We are getting a late start," she said, panting. "I hope Naomi will not be upset with me."

"Not to worry. You look very pretty today. Does your harvest clothing meet with your approval?"

"Yes, Father, they are perfect! But I would rather talk about Orpah." She waited for a response, but he seemed deep in thought. "Father?" She touched his arm. "What happened after I left you yesterday?"

He frowned. "Well as you can imagine, the conversation with Harrash was not pleasant."

"I guess not," she said, kicking pebbles off the path. "Where did you find him?"

"I found him in his garden. At the mention of Orpah's name his face turned bright red and his eyes actually bulged."

"You see! I was right to be worried. He could have attacked you. Were you afraid?"

His eyes narrowed. "Of Harrash? No!" he scoffed. "I was not afraid. I simply told him I was taking Orpah to our field to serve you."

"You did not ask him?"

"Why would I ask him? He does not own her."

"That is true."

"He puffed out his chest like an angry rooster and shook his finger at me."

"What did he say?"

"That I had no right to take her from him. But I reminded him that Orpah's father was one of my supervisors and I had every right to take her as one of my servants."

"Did he try to strike your face, Father?" Ruth giggled, staring at his teeth.

"No," he said, rubbing his jaw in jest. "But I made a point not to stay long enough to find out!"

"Wise choice, Father. When you left did you go to see Orpah's father?"

"Yes. As I neared the field, I noticed a woman running toward me. She had a pail in her hand that was swinging back and forth wildly. If it had anything in it before she started running, it certainly would have spilled by the time she reached me. I kept wondering if she intended to use it on me!"

"Oh, my! What did you do?"

"I was contemplating whether or not to turn and run, but decided against looking like a coward, so stopped in my tracks and waited for whatever was coming my way." Goad looked at Ruth grinning, but said no more.

"And? Then what happened?"

"Just before the woman got to me she dropped the pail and nearly knocked me down in a full embrace."

"Full embrace? Mother will not be happy to hear about this."

"Not to worry. As it turned out—it was Orpah's grandmother."

"Orpah's grandmother! I wish I had been there to see it."

"I wish you had too. It was a sight to see. Needless to say, Orpah had already delivered the news to her family. Her grandmother did not know the specifics, but obviously assumed whatever arrangement I intended was better for her granddaughter than being subjected to Harrash."

"I am excited to see her!"

"You will not see her today."

Ruth stopped and began tapping her foot impatiently. "Why not?"

Goad tweaked her nose lightly and smiled.

"Please do not tease me, Father. I had a difficult night worrying about you. Besides, I waited all day yesterday, hoping you would arrive home *with* Orpah. Now I have to wait even *longer.*"

"You will see her soon enough. She has been through a very difficult time and her mother requested she spend a week at home with her family."

"I hope Harrash did not harm her."

"No permanent damage done. But he was often harsh toward her, from what her grandmother told me." Goad rested his hand on her shoulder. "The week will pass quickly enough."

"I suppose so," she sighed. "When Elimelech and Naomi heard your plan for Orpah, were they happy?"

"They were indeed. They were excited for you and for the extra help they would be receiving. And you know the rest of the story."

As they neared the field, Goad took Ruth's hand. "Be sure to be home in time today and every day to worship with your mother."

She planted a kiss on his cheek. "I will. I love you, Father."

He sighed and began walking home.

When Ruth arrived at the field, she looked back, watching her father until he disappeared from view. Turning, she ran toward Elimelech's home, wondering if the excitement in her heart was the same as Orpah had felt the day before.

Chapter 8

GLEANING

Beads of perspiration trickled down Ruth's face as she clutched her side. When was the last time she had run so hard? She could not remember. Grasping the corner of her tunic, she wiped the salty moisture from her face.

Movement in the field captured her attention. "Mahlon! Good morning," she yelled, watching as he waved his arms overhead and then pointed in the direction of the house.

"Thank you!" she shouted.

He bowed as though she were royalty, exaggerating the movement of his arm at his waist. She rolled her eyes. Was he teasing her, or did he think she put on airs? Examining her plain tunic, she sighed. Perhaps she was being overly sensitive. Forcing a smile, she waved and then continued down the path until arriving at the house. Peering into the main living area, she found Naomi cleaning up after the morning meal. The aroma of honey-roasted almonds lingered.

"I am sorry I am late."

Naomi smiled and motioned for her to enter.

"It is good to see you this morning," she paused, inspecting Ruth's face. "Have you been running?"

"Yes. I felt such a lightness of heart this morning that my feet carried me away."

Naomi chuckled. "Well, you certainly have a way with words. Are you sure you want to work in the field? There are easier chores you could learn to do."

"Yes, I am sure!"

"Really? Have you harvested barley before?"

Ruth shook her head.

"It is very taxing work, especially for a maiden of your stature."

"I can do it. You will see!"

"I believe you can. You certainly did a fine job milking goats. I am confident you will keep up with the other servants."

Naomi handed Ruth a stick with twine wound neatly around it and a small blade she would need for cutting the twine. "You will walk beside me and I will show you how the maidens assist the men in the harvest."

Leaving the house, they crossed the path and headed out into the field. Ruth marveled at the expanse of barley swaying in the strong breeze. Each gust made billows in an endless sea of silver grain.

"Why does harvesting begin when the barley is still white?"

"Because the grain will continue to ripen, even after it is cut. By the time the harvest is complete, the grain will be golden." Naomi pointed toward a group of men who were working deep in the field. "Do you see their sickles?"

Ruth watched the men as they swung their long, curved blades up in the air and down into the barley, the sun glistening along the edges.

"I do. So it is their job to cut the stalks?"

"Yes. Then the maidens follow behind, gathering the stalks and tying them into bundles, called sheaves."

"Father told me they stand groups of sheaves together. The groupings support the stalks and allow air to move freely through the barley."

"That is correct. We usually lean fifteen or twenty sheaves together

74

so the morning dew and rain easily drain off the heads—otherwise they would likely mildew and rot."

Ruth spotted Elimelech and his sons. They were working alongside the other men. She contemplated the pattern of the male servants as they stretched in a long parallel line across the field. Short distances behind the men were the maidens, working in pairs.

They continued making their way through the field until reaching Elimelech and his sons. The three men turned to greet them.

"Welcome, Ruth," Elimelech said, extending his hand.

"Good morning," she replied, shyly studying Mahlon.

"Are you ready to begin harvesting?" Mahlon asked, smiling broadly. Her heart fluttered. "I am."

"Shall we go back to work then?" Elimelech asked, keeping his gaze on his older son.

"Yes, sir."

Mahlon winked at Ruth as the three men turned and took up their positions in the field. Raising their sickles in the air, Ruth watched their blades slice deep into the stalks of grain.

Naomi began gathering barley until her arms were full. Laying the stalks on the ground, she bound the twine around them, tying it securely and then cutting the twine with the small flint blade.

Following her example, Ruth began to gather grain. Upon noticing several stalks left behind by the other maidens, she hurried to where they lay and knelt to retrieve them.

"Please do not gather the barley left behind," Naomi said in a firm voice.

Ruth winced. Releasing the barley, she stood to face Naomi. "But why?"

"We have a mitzvah—"

"What is a mitzvah?"

"It is a principle for living Adonai requires we follow."

75

"What does the mitzvah have to do with gathering stalks left behind? Is it not wasteful to leave the grain?"

Naomi frowned and Ruth lowered her gaze, ashamed her question seemed to disappoint Naomi. As she felt Naomi's hand resting on her shoulder, she lifted her head.

"I am sorry, Ruth. Please allow me to explain. We leave the grain for the poor to glean."

Ruth's mouth dropped. "Your people leave grain behind for the poor? I have not heard Father speak of it. I do not believe this is a mitzvah that our god, Chemosh, requires of my people."

"It is a mitzvah—a command of Adonai. We only go through the field one time to harvest. Any grain which falls to the ground, apart from the first gathering, is left for the poor to come and glean at will."

"Your God provides for the poor?"

"Yes."

"Mother believes Chemosh destroys the needy."

"Adonai's command says:

'When you reap the harvest of your land, you shall not wholly reap the corners of your field when you reap, nor shall you gather any gleaning from your harvest. You shall leave them for the poor and for the stranger: I am the LORD your God.'" *(Leviticus 23:22).*

"Adonai said to leave grain, even for strangers?"

"Yes. He requires us to leave the grain even for those sojourning in the land of Judah."

Ruth's heart quickened. If God rejected all mankind, apart from Abram's seed, why would He provide them food?

"Is there something bothering you, Ruth?"

Fear gripped her. Should she risk asking Naomi if Adonai would accept her? She dug her sandal into the soil.

"Ruth, did I say something that upset you?"

"No, of course not," she hesitated, searching frantically for a question to ask. And then it came to her. "I was just wondering if Adonai requires you follow His mitzvah even though you are not in the land of Israel?"

"Yes. Adonai requires us to follow His mitzvah wherever we may go."

Ruth looked beyond the field to the distant mountains separating Moab from the land of Judah, knowing Naomi must miss the land of her own people. Even so, Ruth hoped the famine would continue. She knew it was a terrible thing to hope for, but she could not help the way she felt. She did not want Naomi or her family to ever leave the land of the Moabites.

"I will ask my father if he will allow families in need to come and glean in this field."

Standing her sheave on the ground, Naomi faced Ruth, holding out her arms. Ruth stepped into her embrace.

"I have always wanted a daughter, my child," Naomi whispered in her ear. "You will be like a daughter to me."

Ruth nodded, swallowing the lump in her throat and vowing in her heart to help Naomi until her family returned to Judah.

As they continued binding sheaves, Ruth was keenly aware of Mahlon's presence. His voice seemed to resonate through the field in laughter and lighthearted conversation. On occasion, she attempted to steal glimpses of him; thankful Naomi seemed oblivious to her curiosity.

"Ruth?"

"Yes, Naomi. What is it?"

Naomi grasped Ruth's hand as she pointed to a tent where the maidens were gathering. They hurried to join them. As they entered the tent, Naomi dipped two goblets into a large cistern filled with water. They drank their fill and then retreated to the corner where Naomi reclined on a pallet. Ruth knelt beside her and felt her forehead.

"Are you feeling ill?"

"No, I am just very tired."

"Is that so?" Elimelech asked, approaching.

Ruth startled. "You are as quiet as a field mouse," she giggled.

"That he is," Naomi said, opening her eyes.

Elimelech grasped Naomi's hands, carefully pulling her to her feet.

Ruth sensed his concern. "I think Naomi has harvested enough for one day."

He smiled. "You are wise beyond your years, Ruth. I believe the two of us are in agreement. I will accompany Naomi to the house and then come back to check on you."

Watching as they walked away, Ruth noted Naomi's bent shoulders. Had she overdone? She hoped not. Lying back on her pallet, she dozed until Elimelech returned.

"And how are you holding up, Ruth?"

Recognizing the look of fatherly concern on his face, she attempted to reassure him. "I am tired," Ruth said with as much strength as she could muster. "But not too tired to continue harvesting." The truth? She was exhausted. But it was a good feeling, one she had never experienced before.

"I am proud of you, Ruth. You have worked in this field and given your time expecting nothing in return. This is the heart of a true servant, and Adonai is always pleased with a servant's heart."

"Adonai desires man to have a servant's heart?"

"Yes. The Torah says:

You shall fear the LORD *your God and serve Him, and shall take oaths in His name. You shall not go after other gods, the gods of the peoples who are all around you (for the* LORD *your God is a jealous God among you) . . ."*
(*Deuteronomy 6:13-15*).

"Adonai is a jealous God?"

"He is. It may sound strange, but Adonai does not want us to share our love with any other god. He commands that He is the only God we are to worship."

Ruth fell silent. Elimelech's God would not tolerate the worship of

Chemosh by His chosen people. But what about her? Did He care if she worshiped Chemosh?

Rolling the name of Adonai over and over in her mind, she sighed. She did not tire of hearing His name. "You serve your God, Adonai, and I will serve you and your family. Adonai will be pleased with me for this."

He chuckled. "Shall we take it a day at a time? By the completion of the barley harvest you may have changed your mind."

"I will not change my mind! I hope you will not change yours." Ruth studied Elimelech's kind face and as she did, her eyes were drawn to the unusual leather pouch tied just above his forehead.

"Ruth," he said as he untied a small flap on the pouch. "I wanted to show you something which is very important to my people."

"I have been wondering what is hidden inside."

Elimelech pulled a small piece of parchment from the pouch and unfolded it, showing it to Ruth. She looked curiously at the unusual symbols inked on it.

"When my people were in the wilderness and just before Adonai allowed us to enter our Promised Land, He gave us mitzvot to live by."

"Naomi just told me about one of your mitzvah that has to do with reaping and providing for the poor."

"That is correct. The mitzvot written on this parchment are reminders of ten very special commandments Adonai gave us on that special day. The most important commandment was to love Adonai and not to worship any other gods."

"But why do you wear the pouches on your head and arm?"

"We wear them because Adonai commanded us to. He said:

"And these words which I command you today shall be in your heart. You shall teach them diligently to your children, and shall talk of them when you sit in your house, when you walk by the way, when you lie down, and when you rise up. You shall bind them as a sign on your hand, and they shall be as frontlets between your eyes." (Deuteronomy 6:6-8).

"What are the other mitzvot written on the parchment?"

"We are not to misuse the name of Adonai; observe the day of Sabbath; honor our father and mother; not murder or commit adultery; not steal or give false evidence against our neighbor or covet what belongs to them . . ." Elimelech's voice trailed off as he appeared deep in thought. She stood watching him as he carefully tucked the piece of parchment back into the pouch.

"Work in the field for a few hours more, Ruth, and then you can help Naomi prepare the evening meal."

She nodded in agreement as he turned and began walking back to join the male servants.

Ruth worked diligently for the next few hours. As the other maidens began leaving the field, she hurried to the house. The aromas of freshly cooked grain filled the air as she entered.

"How did you hold up?" Naomi asked, smiling.

"Very well!"

Naomi eyed the damp hair plastered against the sides of Ruth's face. "Come with me," she said.

Ruth followed her into the bedroom. Naomi retrieved a wooden brush. Approaching Ruth, she turned her backward and removed her head covering.

As Ruth tied the covering at her waist, she felt Naomi's gentle hands gathering her hair.

"Your mother would not be pleased to see your hair in such a state," Naomi said as she moved the brush through her long locks.

"I did not anticipate Mother's disapproval, but you are right. Thank you."

After Naomi completed the thorough brushing, she arranged Ruth's hair and then inserted several combs to hold it in place.

"Much better!" Naomi said, examining her handiwork. "I am sure your mother will be pleased."

Ruth hugged her. "You are sweet. Now I will help you set the table for dinner."

"No, my child, you will go home to your mother."

"But—"

"You have done enough for one day. I am sure Dahlia has a meal prepared and waiting for you."

She nodded. "Very well then, I will go." She kissed Naomi's cheek and headed out to the path. She had only walked a short distance when she felt her stomach rumble. Naomi was right! She was famished. Just as she determined to hasten her step, she sensed someone beside her.

"Mahlon!" she gasped, turning to face him.

Chapter 9

MAHLON

Mahlon walked a mere arm's length away from her. Nervously she ran her palms down her tunic. Mahlon tapped her shoulder, pointing into the distance and then took out running.

"Wait, Mahlon!" she yelled after him. "Where are you going?"

He turned back, motioning for her to follow. "Come on!"

As she began running, a gust of wind blew through her hair, tossing the combs to the ground. Her hair fell to her waist, the sun's rays accentuating its reddish-brown highlights. She blushed.

"Ruth!"

"Wait!" Retrieving the combs, she twisted her hair into a long, thick braid, laying it over her shoulder. Meeting his gaze, she smiled shyly and then continued to run in his direction. She reached him at the stream's edge, winded.

He seemed particularly amused as he took his time inspecting her disheveled appearance. She frowned.

His eyes softened and he smiled. Tossing his sandals to the side, he sat down, dipping his feet into the clear water. He lifted his gaze, staring at her with his big brown eyes. Her heart skipped a beat.

"Please, will you sit with me?" he asked.

She hesitated, scanning the area.

"Please?" he asked again, resting his hand purposefully on the ground.

"If you insist." Shaking her sandals free, she sat beside him on the bank. "But only for a few minutes."

"I am glad Father allowed me to walk you home today. I did not think he would."

"Why?"

"Oh, well, . . . it is nothing you need be concerned about."

"Is that so?" She frowned, attempting to decipher the odd look on his face.

"Yes," he said, smiling. "I wanted to stop at the stream so we would have time to visit."

She swirled the cool water with her toes. "I am glad we did. I love this stream. I stopped here a few days ago when I needed time alone—to think."

"What were you thinking about?"

A mischievous grin crept across her face. "Oh, well, . . . it is nothing you need be concerned about," she said, mimicking him.

He leaned back, laughing. "Is that so?"

His smile faded. Remaining silent, he continued to regard her with a look of admiration. Finally, she could bear it no longer.

"Well, if you must know—I was thinking about how to convince my parents to allow me to spend more time with your family."

"I see." He chuckled. "It appears your plan was successful."

She bit her lip, wondering what her mother would say if she knew she was spending time alone with this handsome Israelite.

"I do not want to talk about me. I want to know more about your people."

"Well then, ask away."

"Why are you not an Abramite?"

"An Abramite?" Mahlon laughed. "Where did you come up with

84

that name?"

"My people descended from Lot's son, Moab, thus we are called Moabites."

"I see, so because I descended from Abram, I should be an Abramite?"

"Well, yes."

"I never thought of it that way, but we are not Abramites; we are Israelites."

"Where did that name come from?"

Mahlon tilted his head as though surprised by her question. "Well, let me see, Abram had a son named Isaac and Isaac had a son named Jacob. It was Jacob whose name Adonai changed to Israel."

"Why did Adonai change his name?"

"Jacob, at the time, was living in a foreign land when Adonai spoke to him, telling him to take his family and all he owned and return to the land of his father Isaac. He obeyed. One night, during the journey home, Jacob sent everyone ahead of him and spent the night alone. My father had me commit the story to memory. Would you like to hear it?"

"Yes, please."

He closed his eyes and began reciting Scripture, saying:

Then Jacob was left alone; and a Man wrestled with him until the break of day. Now when He saw that He did not prevail against him, He touched the socket of his hip: and the socket of Jacob's hip was out of joint as He wrestled with him. And He said, "Let Me go, for the day breaks."

But he said, "I will not let You go unless You bless me!"

So He said to him, "What is your name?"

He said, "Jacob."

And He said, "Your name shall no longer be called Jacob, but Israel; for you have struggled with God and with men, and have prevailed."

Then Jacob asked, saying, "Tell me Your name, I pray."

And He said, "Why is it that you ask about My name?" And He blessed him there. (Genesis 32:24-29).

Filled with excitement, she clasped her hands. "I have so many questions!"

"I would think it out of character if you did not."

"Who was the Man Jacob struggled with?"

"Who do you think He was?"

"I think He was Adonai."

"I agree."

"But did Jacob know he struggled with Adonai?"

"Yes, because after the struggle, Jacob said:

"For I have seen God face to face, and my life is preserved." (Genesis 32:30).

"I love that your people pass down stories from generation to generation."

"It is very important. We are told the stories over and over and memorize them word for word. It is part of our parent's responsibility to make sure all Scripture is committed to heart. So, speaking of names, what does yours mean?"

"It means *friend, companion.*"

"That fits you perfectly," Mahlon said as he cupped his hand in the stream, raising it to his lips. "Do you have more questions?"

"It would be out of character if I did not." She tried to wink at him, but her lids did not cooperate.

He laughed. "I have never known a girl like you, that is for certain!"

"I will assume that was a compliment."

"Of course. Next question."

"Let me see . . . Oh, yes, I remember hearing my father mention *The Twelve Tribes of Israel.* Who are they?"

"Jacob had twelve sons and each son was referred to as a tribe, thus The Twelve Tribes of Israel."

She nodded; fascinated by the calm, steady sound of his voice. It reminded her of the stream, meandering its way through her toes.

Chapter 9 – MAHLON

"Ruth?"

"Yes, Mahlon, is something wrong?"

"I wonder how you feel about my family living among your people."

"I am very happy to have you here. So is my father." She wondered if the tone of her voice sounded reassuring. She hoped so. She meant the words from the depth of her being. There was an excitement and expectancy in her life she had never felt before.

"And your mother, how does she feel about my family living in Moab?"

She looked away. Should she lie to him? She drew her gaze back to his. "She is not all that happy about it." His eyes were sad. Her heart fell. "Please do not worry about my mother." She studied his countenance. Had she convinced him?

"I am not surprised, Ruth. Do not worry about it." He shrugged. "Perhaps we should discuss a more pleasant subject. Would you be interested in knowing what my father's name means?"

"Yes, I would."

"It means *God is my King.*"

"What a wonderful meaning! It fits him too."

"It does. But many in Bethlehem judged him unkindly when he left to sojourn into Moab."

"Why? It is evident he loves and serves Adonai with all his heart."

"They did not want him to leave, even though he had stayed in Judah long after the drought had begun and after many had already left. Only the wealthiest field owners were able to harvest and store enough food to stay in the land. I can remember hearing Father on many a night, when he thought we were asleep, praying to God for direction and mercy. There were days he did not eat or drink as he cried out to Adonai, not only for our family but for all the families in the Promised Land."

"Did Adonai answer?"

"Yes, but not in the way my father expected."

"What do you mean?"

"Adonai spoke to my father in a dream."

"Spoke to him? Like God spoke to Abram and to Jacob?"

"Yes. My father had been crying out to God in anguish over the famine and the plight of our family. Our stores of food were running low. On this particular day, my father dropped to his knees, tore his robes and threw dust upon his head."

"Why?"

"He was beseeching God to answer his prayer."

"And Adonai answered him?"

"Yes."

Hope rose within her.

Could it be true? Adonai answered Elimelech's prayer?

Mahlon stood and extended his hands to her. She accepted. His touch sped the beating of her heart. Feeling his calloused hands as he pulled her from the ground, she thought of her father. She would never marry a man who was not at least as kind as he.

They slipped their sandals on.

"Please continue," she said as they made their way to the path.

"That night as my father slept, he had a dream. In the dream he saw your father's field."

"He actually saw my father's field in his dream?"

"Yes, Ruth. And God told him, 'Sojourn to the land of the Moabites for I have prepared a place for you there.'"

"And your father believed the dream was from Adonai?"

"Yes."

"Even though he had not yet heard from my father?"

"Yes, and when word came that there was a man in the land of Moab seeking a reliable supervisor for his field, my father said yes without hesitation. It was a wonderful day of rejoicing at Adonai's provision for our family."

She considered his words. They were shocking. She wanted to believe them, but still her heart filled with doubt. "Have others heard Adonai speak to them in dreams?"

"Many times. Adonai's Word says:

In a dream, in a vision of the night,
When deep sleep falls upon men,
While slumbering on their beds,
Then He opens the ears of men,
And seals their instruction. (Job 33:15-16).

As Mahlon recited the words from memory, she thought of Chemosh. She was thankful the Moabite god had never spoken to her mother. But the God of Mahlon spoke to His people through His Word and in dreams and visions. Had she heard Him speak? And then the words wandered through her like a whisper: *'If you search for Me with your whole heart, you will find Me.'*

Mahlon motioned for her to sit by the well. She approached a large boulder. Scooting to one side, she left room for him. But instead, he slowly dropped to the ground in front of her and crossed his legs. The expression on his face seemed oddly familiar. Where had she seen it before?

"What will happen to you, Ruth, when we leave Moab?"

"Please do not let your family leave, Mahlon." Her voice quivered. She stood, turning her back to him. "I cannot bear the thought of living in this land without your family."

"I am sorry, Ruth, but someday we will go back to Judah. We have no choice. It is the land Adonai gave to us and when the famine is lifted by His hand, we will return there."

"And you will marry an Israelite."

He stood and gently grasped her shoulders. "I will," he said, turning her to face him. "And you will marry a Moabite."

They remained motionless, their eyes fixed and searching. As tears welled and spilled down her cheeks, he wiped them away.

"You will be as a sister to me, Ruth, and I will love and protect you for as long as we dwell in your land."

She nodded. "And you will be as a brother to me."

There was no need for further discussion. She knew the painful truth: that while they were drawn to each other from the moment they met, they could be no more than friends. But she found solace in the realization of how deeply he cared.

"I will go the rest of the way alone," she said.

He nodded, standing transfixed.

She strolled down the path, glancing back at him one last time, wondering what her future would hold.

He waved and then turned toward his home.

Focusing her thoughts on Adonai, she knew she must learn more of her own people and heritage. Why had the Moabites chosen to worship Chemosh? How could she find the answers without offending her mother? And worse yet, could she bear the truth revealed by them?

Chapter 10

THE STORY OF LOT

"Ruth," Dahlia called down the path. "Please join me in the garden."

Please? Ruth stopped, studying her in the distance. Could it be possible her mother was in a pleasant mood?

Dahlia began to wave excitedly. "Ruth!"

"Yes, Mother, I am coming!" she yelled as Dahlia disappeared from view. She continued running until nearing the garden. Rounding the corner, she slowed her pace, observing her mother resting on a blanket beneath a large palm. Why was she not in the house preparing for worship?

Approaching with caution, she studied her mother's countenance. Her face held a look of contentment, and she marveled at her beauty. Her features were striking. Her long, thick lashes curved upward, the morning sun reflecting the flecks of gold scattered across her deep hazel eyes.

Dahlia motioned for her to sit. "I have been anxious for you to arrive home," she said, smiling.

"Why?" Ruth asked, perplexed by the melodious tone of her voice.

"Cannot a mother miss her only child?"

Only child! How can Mother deny the existence of her son? Is it because she is afraid Chemosh took his life? I best not ask her . . .

Ruth lay on the blanket beside her, tucking her hands beneath her

91

head. "Did the cedar chest Father imported from Egypt arrive?"

"Yes, along with a variety of colorful urns and spices. They also delivered the most exquisite purple embroidered linen I have ever seen."

"I thought the servants would have kept you busy designing your new garments."

"The servants?" she scoffed. "I tire of being tugged this way and that for their endless fittings. I informed them you would stand in for me tomorrow."

"But I—"

"Do not protest! If you rise early, I am sure they can complete the task in a timely manner. Regardless, I can oversee their design more easily with you as my model."

Ruth sighed, realizing there was nothing to be gained in belaboring the issue. Perhaps if she changed the subject her mother would forget!

"Why are you in the garden at this time of day?"

"I have been enjoying the sun and cool afternoon breeze. But I tire of small talk. What did you learn about the foreigners today?"

"Oh, Mother, you would find it all very boring, I am sure."

"Let me be the judge of that."

"I will admit being around them has made me curious about our own heritage."

"Is that so? Well, perhaps some good has come from this day after all."

"Would you mind telling me about our forefathers? I have some vague memory of a man named Lot who lived in a city called Sodom, but I do not recall much beyond that."

"Lot did reside in Sodom. But he did not remain there."

"Why?"

"Because the city was destroyed."

"Destroyed? But how?"

"It is a long story to tell."

"Please share it with me, Mother. There is plenty of time left in the day.

"Well then, let me see . . . As I recall, Abram's God spoke to him, telling him that the cities of Sodom and Gomorrah were filled with morally corrupt men and because of that, He was going to destroy them. But Abram pleaded on Sodom's behalf."

"What did Abram say?"

"He asked his God if He would destroy the righteous with the wicked.

Righteous? Where had she heard that word before?

"What was God's response?

"He said if He found even as few as ten righteous men, He would spare the city."

"Did He?"

"No. There was only one man found to be righteous."

"Who was it?"

"Our ancestor, Lot."

Her heart leapt, remembering where she had heard the word. It was Abram! Adonai deemed him a righteous man.

"Lot!" she hesitated, determining to choose her words wisely. "What happened to him?"

"The story is told that two angels visited Sodom and found Lot sitting at the gate. He rose to meet them and then bowed himself to the ground."

"Why would he bow to them?"

"He recognized they were angels sent by Abram's God. He insisted they come to his house where he prepared a feast for them. While the angels were there, the men of the city came and banged on the door, insisting Lot send the men out so they could know them in a carnal way."

"Mother! Are you saying what I think you are?"

"Yes, my child. As I said, Sodom was a wicked city. But Lot refused to hand them over, begging the inhabitants to reconsider. But the crowd became even more riotous, accusing Lot of acting as judge and threatening to deal worse with him than the men he attempted to protect. It was at that point the angels intervened, pulling Lot inside the house and striking his attackers with blindness. When morning came, the angels took Lot, his wife and two daughters and set them outside the city, as Abram's God had chosen to spare their lives. So Lot escaped destruction."

"What happened to his son, Moab?"

"Well," Dahlia said, hesitating. "The truth is, Moab had not been born."

"Lot's wife bore Moab after they escaped?"

"No. Lot's wife died."

"Died? Why? I thought God spared them?"

"He had, but she did not heed the angels' warning. They were told to leave and not look back, but she disobeyed. The moment she did, she turned into a pillar of salt."

"She did not fear Adonai if she refused to heed His angels' warning."

"It would appear so. It was not a wise choice on her part. That is why we should obey Chemosh without question."

How could she justify comparing Adonai to Chemosh? Absurd!

"Mother, you believe the God of Abram was powerful enough to destroy an entire city?"

"Of course. The destruction of Sodom is common knowledge among our people. Although we do not worship their God, we do not deny His power."

Ruth shook her head in disbelief, confused by her mother's reasoning. "So what happened to Lot? I assume he remarried."

"No, my child," she said, hesitating. "He did not."

Ruth pondered the troubled expression on her face. "What are you saying, Mother?"

"I suppose you are old enough now to know the truth," Dahlia said, avoiding Ruth's questioning stare. "The fact is, Lot fathered two sons—by his daughters."

His daughters! Ruth felt a pain in the pit of her stomach. What must Naomi and Elimelech think of their past kinsman?

Ruth sat, staring at her mother—her mouth agape. "Why would he commit such a grievous act? He must have been a cruel father!"

"Not at all, Ruth! It was his daughters who deceived him."

"Mother! How could that be—"

"Wait, Ruth! Let me explain. They justified what they did, because they believed apart from their act of deception, they would never bear children."

"Why would they believe such an absurdity?"

"Lot was afraid, so he took his daughters and went to live in a cave in the mountains. Because of his decision to live in seclusion, his daughters believed they would never marry and thus there would be no son to carry on his lineage."

"But how did they carry out such a grievous act without his consent?"

"They gave him wine and he became like a drunkard; not knowing when his daughters lay with him or when they arose. Both daughters bore him a son. The oldest daughter named her son Moab. We are his descendants."

"Well, Mother, I am sure he was devastated by their act of betrayal."

"Do not judge too harshly, Daughter. Had you been in their situation, you may have acted the same."

"No, Mother, if faced with their reality, I would choose to die childless!" Ruth shook her head, grimacing. "Our ancestry does not hold much honor."

A look of defiance covered Dahlia's face as she sat up, glaring. "Do you think Elimelech's family has any higher honor than ours? Well if you think so, you are mistaken!"

"I am sorry, Mother, I should not have—"

"Enough!" Dahlia held up her hand. "So you question our ancestry, do you?" Well, have they told you about Abram? Have they told you he was willing to sacrifice his only son to his God?"

The words pierced Ruth's heart. Adonai required His people to sacrifice their young? Unfathomable!

"Mother! That cannot be true!"

"You heard me! Why do you not ask *those foreigners* you seem so taken with? Our heritage holds as much honor as theirs!"

As she rose, Ruth attempted to join her.

"Stay here," Dahlia sighed. "I think it best if I worship alone today." She managed a terse smile as she touched Ruth's cheek. "I am sorry if you believe me harsh. The truth can be difficult to bear, but you must not think those Israelites' heritage has more worth than our own."

Ruth grasped her mother's hand as she peered up into the palm tree. "Do you ever wonder, Mother, if there is a Great Designer?"

"Great Designer? Ruth, I have no idea what you are talking about."

"I was just thinking about all the manmade finery Father has provided, like the necklace you wear, intricately sculpted from gold. Or the vases scattered throughout our home, skillfully crafted from ivory. It is apparent they were fashioned by the hands of master craftsmen."

"True," she responded. "What is your point?"

"Well, for instance, look at the branches of this palm. Do you not see their intricate design?"

Dahlia yanked her hand free. "Intricate design of tree branches!" she huffed. "I declare! You worry me sometimes, Ruth!"

"I am sorry, Mother. I was just having a random thought."

"Well, you best learn to keep those to yourself!" Dahlia grasped her robes and swept them around as she stormed to the house.

Watching her walk away, Ruth was overcome with sorrow. How could someone as refined as her mother appreciate the craftsmanship of manmade things yet fail to see the miraculous design of nature? Even their own bodies must surely be the work of The Master's Hand, perhaps the same One who lay out the pattern of the branches towering above her.

Chapter 10 - THE STORY OF LOT

Lying back on the blanket, Ruth thought of Abram and Sarai and how their God, El Shaddai, promised them a son from their own bodies. And Abram trusted, believing his descendants would one day be a great nation.

As her thoughts wandered to Lot, her heart filled with hope. El Shaddai sent angels to rescue him from Sodom because He considered Lot a righteous man. But what did that mean? If He saw Lot as righteous, why was he not included in the blessings of Abram? Perhaps he was after all? Naomi had said that through Abram *all the families of the earth would be blessed*! Lot had been spared because of Abram's plea on his behalf. Could that blessing extend through time to a Moabite?

As the aromas of roasting lamb, herbs and freshly baked bread drifted across the garden, her stomach growled. She was famished! Should she sneak into the kitchen and grab a bite to eat before dinner? Perhaps it was not worth the risk.

Rolling on her side, she yawned, recalling her mother's accusation against Abram. She knew some radical worshipers of Chemosh were known to conduct human sacrifices, but she never considered Adonai would require the same. She shook her head. No, there may be some truth to the story, but could it be the whole truth? She knew Elimelech's family could answer her questions, but dare she ask and risk offending them—losing their friendship? And if their God required them to sacrifice their young, did she want to know more of Him?

Wearied by her mother's accusations against the Israelites, she forgot her hunger. Closing her eyes, she drifted to sleep.

Chapter 11

THE SACRIFICE

Ruth ran through the open doorway, slipping along the stone floor and narrowly avoiding the table where Elimelech's family was gathered.

The three men rose as Ruth stood before them, adjusting her head covering.

"You are out and about early this morning, Ruth!" Elimelech said, motioning for her to join Chilion on the bench.

"I could not wait to get here," she panted as she struggled to catch her breath. "Although my mother's plans almost prevented my early arrival."

"Plans?" Naomi questioned as she set a plate of food in front of her.

Ruth held a slice of freshly baked bread to her nose and took a deep breath. The warm aroma of the grain made her mouth water. "Mmmm," she said, taking a bite. "Delicious! Mother wanted me to—" she stopped mid-sentence to swallow. "I am sorry! It is unbecoming a maiden to talk with her mouth full."

"Yes," Naomi chuckled. "We know. Please continue."

Ruth laid the bread on the plate. Her face beamed as she met their inquisitive stares. "Mother wanted me to stand in for her fitting this morning, but I roused the servants a bit too early for her liking."

"Ah, wise planning on *your* part," Mahlon said, grinning.

Ruth ignored his assessment, fixing her eyes on Naomi. "Mother sent the servants back to their quarters saying we would postpone the fitting."

"To what may we attribute your early arrival then? Are you excited to harvest more barley?" Chilion interjected as the table erupted in laughter.

"Not exactly," she said, stalling as she attempted to muster her courage. "Mother told me something about Abram." Looking at Elimelech, she winced.

"What did she say?" Elimelech asked as his face grew serious.

Ruth looked at each of them in sequence—suddenly apprehensive of repeating her mother's accusation.

Mahlon sat up in his chair. "Go on, Ruth, what did your mother say?"

"Well, Mother said Abram was willing to sacrifice his son to your God." The family sat silent. Ruth's voice shook as she attempted to continue, "But I could not believe—"

"You could not believe what?" Mahlon asked.

She took a jagged breath. "The truth is, some who worship Chemosh sacrifice their young, but why would your people do the same?"

"Ah! I see," Elimelech responded. "It is acceptable to question, Ruth, but perhaps you should hear the whole story of Abram and Sarai before deciding what you think."

Elimelech turned his head in Mahlon's direction and nodded.

Mahlon acknowledged his father, as he began the story.

"And Adonai said:

"*As for Me, behold, My covenant is with you, and you shall be a father of many nations. No longer shall your name be called Abram, but your name shall be Abraham; for I have made you a father of many nations.*" (*Genesis* 17:4-5).

"God changed Abram's name to Abraham?" Ruth asked.

"Yes, He did," Mahlon said as he looked at his younger brother and smiled.

Chilion eyed his father with excitement and then turned toward Ruth, saying:

And God said to Abraham: "As for you, you shall keep My covenant, you and your descendants after you throughout their generations. This is My covenant which you shall keep, between Me and you and your descendants after you: Every male child among you shall be circumcised; . . . he who is born in your house or bought with money from any foreigner who is not your descendant." (Genesis 17:9-10; 12).

"So Adonai also required foreigners among them to be circumcised?" Ruth asked.

"Yes." Chilion responded.

Ruth shifted on the bench, delighted by the realization that foreigners were included in Adonai's command.

Elimelech continued the story, saying:

"And so Abraham did as Adonai instructed, circumcising all males in the camp. This also included a son Abraham had by Sarai's slave girl."

"Abraham already had a son?" Ruth asked.

"Yes," Naomi said, "Sarai knew she was to bear a son, but she grew discouraged and began to doubt. So she decided to give her slave girl, Hagar, to her husband, hoping to obtain a son through her. Abram did as Sarai requested, going in to Hagar. She bore a son and they named him Ishmael. After Ishmael was born, Abraham cried out:

And Abraham said to God, "Oh, that Ishmael might live before You!"

Then God said: . . . "And as for Ishmael, I have heard you. Behold, I have blessed him, and will make him fruitful, and will multiply him exceedingly. He shall beget twelve princes, and I will make him a great nation. But My covenant I will establish with Isaac . . ." (Genesis 17:18-19; 20-21).

"What happened to Sarai?"

Naomi responded, saying:

Then God said to Abraham, "As for Sarai your wife, you shall not call her name Sarai, but Sarah shall be her name. And I will bless her and also give you a son by her; . . . and you shall call his name Isaac; I will establish My covenant with him for an everlasting covenant, and with his descendants after him." (Genesis 17:15-16; 19).

"Just as God promised, the following year Sarah gave birth to a son and they named him Isaac."

"And Abraham circumcised him on the eighth day, as God commanded," Mahlon added.

"So how could Abram—I mean Abraham have come to the place in his life where he would consider sacrificing his son?"

"Ruth, how do we come to know a person's true character?" Elimelech asked.

She thought for a moment, remembering Lot's daughters. "Adversity can reveal someone's character."

"You are wise in your answer," Mahlon said. "We believe that Adonai tests those He loves. And that is exactly what He did to Abraham. He tested him."

"Continue the story," Elimelech said, looking at his youngest son.

Chilion acknowledged him, saying:

Now it came to pass after these things that God tested Abraham, and said to him, "Abraham!"

And he said, "Here I am."

Then He said, "Take now your son, your only son Isaac, whom you love, and go to the land of Moriah, and offer him there as a burnt offering on one of the mountains of which I shall tell you."

So Abraham rose early in the morning and saddled his donkey, and took two of his young men with him, and Isaac his son; and he split the wood for the burnt offering, and arose and went to the place of which God had told him. Then on the third day Abraham lifted his eyes and saw the place afar off. And Abraham said to his young men, "Stay here with the donkey; the lad and I will go yonder and worship, and we will come back to you." (Genesis 22:1-5).

"God was testing Abraham, was He not?" Ruth asked, looking at Elimelech.

Elimelech smiled and his voice filled with emotion as he proceeded with the story:

So Abraham took the wood of the burnt offering and laid it on Isaac his son; and he took the fire in his hand, and a knife, and the two of them went together. But Isaac spoke to Abraham his father and said, "My father!" (Genesis 22:6-7).

Elimelech's voice caught. Naomi reached across the table, gently touching his hand and then she continued the story, saying:

Isaac spoke to Abraham his father and said, "My father!"

And he said, "Here I am, my son."

Then he said, "Look, the fire and the wood, but where is the lamb for a burnt offering?"

And Abraham said, "My son, God will provide for Himself the lamb for a burnt offering." So the two of them went together.

Then they came to the place of which God had told him. And Abraham built an altar there and placed the wood in order; and he bound Isaac his son and laid him on the altar, upon the wood. And Abraham stretched out his hand and took the knife to slay his son. (Genesis 22:7-10).

All fell silent for a time as tears welled in Ruth's eyes. "Abraham trusted God and Isaac trusted his father, even to the point of death!"

"Yes," Mahlon said as he looked at his father and then at Ruth saying:

But the Angel of the LORD called to him from heaven and said, "Abraham, Abraham!"

So he said, "Here I am."

And He said, "Do not lay your hand on the lad, or do anything to him; for now I know that you fear God, since you have not withheld your son, your only son, from Me."

Then Abraham lifted his eyes and looked, and there behind him was a

103

ram caught in a thicket by its horns. So Abraham went and took the ram, and offered it up for a burnt offering instead of his son. And Abraham called the name of the place, The-LORD-Will-Provide; as it is said to this day, "In the Mount of the LORD it shall be provided."

Then the Angel of the LORD called to Abraham a second time out of heaven, and said: "By Myself I have sworn, says the LORD, because you have done this thing, and have not withheld your son, your only son—blessing I will bless you, and multiplying I will multiply your descendants as the stars of the heaven and as the sand which is on the seashore; and your descendants shall possess the gate of their enemies. In your seed all the nations of the earth shall be blessed, because you have obeyed My voice." (Genesis 22:11-18).

The family remained silent as Ruth clasped her hands together and closed her eyes, mulling over all she had heard.

Finally gathering her thoughts, she spoke. "Adonai's testing revealed to Isaac his father's trust in God and sealed the covenant He made with Abraham," Ruth said as hope filled her. "And Abraham's trust would bring future blessings to all nations." Wide-eyed, Ruth studied them, awaiting affirmation.

"That is right!" Elimelech said.

"Adonai never planned to allow Abraham to take his son's life, did He?"

"I do not know the answer to your question. I can only tell you that Abraham's own words reveal his belief that God would spare his son."

"Yes, they did!" Ruth said, remembering. "Because Abraham told his servants that he and Isaac would go and worship and then they would return to them?"

"True," Elimelech responded. "And when Isaac asked his father where the sacrifice was, Abraham told him that God would provide the lamb for the offering."

"I also believe Adonai wanted our people to know the extent of Abraham's and Isaac's trust because He expects the same trusting from us," Mahlon said.

"And because your people pass the stories on from generation to generation, you will not forget," Ruth added.

Elimelech smiled, as he stood. "I would say it is time for my family to reap a harvest!"

Ruth clapped her hands as she rose to join them.

"And Ruth," Elimelech paused as the smile faded from his face. "I believe it is time for you to go home."

"Go home?" Ruth asked in shock. "Have I offended your family?"

"No, my child, but I fear you have offended your mother."

"How?"

"By now I am sure she realizes your motive in rousting the servants from their much needed sleep. You can be sure that if you do not go back home now, doing as your mother requested, you may not be allowed to return."

Ruth looked in protest at Mahlon, but he kept his eyes focused on his father. Then she looked at Naomi, but found no sympathy in her steady gaze.

"Yes, sir," she said as she dropped her shoulders and began walking toward the door.

"I hope we will see you tomorrow," Elimelech said.

Ruth turned back to face him, wiping a tear away. "You do?"

Elimelech's eyes were filled with compassion. "Of course, Ruth. We will be praying for your return."

Ruth walked to Elimelech, wrapping her arms around him. "Thank you for praying for me. I fear you are right. I will obey Mother and hopefully she will allow me to come back."

Ruth glanced at Mahlon and then turned, running from the house as fast as her legs would carry her.

Chapter 12

ORPAH

Ruth awoke to an unusual stillness in the house. She dressed and then quietly left her bedchamber, entering the main living area. She expected to see her mother sitting in the chair near the door, but it was empty. Leaving the room, she walked to the back of the house. The servants, who would normally be in the kitchen preparing breakfast, were nowhere to be seen. At a halting, furtive pace, she crept toward the window, but stopped abruptly, recognizing the hushed voices of her parents arguing in the garden.

Fearful, she looked for a place to hide, settling on the small wine cellar located near the back door. The room smelled musty as she weaved her way through the skins hanging from the ceiling in neat, narrow rows. Retreating to the corner, she stood motionless. What could her parents be discussing? It must surely involve her, but why? She had come home early the previous day, submitting herself to endless hours of fittings. The remainder of the day the two spent sampling various dishes the servants made using the spices her father imported. Her mother seemed content at day's end. Could her assessment have been wrong?

Suddenly the idea of hiding from them seemed ridiculous. She made her way back through the wine skins as her parents entered the kitchen;

her mother's face was filled with fear.

Alarmed, she stepped backward. "What is wrong?"

Her father's lips were thin and pursed. "Something has happened to Orpah."

Ruth felt suddenly nauseous and her knees started to give way. Dahlia hurried to her side, grabbing her by the waist to steady her. Her father, however, remained near the door.

"Tell me what happened!"

"I will, if you remain calm!" Dahlia said. "I do not want you fainting."

Ruth closed her eyes, attempting to slow her breathing.

Dahlia led her to the table, gently guiding her into the chair. "Someone entered Orpah's home while the family was sleeping last night and carried her away."

"They found her this morning near the well," Goad said.

"Is she dead?"

"No. But she is near death!"

"But who would do such a thing?"

"Chemosh!" Dahlia whispered, glaring at Goad.

"No, Dahlia, I told you this is the work of Harrash! Of that I am certain."

"I warned you Chemosh would not tolerate those foreigners in our land, and Ruth spending time with them!"

Ruth looked at her mother in horror, covering her ears. "No! Surely I have not been the cause of this?"

Dahlia did not respond.

Ruth clinched her fists, her eyes narrow and piercing. "Where is she? I want to see her!"

"You cannot see her now," Goad said.

"But why?"

"For her safety, we have hidden her," he replied, his face softening.

Ruth sensed her father's anguish. An image of him standing over his dead son's body flashed through her mind.

Overcome with sorrow, she approached him. "Oh, Father, I am so sorry."

He hugged her. "This is not your fault, Ruth. We will keep her in seclusion until we find and deal with whoever has perpetrated this horrendous act."

"Will she live, Father?"

"I hope so, but she was badly beaten and is still unconscious."

"I *have* to tell Elimelech." Pulling away from his embrace, she attempted to move toward the door but he blocked her way. Turning she gave her mother a pleading glance, but her brow was furrowed.

"You will not be going back to see those foreigners," Dahlia said.

"But I have to! They are expecting me!" Ruth turned to her father, but his face remained stern, his silence—palpable. "Father," she begged, wiping tears from her face. "They will worry if I do not come."

"No, Ruth. You will not go to see them. Have I made myself clear?"

Ruth looked at her mother, imploring her to speak, but she remained mute.

Crossing her arms, she stomped her foot on the floor. Goad frowned, his eyes set and unyielding. Her heart beat erratically as she held his inscrutable glare and then she spun around and ran from the room.

She approached the hallway leading to the room of worship. Dropping to her knees, she crawled along the floor, feeling for the rug resting beneath the stone idol. Upon reaching the table, she lay prostrate before him. Listening, she heard her parents as they continued to argue until at last, her father's voice became muffled and faded.

The house was silent.

Ruth noticed flickers of light. She turned to see her mother lighting the lamps. Ruth leaned forward again closing her eyes, attempting to block the shadow of Chemosh dancing across the ceiling and down the wall. Even with her eyes closed, she could not escape the images of him as he hovered overhead.

Ruth felt the brush of Dahlia's hand as she knelt beside her and then lay face down on the floor. She began to chant. As the guttural hum of her voice grew louder, Ruth felt an evil presence in the room. Her chest grew tight and her body ached as she struggled to breathe. Gasping for air, she rose to her feet and bolted from the room. She rushed out the door and into the courtyard, scanning the area in search of her father, but he was nowhere to be seen.

Even if he were there, it did not matter. She did not care if she disappointed him! She looked back at the house. She would not stay there one more moment and they could not stop her!

Grasping her robes, she ran down the path, determined to see Elimelech's family one last time.

✡   ✡   ✡

As the field came into view, she clutched her side, gasping for air. "Mahlon!" she screamed.

He dropped his sickle and hurried in her direction.

"Oh, Mahlon," she cried as he came near. "I had to see you," she said, burying her face into his chest.

"You must go home, Ruth." His voice was calm and steady as he pulled her arms away.

She lifted her gaze. "But I wanted to tell you about Orpah."

"We already know. Your father was here earlier today."

"I am worried about her, and . . ."

"And what?"

"Mother said I could not come back."

"Perhaps she will change her mind."

"You do not know my mother! She will not relent!"

"Perhaps not, but until then, you must honor your parents' wishes. In this you have no choice."

Ruth backed away from him. Why was he treating her as if *he* were her father! She would not stand for it!

"I want to say goodbye to your parents!"

"No, Ruth. Go home. I am sure you will see them again."

"How do you know?"

"I know your parents love you very much and they are trying to make the best decisions where you are concerned. As long as you live in their home, you must obey their wishes."

"Where is Orpah?" Ruth asked with an air of defiance.

"I cannot say," he said, his voice low.

"Did Father tell you where she is?"

"I am sorry, Ruth, I cannot answer your questions."

"Cannot or *will not*? Everyone is treating me like a child. If you know where she is, I command you to tell me!"

She studied his countenance but it was resolute. There was no use asking again.

"Please tell your family goodbye for me," she said in a sarcastic tone. "And please pray to your God that He will protect me from the wrath of my god!"

Mahlon winced. She knew she caused him pain, but she did not care! Perhaps she did not ever want to lay eyes on *this* foreigner again! She turned, holding her head high as she stormed away.

"Ruth!" Mahlon called after her.

She ignored him.

✿   ✿   ✿

As Ruth neared home, she saw her mother standing in the courtyard. She contemplated lying as she approached. But why should she? Nothing mattered now anyway.

"Ruth, where have you been?"

"If you must know, I went to see Naomi and Elimelech."

"You disobeyed your father's wishes!"

Ruth narrowed her eyes. "I did. But I am sure you will be elated to

111

hear I did not make it."

Dahlia tilted her head, questioning. "Did your father stop you?"

"Father? Oh, no! I wish it had been him. It was Mahlon, their oldest son. He refused to let me see them!"

"He would not allow you to see his parents?" Her look of disbelief dissolved into a broad smile.

Ruth turned and marched across the courtyard, disappearing beneath a large willow tree. Grasping one of the long slender branches hovering just above the ground, she pulled it free.

"Come back here this instance!" Dahlia commanded. "I have not finished speaking with you."

She emerged with a look of triumph as she strolled to her mother, swinging the branch back and forth over the ground.

"This son of theirs—Mahlon?"

"Yes. I wish you would not repeat his name."

"Why did he refuse you?"

"He told me I should obey *all* you and Father say as long as I live with you. Then he sent me away—as if I were a child!"

Dahlia shook her head in disbelief. "Well, I am impressed with the young man."

"I am not. He should answer *my* questions! After all, he works for us, not the other way around!"

"Is this my daughter speaking?" Dahlia asked, smirking.

Ruth let out a heavy sigh as she lowered her head, staring at the ground. "Mother," she said softly as fear rose in her heart. "Do you suppose Chemosh is still angry with me?"

Dahlia hesitated.

"Mother?" Ruth asked again. "Please answer my question."

"I will admit the possibility has crossed my mind."

She grimaced. "Do you think he tried to kill Orpah because of me?"

Dahlia looked as if at a loss for words. Approaching Ruth, she rested her hand on her shoulder. "I believe Chemosh has been somewhat appeased by your worship of him this morning. I also prayed on your behalf that he would relent from punishing you or Orpah any further."

Ruth began to tremble as she realized the repercussions her friendship might cause Mahlon. "If Chemosh has the power to punish Orpah for my actions, then perhaps he will punish Elimelech's family also."

"Perhaps," Dahlia said, her face awash with dread.

"I understand. I need time alone, Mother, please."

Dahlia pointed toward the house. "Go on inside. I will be here in the courtyard if you need me."

"Thank you." Ruth forced the words. It hurt to say them but something inside her knew Mahlon was right. Retreating to the corner of the room, she leaned her back against the wall, and then slid to the floor.

Mahlon said she was to honor her mother and father. She decided at that moment to obey his request. She knew her motive was not completely pure. But staying away from their family might also protect them from Chemosh. There was no other solution. She would never see the foreigners again. She would stay away from them because she loved them. Adonai could not be her God.

Dahlia entered the house, walking past Ruth without making eye contact.

"Mother?"

"Yes," Dahlia said, facing her.

Ruth determined to speak loud enough for Chemosh to hear. "I will not go back to see Elimelech's family. I will stay here. I am sorry I disobeyed you and Father. Will you forgive me?"

Dahlia knelt beside her.

"Yes, of course, Daughter. I forgive you."

"Thank you, Mother," she sighed. "I am so tired. Do you mind if I go to bed?"

"But it is still morning."

"I know, but my body aches and I feel weak."

"I am sure it is only from worry, but I agree, you should rest."

Ruth entered her room. Nestling into bed, she recounted Mahlon's rebuke. How dare he speak to her that way! She wanted to stew in her anger, but it was no use. She knew he was right.

As her lids grew heavy, sleep overcame her. In her dreams, she saw Chemosh looming over Elimelech's home. She tried to push the images from her mind, but could not. In fitful sleep, she tossed and turned, attempting to remember the words whispered in her soul; but there was only silence.

Chapter 13

APPEASING CHEMOSH

Ruth followed the old servant woman from the house. She was her mother's personal maid and had been for as long as Ruth could remember. As to why her mother kept her around, however, was a mystery. She certainly did not meet her mother's high physical standards with her rough, pitted skin. Even her posture caused one's heart to ache as it curved like the gnarled trunk of an ancient tree.

"Wait, Miss Ruth," the old maid said, hobbling to a tall palm towering deep in the garden. Pulling a lightweight linen sheet from her shoulder, she gave it a shake and then released it. It rippled in the warm, morning breeze and then fell neatly on the ground. "Why do you not want to dress this morning?" the woman asked in a hushed voice.

Ruth lay back against the linen. Every pebble and blade beneath it bore into her weary body. "I am still not feeling well, Lilia."

The old woman glanced back at the house and then began pacing in short, faltering steps. "You should tell your mother you are ill."

"I do not want her to know. And please stop moving about. You are making me dizzy."

"Miss Ruth, your dizziness cannot compare to my indigestion," she said, kneeling next to her. "Does your head still cause you pain?"

"Yes, it does."

She pressed her leathery palm against Ruth's brow. "You feel warm," she said, rubbing her hand on her tunic. "Your mother will not deal kindly with me if she finds I have kept this from her."

"She will not know, unless you tell her."

"But if you refuse to dress again today, she may become suspicious."

Lilia's reproof grated on Ruth's frazzled nerves, but she was too tired to put up a fight.

"I agree, Lilia. When I am done resting, I will do as you request. Now, will you please leave me?"

Lilia bowed as she backed toward the house, continuing to rub her hand on her tunic as she went.

Ruth closed her eyes. It had been a difficult three weeks staying away from the foreigners and she had not felt well since the day she bolted from the room of worship. She hoped it was not Chemosh's doing. But even if it was, what did it matter? She had nothing left to look forward to.

"Get up, Ruth," Goad said in a stern voice.

"Father, Mother!" she said, scrambling from the blanket. "How long have you been standing there?"

"Not long. Are you well?" Dahlia asked. "You look a little pale this morning."

"I am fine, just feeling lazy."

Goad frowned. "I have endured enough laziness from you these past weeks to last a lifetime. Go get dressed for the day. You are coming with me."

"Where are we going?"

"To Elimelech's," Dahlia said, smiling.

Ruth stumbled backward, catching her foot in the linens as her mother grabbed her arm. "But you said I could never see them again!"

"Well, your mother has changed her mind."

"But I cannot! I *will not* go!"

116

"Do not be ridiculous!" Dahlia said. "You will go because I am giving you permission to."

"But Chemosh may punish them if I do."

"On the contrary. I have come to believe Chemosh has been appeased."

"The near death of Orpah has appeased him?"

Another wave of pain surged through Ruth's head. She groaned.

"What is wrong?" Dahlia asked.

"I am afraid."

"I do not understand why, but we will discuss the matter on the way to Elimelech's," Goad said as worry lines furrowed his brow. "Now get ready. I want to leave as soon as possible."

"Yes, Father." Ruth dropped her shoulders in resignation and walked to the house.

Nearing the room of worship, she stopped, vacillating. Should she attempt to explain this turn of events to Chemosh? She carefully made her way across the dark room. Upon reaching the table, she felt for the statue, moving her fingers over the cold stone. When she reached the top of its head, she felt the spikes of his crown. Trembling, she bowed her body.

"Please know I had determined never to see those foreigners again, but Father insists I go with him to his prized field today. And, well, the foreigners will likely be there. But I care not to see them. I just wanted to make sure you know. There is no need to harm them on my account. I will return home as quickly as I can." She lay still, waiting for a response. Finally she rose and fumbled her way outside the room.

She stood in the hallway, determining what she should wear. Remembering her mother's new robe, she crept to the fitting room, retrieved the garment and hurried back to her bedchamber. She laid the robe across the bed, admiring the intricate detail of the purple and gold stitching. Her mother was right; it was the most beautiful fabric she had ever seen.

If she were forced to go with her father, she would do so on her own terms, as a wealthy Moabite maiden. She must keep her distance from the foreigners. This robe would accomplish that without uttering a word. And then there was Mahlon. How could she face him? He wounded her pride and though she knew he was right, she was still upset with him. Resigned to her fate, she dressed quickly.

She brushed and arranged her hair, allowing locks to fall and curl around her cheeks. Selecting a gold bracelet, she slipped it on her wrist and made her way into the courtyard. Her father was leaning against the trunk of a sycamore tree, staring down the path. She approached him from behind and covered his eyes.

Grasping her hands, he chuckled and turned to face her. "My, but you are dressed in your very finest today! You look stunning, Daughter," he said, hesitating. "But you know Elimelech's family will wonder why you are dressing in this manner. Are you concerned your robes may make them uncomfortable?"

"Not at all. I have accepted my position in life and they need to do the same. I thought I could get away with hiding who I am, but Chemosh may punish them if I do. I do not want that to happen."

They proceeded down the path, but with each step, Ruth's chest grew tighter and pain shot down her arm. Goad glanced at her several times as she tried desperately to remain calm. Nearing the well, Goad motioned for her to join him.

"Ruth, you do not need to fear Chemosh," he said, leaning against a large boulder.

"Mother fears him. You do not?"

"I believe there is a greater power, but I do not believe Chemosh is necessarily that power."

"Can you say with certainty Chemosh did not attack Orpah?"

"No, I cannot."

"Why does Mother believe so strongly?"

"I do not know, but she does—as surely as the sun rises and sets."

"How did you convince Mother to allow me to come with you?"

"I reasoned with her."

"How?"

"I told her that Chemosh allowed Orpah to live, so that must mean he had been appeased," he said with a prankish smile.

"You lied to Mother!"

"Did I really? Ruth, why did Orpah live? If Chemosh had the power to kill her and wanted her dead, she would not have survived."

"I guess that could be true. But how can we know? I am afraid to go to Elimelech's because it may cause Chemosh to harm them, too."

"If Chemosh was angry with their family, why would he allow them to care for Orpah?"

"Naomi took care of Orpah after the beating?"

"No, not exactly. Chilion found her near this well the morning after her abduction."

"Chilion?"

"Indeed. He came to the well early that morning. When he arrived, he heard groaning coming from the brush behind the well. He followed the sounds until he found her. She had been badly beaten and left for dead."

"Did he know it was Orpah?"

"No, he did not. He carried her home, staying off the main path to avoid being seen."

"Chilion's parents allowed him to bring Orpah home, not knowing who she was or what kind of trouble she was in?"

"They did. Then Elimelech sent Chilion to me, requesting I come quickly. When I arrived, I was shocked at the condition of the girl, not realizing at first it was Orpah. After recognizing who she was, I returned home to tell your mother. Dahlia was afraid, and rightly so, that you might also be harmed."

"Was that why you were arguing with Mother in the garden?"

"Yes."

"Why did you wait so long to tell me who rescued her?"

"We wanted to keep her safe *and* you as well."

"Where is she now?"

"She is still at Elimelech's. Once I knew it was Orpah, I sent for her parents. When they arrived and saw her condition, they agreed it would be best for her to remain hidden there."

"I would have taken my daughter home and cared for her. Would you not have done the same?"

"No, Ruth, they were fearful, and justifiably so. Had the person who attacked her discovered she survived, they would likely have returned to finish the job."

"I suppose so. How is she now?"

"She is weak, but hopefully will make a full recovery, thanks to Chilion."

"Chilion?"

"Yes, Chilion. From the moment he arrived home with Orpah, he has taken charge of her care, refusing to leave her."

"What about the man who attacked her? Has he been caught?"

"No, and unfortunately Orpah cannot remember anything about the night of the attack. I am convinced it was carried out at the hand of Harrash or one of his servants."

"Are the townspeople aware she survived?"

"Now they are. Yesterday, we brought Harrash before the village council and confronted him."

"What did he say when you accused him of the attempt on Orpah's life?"

"He insisted he had nothing to do with it, but was given notice by the council that if anything else should happen to Orpah or her family, he would be held responsible." Goad stood, waiting for Ruth to join him as they continued down the path.

Rounding the bend, Ruth waved excitedly.

"Naomi!" she yelled. Turning she grasped her father's arm. "Come, Father."

"No," he said smiling. "This journey you must make alone."

"I am not a little girl any more, am I, Father?"

"Far from it." He kissed her forehead and walked away.

Ruth looked at Naomi. Her arms were extended and waiting. *Have you forgotten your vow, Ruth? Turn back while you can!* Ignoring the warning, she lifted her robes and ran.

"My daughter," Naomi said as Ruth came near. "I have never seen a more beautiful sight in all my days."

"Oh, Naomi, I have missed you!" she said, hugging her tightly. "How is Orpah? Is she regaining her strength?"

"Yes. Her recovery has been slow, but I believe she will survive, Daughter. Now that you are back with us, my joy is complete."

Ruth sighed. How could she tell her the truth? But she must. "I have only come to see Orpah."

A look of confusion covered Naomi's face as she took Ruth's hand, pulling her toward the house.

Ruth looked back down the path, watching her father round the bend and disappear from view. She knew he sensed a change in her since the arrival of the foreigners. It must have been a painful realization for him, knowing Ruth needed more from life than he could provide. She was thankful that he understood her so well. He knew how much she missed Elimelech's family and sought to restore their relationship. She appreciated the gesture but what did it matter? She could not have what she desperately wanted. But one fact was certain, she had stepped into adulthood and there was no going back.

As they entered the house, Mahlon stood. Stepping away from the chair, he smiled, keeping his eyes focused on her. Her attempt to put him in his place had not gone as planned. Unable to bear his approving eye, she looked away.

Seeing Elimelech sitting in the corner of the room, she went to him and knelt at his feet. She studied his kind eyes and then rested her head in his lap. The pain she fought all morning subsided as she felt his hand on her head. Within moments she sensed the family as they gathered around her.

Closing her eyes, she listened intently to Elimelech's warm, soothing voice as he prayed, "Thank you, Adonai, that we have found grace in Your sight. Thank you for considering our prayer and bringing Ruth back to us. Amen."

Ruth rose to her knees, wrapping her arms around Elimelech's neck and then stood and hugged Chilion. She turned toward Mahlon, furrowing her brows—then awkwardly held out her hand to him. He took it into his and squeezed it. His touch warmed her heart and she pulled her hand away. Mahlon's face seemed to fill with surprise, giving way to sadness, but Ruth did not care. She would make no attempt to embrace him. He treated her like a child, refusing to answer her questions when they last met.

"Where is Orpah?" Ruth asked Naomi.

"She is resting in the garden," Mahlon replied.

"May I go to her?" Ruth countered, keeping her gaze on Naomi.

"Yes." Naomi said, looking at Mahlon.

"I will take you to see her," he said.

Not Mahlon! I do not want to be near him. Ruth looked panic-stricken in Elimelech's direction. He stood, motioning for his son to go.

Do not offend them, Ruth! Remember you will not see them again after today.

She quickly left the house and hurried down the path toward the garden.

"Ruth, wait!" Mahlon said as he caught up with her. "Are you still upset with me?"

She halted abruptly, turning to face him. Then she eyed him closely, allowing her brows to form a frown that would surely convey their meaning without uttering a word.

"*Please* answer me . . . You are angry! Why?"

"You *know* why I am angry! Why do you bother to ask me such a question?"

"Is it because I did what God's mitzvah requires me to do?"

"Do not use God's mitzvah against me!"

"I am not using it against you, Ruth. I have no choice but to honor my father and mother. How could I not expect you to honor yours?"

"I told you, Mahlon, I am not a child."

He smiled. "I am well aware you are not a child—you can be certain of that."

"Do not look at me like that, Mahlon!"

"Look at you like what?"

"The way you are looking at me now!"

He laughed and Ruth flushed with irritation.

"Ruth, please do not be angry with me. I have missed you and have prayed that Adonai would bring you back to us. He has answered my prayer."

"Perhaps it is not Adonai that allowed me to come back, but the god of my people, Chemosh."

Mahlon studied her intently. "I will not talk against your god if you do not wish me to, Ruth. I only ask that you understand the requirements of my God where I am concerned. Please know I had no choice but to send you home."

She lifted her head in the air as she had seen her mother do. "The truth is, I tire of this conversation as none of it matters to me."

"But, Ruth, I—"

"Please tell me about Orpah. My concern for her is the only reason for my visit today. How is she?"

"She has almost recovered but has no memory of what happened to her. She will be staying here with us and will be moved to the servants' quarters tomorrow. Father thinks that is best, considering."

"Considering what?"

"Chilion loves her."

"Loves her? When did that happen?"

"I think it happened when he found her. I do not know what Father is going to do about it. Chilion has not said as much, but it is obvious by the way he talks about her and cares for her."

"She was to be *my* servant, not yours!"

"Your servant? That does not sound like you, Ruth."

His assessment sliced through her like a knife.

"I am sorry, Mahlon, truly I am. I never really wanted her to serve me."

"I know, Ruth. This has been very difficult for all of us. You were excited to have a companion—and she will be."

Ruth fought tears as she turned away. He did not understand and she would not tell him. "I want to go home, Mahlon. Do you understand? I cannot see Orpah."

"But why?"

"I am afraid!" Ruth screamed as she began to run toward home.

Mahlon ran after her. Grabbing her by the arm, he turned her to face him. "You cannot run from life, Ruth! You must face your fears."

"I *have* faced my fears! I cannot see Orpah *or* your family!" She jerked her arm free. "If you value your father's welcome in this land, do not attempt to follow me!"

Ruth turned and began running again. She could hear Mahlon calling her name. As she neared the well, she pushed her body harder, fearful he might attempt to reach her. But the harder she tried to run, the weaker her legs felt. Her breathing became more labored and the pain in her head more intense.

She stopped, standing motionless and then screamed. Her body was on fire and the path began to spin beneath her.

"I cannot see!" she cried out in agony as she collapsed. "Mahlon, help me!"

Chapter 14

THE PIT

Ruth could hear Mahlon's anguished cries in the distance as he called out her name, but she was powerless to answer him. Her body lay unresponsive to her efforts to move or speak.

As he drew near, Ruth heard the steady drumming of his sandals on the path. Gravel scattered across her as he skidded to a halt and dropped to his knees, lifting her limp body into his arms. As he held her tightly against his chest she felt the rapid beating of his heart.

"Please do not leave me, Ruth!" he cried.

His hand felt cool upon her forehead. Rocking her back and forth, he moaned in response to her shallow, uneven attempts to breathe.

"Do not let her die, Adonai!" he begged as he lifted her from the ground, struggling to stand.

As he ran, her body bounced back and forth in his arms in lifeless response to each movement he made. He collapsed on the path and then wrestled to lift her as he rose to his feet.

Her heart ached for him and for the anguish she had caused. She wanted to tell him she was sorry for the way she acted. She had not meant to hurt him. But now he would never know. Was this what it felt like to die? Her life was ebbing away and she was powerless to stop it.

"Goad! Dahlia!" Mahlon yelled as he neared her home. "Help me!"

"Ruth!" Dahlia screamed, running toward him. "Quickly, bring her to her bedchamber."

"I am so sorry," Mahlon said as he entered her room and placed her ashen body on the bed.

"Who are you?"

"I am Elimelech's son, Mahlon."

"What happened?"

"I am not sure. She seemed fine at first, but as we were going to visit Orpah she said she was afraid."

"Afraid of what?"

"I have no idea. We were almost to the garden when she turned and began running home. I followed her, begging her to come back, but she refused. Then she suddenly dropped to the ground," Mahlon said as his voice broke.

Ruth felt her mother's hand on her forehead.

"She is burning up! What am I to do? Goad left over an hour ago and will not be home for several days!"

"I will go and get my mother, Naomi."

"Yes, you must. Go quickly!"

Ruth's body began to shake.

"Dahlia," Mahlon said, his voice firm, "lie down by Ruth. Do not leave her. I will return as soon as possible."

"I understand. Now go!" Dahlia yelled as she climbed over Ruth's body.

Ruth heard Mahlon as he ran from the room.

"Do not die, Ruth," Dahlia wept as several servants came rushing in. "Leave us!" Dahlia commanded.

Dahlia locked her arms around Ruth. They felt like a vice on her chest, crushing her lungs, squeezing her heart. Her breath was like ice against Ruth's neck. She tried to push her mother away, but her hands lay limp on the bed.

Dahlia began to chant—saturating the room with her guttural wailing. The sounds encircled Ruth's body like a web, hissing . . . growling—tormenting!

Stop, he is killing me, Mother, stop!

But Dahlia continued on, unaware as Ruth gasped for breath. The room grew frigid as she sank deeper and deeper into an abyss of darkness.

As Ruth slipped from consciousness, her mother's voice faded. Visions of an evil spirit began hovering over her bedchamber. It was massive, flowing like smoke in crimson and black. She screamed, plunging her fists into its formless shape. It laughed, mocking her—its sounds echoed—building and slamming into her in waves of pain.

Cowering before the being, she cried out in agony, "I know who you are! You cannot deceive me . . . you are no god . . . you are a DEMON! You are Chemosh! I will not bow to you!"

The terror she once saw in her mother's eyes filled her as she fought to escape him. His voice was deep and sardonic as he mocked her. "Sweet Ruth . . . kind Ruth . . . DEAD Ruth!" he screeched, lifting her from the bed.

Looking down, Ruth saw her mother clutching her body as Chemosh carried her through the ceiling and into darkness.

The land sailed below her in flat tones of black and gray. He carried her higher and higher until the mountains looked like charcoal etchings on parchment.

"Do you see the fire, child?" he cackled.

A red and blue flame flickered beneath them like a dot on canvas. Suddenly, he dropped her. She screamed in horror, flailing toward the flames. Then he swooped her up, hovering in place high above the fiery pit.

"Let me die," she begged.

"Oh, you will, soon enough!" he bellowed. "Do you see them?" He laughed as the putrid smell of hot sulfur and burning flesh shot upward. "Can you hear them?" he mocked.

The cries of men and women bound and howling their mournful laments emanated from the pit.

"Let them go!" she begged as the flames reached for her like hands hungry for the taste of death. Closing her eyes, she attempted to block the images below and then cried out in horror as she felt her body falling. "No!" she cried. "Stop!"

"Stop?" he mocked, his voice saturated with glee. "Ah ha ha! Soon you will be mine, Ruth, for all eternity!"

Repeatedly he dropped her then scooped her up until she could feel the heat radiating upward.

"Help me!" she cried as he released her body for the last time.

"Goodbye, Ruth!" he bellowed.

"Someone help me!" she wept in agony as the flames engulfed her body, scorching her skin.

"Ruth, can you hear me?" Naomi cried, her voice slicing through the torment.

Naomi! Is that you? Help me! Please help me! But she had fallen too far . . . it was too black . . . too late. Giving in to the flames, she welcomed death as Naomi began to pray.

"Adonai, Elohim, do not allow Ruth to be taken from us! Jehovah Rapha save her!"

Naomi raised her palms above Ruth and slammed them into her chest as her body convulsed.

Ruth heard Chemosh shriek and then he was silent. Gasping, she felt her lungs fill with air.

"She is breathing!"

"Quickly, Dahlia, bring wet cloths."

Dahlia ran from the room and returned with several servants carrying vases filled with water.

"Mahlon, you must leave."

No! Naomi, I need him . . .

"But I want to stay, Mother."

"There is nothing more you can do here. Go outside. We must remove Ruth's garments and bathe her to bring the fever down."

"Please, Ruth, come back to me," Mahlon said as she felt his lips on her forehead.

Goodbye, Mahlon. I love–

"Leave, Son, we have no time to waste."

"I will wait in the courtyard," he said, running from the room.

Ruth felt Naomi and her mother's hands as they worked together to remove her garments. As they touched her body with the cloths, her skin burned. She screamed in agony and begged them to stop, but still no sound came from her.

Desperate, Ruth prayed, *Adonai, please let me live. I cannot bear to leave them.*

As she drifted toward a peaceful presence, she heard a familiar voice washing over her saying, *Fear not, Ruth, for I Am That I Am has heard your plea.*

She tried to sit up as she recognized the familiar sound of His voice.

"Lay still, Ruth," Naomi said. "We are trying to bring your fever down."

"She moved!" Dahlia said, weeping. "Naomi, will she live?"

"I pray she will. We should know within a few days."

"Will you stay here with me until Goad returns? I am afraid to be alone."

"Yes, of course I will stay."

As they continued to bathe Ruth, an all-consuming fatigue overcame her as she drifted to sleep.

Ruth rolled to her side and struggled to sit.

"Wait, Ruth," Dahlia said, rushing to her. "Let me help you."

She felt her mother's arms around her. "I see light," she said and then giggled at the garbled sound of her voice.

"Goad," Dahlia called, "Come quickly, Ruth is awake!"

"Naomi?" Ruth whispered, reaching out for her hand.

"She left this morning because she was convinced you were out of danger. She requested we bring you to see them as soon as you are strong enough."

"And Father?" she asked, weakly.

"I am here, Daughter," he said, taking her into his arms. "You gave us quite a scare."

Ruth touched his face, running her fingers over his forehead and feeling his mouth as her eyes fluttered open. "I see you!" she said, patting his cheek. "But you are a bit blurry."

Goad laughed. "Give your eyes time to focus."

"What happened to me?"

"You have been very sick," Dahlia said, her voice trembling. "We were afraid you would not make it."

"Naomi and your mother stayed by your side for the past three days, watching over you like mother hens."

Ruth sighed, "It has been three days since I fell ill?"

"Indeed."

"I am sorry Naomi left before I could thank her."

"You love her very much, do you not?" Dahlia asked.

Ruth sensed regret in her voice. "Yes, Mother, I do."

"Something miraculous happened when Naomi came to you."

"What?"

"I thought we had lost you. You were so ashen and had stopped breathing. Naomi arrived and upon seeing your condition, prayed to her God."

"She prayed for me?"

"Yes, and then she struck your chest. Do you remember?"

"I do, but I thought it was all part of my dream."

"Dream?"

"Yes, Mother, but I am too tired to talk about it."

"You can tell us later," Goad said. "Right now you need to rest."

"I am sorry, Ruth, that I prevented you from seeing their family."

"Do not worry, Mother, I understand why."

"Mahlon carried you all the way here, Ruth, and then willingly left to bring his mother at my request."

"Has he been back?"

"No," Goad said. "As soon as you are strong enough, we will take you to see him."

"I am not sure I want to go back."

"Why?" Goad asked.

"I do not want to talk about it. Please understand."

Goad looked at Dahlia, shaking his head.

"But Ruth," Dahlia said.

"No, Dahlia, this is not the time. Rest, Daughter," he said, kissing her forehead.

As they left the room, Ruth thought of Mahlon, realizing the depth of his love for her.

I will not allow him to burden his parents with the truth, Adonai! Your mitzvah is more important than any selfish desire we have.

Adonai, I will stay away from Elimelech's family. It will be my sacrifice to You for sparing my life. Just as Abraham did not withhold his son from The One True God, so I will not rob Elimelech or his son of their blessing. But how can I accomplish such a feat unless I never see Mahlon or his family again?

Chapter 15

THE STREAM

Ruth kicked the linens off her bed. There was no use trying to sleep. Seven days passed since she regained consciousness. Still she wrestled with the vision, wondering if the dark world she fought to escape truly existed. Restless, she walked through the house in search of her mother and found her sitting at the table.

"Mother, do you mind if I go for a walk?" Ruth asked as Dahlia observed the servants preparing the morning meal.

Dahlia eyed her. "Are you strong enough?"

"I am."

"Let us eat and then I will join you."

"But I want to go alone."

"Why?"

"These past few days I have not felt like myself. Perhaps getting out of the house will clear my mind."

"Does this have anything to do with Mahlon?"

"Mahlon? Mother, no, please do not make this about him."

Dahlia rose from the table. "Come, Daughter." She reached for Ruth, turning her full circle, assessing her condition. "A leisurely stroll with a nice view will do you good and I know just the spot."

"Where?"

"Remember the field that lies just west of our home. It has the lovely stream that runs along its southern boundary."

"Yes, I know the one. You and Father used to walk there."

"We did." Dahlia smiled. "If any place can bring you solace, it will. Do you remember the way?"

"I do. Thank you, Mother." She kissed her cheek, realizing she was surrounded by all that was familiar . . . her parents, her home and the servants. So why did she feel so empty?

"Are you sure, Daughter, that you are up to going by yourself? I will gladly go with you."

"Thank you, Mother, but no. I need time alone and I am definitely strong enough for a leisurely stroll."

"Very well." Dahlia raised her hands, clapping as she addressed the servants. "Prepare Ruth some dried fish, fresh bread and a skin of goat's milk—and add a few dates."

The servants bowed as they hurried about, preparing her provisions.

"I expect you to eat, Ruth. You must keep up your strength."

"I will."

A servant handed Dahlia a small pack. "Did you include a linen sheet?"

"Yes," the servant responded.

Dahlia inspected the contents and then lifted the pack in the air, testing its weight. Motioning for Ruth, she positioned it on her back, wrapping the straps about her waist and tying them in a knot. "Too heavy?"

"Not at all." Ruth smiled at the servant. "Thank you."

The servant nodded as Dahlia tilted her head, motioning with her eyes for her to return to work.

"Enjoy your walk, but be home by mid-afternoon, and stay on the path until you see the stream."

"I will," Ruth said, waving.

✡   ✡   ✡

Arriving at the stream, she selected a spot under a grove of poplar trees. Tossing the sheet along the bank, she removed her sandals and dipped her feet into the cool water.

Thank you, Adonai, for answering Naomi's prayer—and mine too.

She lay down, looking up at the sky through the tree branches. Searching the lazy clouds and breathing the fresh air, she sighed as the confusion that plagued her lifted.

She wondered if He could read her thoughts. And if so, could she tell Him how she really felt?

Closing her eyes, she lifted her heart in prayer to Him.

Adonai, why did You rescue me from death and the fiery pit? I do not mean to sound ungrateful. I am very thankful You rescued me from Chemosh. But what does it matter in the end if I am destined to be separated from You?

Startled by the sound of rustling across the stream, she scrambled to her feet. Shading her eyes, she squinted, searching the grove. "Who is there?"

"I could ask the same," came a muffled response.

Her heart pounded. Should she run? It could be Harrash or one of his men. She stood tall, positioning her fists on her hips as she prepared for a confrontation.

"I am Ruth—Goad's daughter! Do not come any closer or you will answer to him with your life!"

He laughed.

"Mahlon?"

"Yes, it is me," he said as his voice grew louder.

Scanning the trees, movement caught her eye as Mahlon's head peered from behind a massive sycamore. He smiled and then ducked his head from view.

"Come out where I can see you," she said, tapping her foot.

"I will not! I fear for my life."

"Is that right?" She giggled. "Very well, I grant you safe passage this time."

Mahlon stepped from behind the tree, bowing. "May I have permission to join you?"

"If I said no, would you leave?" She tilted her head, grinning.

"Not without an argument," he said. Removing his sandals, he crossed the stream and sat on the bank, dipping his feet in the water. He patted the ground next to him. "Are you going to join me?"

She took several steps away, eyeing him. "How did you know where to find me?"

"Find you? I had no idea you would be here."

"Mother did not tell you?"

"Your mother? Why would she tell me?"

"Never mind," she said, sitting a safe distance from him.

"Please trust me, Ruth. This was not planned."

"Well enough. I believe you. Regardless, I wanted to thank you for carrying me home."

"You are welcome," he said, avoiding her gaze.

"What is wrong, Mahlon?"

He looked at her squarely. "Are you sure you want to know?"

She hesitated, studying him. "If it has to do with the day I ran from you, then yes."

"You were so angry with me."

"Please forgive me. I acted like a spoiled child."

"Done. So what made you so fearful that day?"

"Chemosh."

"Chemosh? Why?"

"Mother said he might harm your family."

"We are not afraid of your god, nor do we serve him."

"I know that now."

"Ruth . . ." Mahlon's expression turned serious.

"Yes. What is it?" she asked, suddenly recognizing the look of love and longing in his eyes.

Surely he would not risk his family's inheritance by declaring his feelings! Remembering her promise to Adonai, she stood, turning away. "Do not say it, Mahlon!"

"Say what?"

She spun around, facing him. "What I think you are going to say!"

He sighed. "You cannot read my mind, Ruth." Pulling a long slender blade of grass from the ground, he twirled it between his fingers and then glanced at her sideways. "I have been thinking . . ."

"Best not to do that."

Dropping the blade, he shook his head and stood. "What is wrong with you?"

"A lot, actually! I simply must *know* the truth."

"I am *trying* to tell you the truth, but you will not let me!"

"This is not about you, Mahlon."

His countenance fell. She had injured him again with her harsh words, but she had no choice.

"Well, if it is not about me—then what is it?"

"Will Adonai ever accept me as one of His chosen people?"

Mahlon approached her. "I do not know," he said, pausing.

"Why?"

"The answer lies with my father, but I feel unable to ask him as he may question my motive in doing so."

Ruth threw her hands in the air. Why had she allowed him to cross that stream! She should have stayed home.

"Are you still angry with me?"

"No, Mahlon!" She crossed her arms. "You must understand! I want nothing more from you than friendship." There she said it plain and simple!

"But Ruth—"

"Will He accept me?"

Mahlon lowered his head. "I was hoping you would not ask that question until I had an answer for you. But since you insist, I will tell you what I know." He paused to study her and then continued. "Do you remember when God took Abraham into the land of Canaan and promised him that one day the land he was standing on would belong to his descendants?"

"Yes, I do, but at the time of the promise, Abraham had to leave because of a famine, so he took Sarah and sojourned into Egypt."

"That is right. Many years later, and after Abraham and Sarah died, God spoke to the Israelites and told them it was time for them to leave the land of Egypt and travel to the Promised Land. On the way, they asked the Moabites for help, but they refused and even worse, they hired a false prophet named Balaam to put a curse on my people."

"Was Adonai angry?"

Mahlon's eyes filled with sorrow. "Yes, He was."

"What did He say?"

Mahlon began reciting Adonai's words from memory:

"An Ammonite or Moabite shall not enter the assembly of the LORD; even to the tenth generation none of his descendants shall enter the assembly of the LORD forever, because they did not meet you with bread and water on the road when you came out of Egypt, and because they hired against you Balaam . . . to curse you." (Deuteronomy 23:3-4).

The color drained from her face. "Why would God reject me because of a mistake my people made so long ago? I had no part in denying food and water to His people."

"I am so sorry, Ruth."

"But my father allowed Elimelech to come supervise our field!" Ruth stared at him waiting for a response, but he remained silent. She turned her back to him.

"Do not . . ." Mahlon said, reaching for her as she ran from him.

With every step, her body grew weaker. As her legs gave way, she felt his hands against her waist. He steadied her and then gently turned her to face him.

As he released his hold, she lowered her head. "Ruth," he said in a soft voice, lifting her chin. She trembled at his touch. "You will never run from me again."

"Please let me go."

"You may go, but you may not run."

Anguished, she closed her eyes, nodding. "Do not tell me more. I cannot bear it."

"Look at me," he said.

She opened her eyes in obedience. His tender gaze pierced her soul. She tried to hide her feelings for him, but it was futile. He touched her cheek; her heart fluttered.

"I do not have all the answers, but I do know God did not allow you to die. He heard my mother's prayer."

"And mine," Ruth said, stepping away.

"How could you pray? By the time Mother arrived, you were dead."

"Oh, Mahlon, it is true! I was trapped inside my body unable to move or speak, but I could hear everything around me."

"You heard me on the path?"

Ruth blushed. "Yes."

"And in your bedchamber?"

"I heard everything. Before your mother arrived I had a vision. It was of Chemosh. He entered my room, picked me up and carried me to a place where men and women were being sacrificed. There was a fiery pit—"

Mahlon looked at her, his mouth agape. "A fiery pit!"

"Yes. And as I fell into the flames, my heart stopped. It was then your mother entered my room. I could hear her praying for me, but it was too late. I could not find my way back to her. My body was burned. My flesh was gone. I cried out to Adonai."

"What did you say?"

"I asked Him to let me live." She stared into the heavens. *Forgive me, Adonai, I cannot tell Mahlon the whole truth—that I could not bear to leave him.* "And then I heard a voice speak to me."

"Who was it?"

"He said His name was I AM THAT I AM."

Mahlon stumbled backward.

"And He said, 'Fear not, Ruth, for I AM THAT I AM has heard your plea.'" Ruth shook her head. "But Mahlon, why would God bother to save me if I am destined to be separated from Him?"

"I do not have the answers, but I will try to find them for you, of that I promise." Mahlon motioned in the direction of her home. "May I walk with you?"

"No, I will stay here awhile longer."

"Then I will wait here with you."

"No, please leave. Mother sent a meal and I promised to eat before returning home."

"When will you come back to us?"

She hesitated. "Come back? . . . I cannot."

"Yes, you can!"

Why does he press me, Adonai? I cannot tell him the truth!

"My mind is made up, Mahlon."

"Your decisions affect others also, you know! My parents will be heartbroken if you refuse to see them."

"I am so sorry, but I do not know what else to do."

"You will come back for *them*, Ruth—and them alone."

Turning, he walked away.

"Mahlon," Ruth called after him.

He held his hand in the air and continued toward the path. Ruth watched him, wondering if he would look back. He did not.

Sighing, she walked to the bank and retrieved the pack. Pulling the cords free, she removed the bread and fish. On any other day the fish would have tasted delicious, but as she took a bite, she found it dry and difficult to swallow.

As she continued to eat, she considered Adonai. Could One as powerful as He not look into the future and know she would be waiting for Him there?

Adonai, it was Your voice I heard in the wind and in the vision. Please give Mahlon the answers to my questions. I long to know the truth. I will accept what he says, trusting the answers come from You.

Retrieving the skin of goat's milk and dates, she finished the meal and gathered her belongings.

Strolling along the path, she was awestruck by the realization that she almost died! Even more amazing—God spared her! Was it because He loved Naomi and she pleaded on her behalf, as Abraham had done for Lot? Or did He care for her even though she was not one of His chosen people?

One result was certain, Ruth no longer feared Chemosh. The demon took her to the brink of death—but Adonai, by His *greater* power, delivered her. Regardless of why, she was grateful.

She thought of Naomi and Elimelech. Mahlon was right; she must consider how her decision would affect them. They loved her, needed her and accepted her. Mahlon freed her to return without fear of jeopardizing his inheritance. Her decision was made. She would tell her parents and never look back.

Chapter 16

HIS HEART'S YEARNING

Ruth sat in the main living area of their home, stitching intricate lace-like patterns along the edge of a tunic. A brisk morning breeze blew through the windows, leaving her hair in disarray. Removing the comb, she let her locks fall and then tied them with a cord at the back of her neck.

Retrieving the tunic, she continued stitching. She sighed as she pushed the slender, wooden needle through the linen. It had been two weeks since she last spoke to Mahlon. He requested she return to the field for his parent's sake. Still, she had not mustered the courage.

Closing her eyes, she ran her fingers across the web-like patterns of thread—intrigued by the feel. It had taken several days of pleading to convince Lilia to teach her to sew. The old woman finally gave in to her request, but not before accusing Ruth of sending her to an early grave.

"Do you mind if we join you?" Goad asked as he and Dahlia entered the room. A servant followed behind, carrying a small sewing basket.

"Of course not," she said.

Dahlia situated herself in a chair near Goad, removed a hand cloth from the servant's basket and began stitching.

The servant approached Dahlia with caution, kneeling at her feet. "No, ma'am, push the needle from the bottom—"

"I can see that!" Dahlia chided. The servant pulled her hand away as Dahlia looked in Goad's direction.

He frowned.

"Thank you for pointing it out, though," she said, peeking at Goad over the cloth, smiling demurely.

He beamed at the servant as he leaned back in his chair. Ruth eyed him, questioning, but he ignored her. Yawning, he clasped his hands behind his neck and closed his eyes.

Ruth shook her head in confusion. What had gotten into her parents? Today her mother was learning to sew! And then there was her father. The day before he had installed a door at the hallway's entrance, blocking the room of worship from view!

As she focused on her stitching, her thoughts turned to Adonai. Each day she prayed but He remained silent. Was He cruel like Chemosh? The thought wrenched her soul as her heart filled with sorrow. Somehow she knew it could not be true. If He created all mankind; He was also LORD over them. He judged the Moabites, finding them unworthy. How could she determine His judgment unjust?

"Ruth, you seem deep in thought today," Goad said, leaning forward.

"Actually, I am."

"What are you thinking about?" Dahlia asked.

"Going to see Elimelech's family."

Dahlia smiled. "We hoped you would."

"I thought you did not like them, Mother."

"They saved your life and the truth is, I know when I have lost."

"Lost what?"

"When I met your father, my parents did not approve. At the time he was a lowly servant—"

Goad laughed. "Dahlia, be kind."

She shook her head and continued, "My parents knew they could not convince me otherwise, so eventually they relented."

"Relented? What are you talking about?"

"Mahlon, of course."

Ruth dropped her needlework. "Mahlon?" Had his affection for her been that apparent?

"It is obvious he cares for you."

"He does, but only as he would a sister."

"Is that so?" Goad raised his brows, looking unconvinced.

Ruth stood, tossing the tunic into the chair.

"Perhaps you are right, Daughter," he said.

"But the day he carried you home, he seemed so—taken with you."

Ruth rolled her eyes. "Mother, please! That is ridiculous. He is not *taken with me.* Far from it!"

Goad kept his eyes focused on Ruth. "I am sure he was simply overcome by the moment, was he not?"

"Yes, Father, I am sure that is all it was." Ruth walked to the bench on the opposite side of the room. She sat straight, facing them with her hands clasped in her lap. How had she gotten herself into this situation? And now she stooped to lying to her parents!

"Then why will you return?" Dahlia asked.

"Because I want to learn more about their God."

"Their God is more important to you than Mahlon?"

"Mother, stop!"

"But I assumed you might want to . . ." she paused, glaring at Goad. He shook his head and frowned.

Crossing her arms, she turned to Ruth. "Do you not desire to marry him someday?"

"*Marry* him!" Ruth stood. "Where did you get such an absurd idea? Certainly not from me!" She stared at her father. "Elimelech will choose a wife for his sons from among the Israelites." Turning, she faced her mother. "Besides, if I marry it will be to a Moabite. Perhaps I will even agree to a Moabite of your choosing."

147

"Not likely!" Goad chuckled.

"But Goad," Dahlia said. "I do not understand."

"It seems your daughter has some of your stubbornness in her. You would do well and save yourself heartache by accepting her decision."

"Ruth, I think you do the opposite of what I want just to frustrate me!"

"That is not my intent, Mother. Please give me your word you will not get any ideas in your head where Mahlon is concerned."

"She made herself clear, my love."

Dahlia threw the cloth in the basket. "Oh, what is the use!"

"I know this is difficult," Ruth said.

"I just want you to be happy."

"How can I be, unless I am accepted by their God?" There she said it!

Dahlia bit her lip. "You will not be worshiping Chemosh with me?"

"Is it my decision?" Ruth glanced toward the room of worship.

"I am afraid for you—"

"But we accept your decision. Do we not, Dahlia?"

"I suppose so."

"Thank you, Mother. Father, would you object to my walking to Elimelech's?"

"Perhaps you should wait until tomorrow. It will be dark soon."

"Please? There is still enough daylight if I hurry."

"If you must go, take your time. I certainly do not want you running."

"I will try to be home before the sun sets." She picked up her head covering and tucked her hair beneath it as she left the house.

✿ ✿ ✿

The sun was beginning to set and the air was filled with the aroma of ripened grain as Ruth watched the servants loading sheaves of barley onto carts. Wiping moisture from her brow, she removed her head covering, allowing the wind to lift her hair and cool her skin.

Suddenly she was filled with regret. Why had she wasted so many days before returning? "Where is Elimelech's family?" she called to one of the servants.

He turned, pointing down the path in the direction of the wheat field. Nodding, she proceeded.

With each step, her apprehension grew. What if they were not happy to see her? What if Mahlon attempted to ask his father about the Moabites and it had not gone well? Perhaps her father was right, she should have waited one more day.

Arriving, she slowed her pace and then paused, surveying the field.

"Ruth!" Elimelech called.

She looked in the direction of his voice as she heard his familiar laugh.

"You have come!" he yelled, holding out his arms.

He was happy to see her! Why had she thought otherwise? Waving, she grasped her tunic and hurried toward him, pushing her way through the dense wheat.

Suddenly she heard him groan.

"Ruth—" he gasped, clutching his chest.

"Elimelech!" she screamed as he fell to the ground. "Help! Somebody, help!" she cried. "What is it, Elimelech? What is wrong?"

"Get Mahlon," he said, gritting his teeth as she pulled him into her lap.

She attempted to lift him as she peered through the wheat, searching the field.

"They are coming," she said, observing his family and servants frantically weaving their way through the rows. "Oh, Elimelech! I am so sorry!"

He continued to gasp as Ruth watched his skin turn gray, his lips blue.

Suddenly, Naomi was standing over him. Stooping, she gently touched his face. "No, Elimelech," she cried.

"What is wrong, Father?" Mahlon asked, kneeling beside him.

"Chest, tight—hard to breathe."

"Quickly, we must get Father to the house," Mahlon said, addressing the servants. "

Gathering around him, they grasped his arms and legs; carefully lifting him into a nearby cart.

As they made their way to the house, Ruth followed behind, keeping her distance. Mahlon turned his head toward her several times, his eyes filled with anguish.

Why had she come back? Would this have happened if she had stayed away?

"Please, do not leave me, Elimelech," Naomi cried as she took his hand.

"I love you," he managed, his voice weak and broken.

Arriving at the house, the family followed the servants as they carried Elimelech to his room. They left with their heads bowed.

Ruth observed Orpah huddled in the corner, recognizing the fear in her eyes. Her arms were clamped around her knees and she rocked back and forth in trancelike repetition. Ruth sat beside her as Orpah buried her head into Ruth's shoulder.

"Chemosh?" she whispered.

"No, Orpah."

The sound of Naomi's soft cries mingled with Elimelech's deep voice traveled across the room in muffled tones. Moments later Mahlon and Chilion left the house without acknowledging them.

Naomi was alone with Elimelech almost an hour. When she emerged, her face was red and streaked with tears, but resolute. She stood squinting into the darkened corner where Ruth sat.

"Elimelech asked for you, Ruth."

She stood. "But why would he want to see me?"

"Because he loves you," Naomi said, motioning for Ruth to enter.

Chapter 16 – HIS HEART'S YEARNING

She approached the doorway to Elimelech's room as Naomi left the house. The lamp's flame flickered, casting shadows across his ashen frame. His body, strong and muscled only a few hours ago, now seemed frail—his attempts to breathe; shallow and uneven.

Slowly she came near, kneeling beside him. She touched his shoulder as he reached his hand toward her. He opened his eyes and Ruth wondered at their dull appearance. She sniffled, wiping her tears with the edge of her tunic.

"Do not mourn for me," Elimelech said in a raspy voice. "A man named Job once taught our people saying:

"Naked I came from my mother's womb,

And naked shall I return there.

The LORD *gave, and the* LORD *has taken away;*

Blessed be the name of the LORD.*" (Job 1:21).*

Ruth's body shook with grief. He seemed so distant, as though on a journey from which he would not return.

"Why Elimelech?"

"Adonai knows and determines all. Who are we to question? I trust Him, Ruth, with my life."

She kissed his forehead.

"I want you to remember a Scripture that is close to my heart."

"I will try."

Elimelech closed his eyes, reciting from memory:

"For I know that my Redeemer lives,

And He shall stand at last on the earth;

And after my skin is destroyed, this I know,

That in my flesh I shall see God,

Whom I shall see for myself,

And my eyes shall behold, and not another.

How my heart yearns within me!" (Job 19:25-27).

She lifted his hand to her lips and then held it against her cheek.

151

"Thank you for accepting me, Elimelech."

He nodded. Releasing her hand, he turned his head away.

She wanted to tell him she was sorry she had not come sooner, but perhaps it no longer mattered. She rose, returning to the corner where Orpah waited.

"Do you want to see Elimelech?"

"No, I cannot," she said, placing her hands over her ears.

Walking to the door, Ruth watched Mahlon as he hugged his mother and then headed in their direction.

Returning to the corner, Ruth sat waiting as Mahlon glanced her way. He entered his father's room. Her heart ached as she heard Mahlon's muffled cries. He wanted her to come two weeks ago, but she refused. Perhaps if she had done as he requested, Elimelech might have lived.

Chilion entered the house and approached Orpah, whispering something in her ear. Then he joined his brother.

Ruth could hear Mahlon and Chilion talking to their father in hushed voices. When Mahlon left the room a short time later, he walked from the house without a word.

Approaching the door, Ruth surveyed the field—observing the silhouettes of Naomi and her son comforting each other as they stood beneath the starlit heavens. She thought of her own father. He would surely be worried by now. Perhaps he would even be on his way to the field.

Tormenting thoughts of rejection began to flood her as she remained still by the door.

You see, Ruth, you do not belong here. Mahlon's father is dying because of you! Run! Run away while you still can!

Ruth looked back at Orpah.

"What is wrong, Ruth?"

"I must go home and speak to my father."

"Why?"

"Because he will know what to do."

"Please do not leave me. I am afraid!"

"One of us must stay. It is better that I go. Be strong, Orpah, do you hear me?"

"I will try."

Standing tall, Ruth took a deep breath. She would not run from her fears! Never again!

Walking into the field, she stood before Naomi. "I am going home to get Father."

"Thank you, Ruth," Naomi said, hugging her. "We appreciate your kindness more than words can express."

"No, Naomi, it is your family who has been most kind to me."

As she turned, Mahlon stepped toward her, but Naomi restrained him.

Lowering her head, she hurried down the path until she knew they could no longer see her, and then she ran.

Nearing the well, she stopped, attempting to catch her breath. Looking into the night, she recalled Elimelech's words.

After my skin is destroyed—with my eyes I will see God.

Chemosh dropped her into the fiery pit, burning her body, but Adonai spared her life. Why had He not spared Elimelech's?

"Why?" she asked, raising her fists toward the heavens. "Why did You bring him here?" she screamed. "Why did You not leave Elimelech in Bethlehem where he would be safe?" She dropped to her knees, weeping. "What will happen to his family now?" she cried.

She fell forward, lying prostrate on the ground. Tears mixed with dirt smudged her face as her body lay wracked in anguish. And then it was as though a dense fog lifted from her heart and she understood what Elimelech tried to tell her. His body was dying, but as a result, he would see God!

"Please forgive me, LORD, God of the Israelites, for questioning Your love for Elimelech and his family."

Then she repeated the Scripture Elimelech shared:

"Naked I came from my mother's womb,

And naked shall I return there.

The LORD gave, and the LORD has taken away;

Blessed be the name of the LORD." (Job 1:21).

Her legs cramped as she pushed herself to her knees and stood. Remembering her promise to Naomi, she took a deep breath and continued running toward home.

Chapter 17

HER FATHER'S KINDNESS

Ruth could see the lamps lining the windows of her home flickering in the dark as she bent over, clutching her side. It was no use; she could not take another step. "Father! Mother!" she screamed. "Come quickly!"

Her lungs burned as she waited, gasping for air.

Goad appeared in the doorway. "Ruth!" he yelled, running from the house.

"What is wrong?" Dahlia called, following him.

"Please hurry!"

He reached her; hugged her tightly and then held her at arm's length. "I was just leaving to come for you. Are you ill?"

"Oh, Father, it is not me. It is Elimelech!"

"Elimelech? What happened?"

"He is dying!"

He stepped backward. "Dying? Surely not!"

"He is. Nothing can be done to save him."

Dahlia brushed a lock of hair from Ruth's brow. "How can you be sure?"

"I was with him in the field when he collapsed." Ruth covered her face, trying to block the images of Elimelech as he lay on the ground.

"Now, Daughter," Dahlia said, touching her hand. "I am sure it is not as bad as you imagine."

"But it is. If you had been there to see the look in Mahlon's eyes—and Naomi's, you would understand. He will not survive."

Goad pulled her hands free. "I am sorry, Ruth," he said, his voice rough with emotion. "I know how much he means to you."

"What will happen to his family now?"

"Do not worry. We will help them," Goad said, looking at Dahlia.

"Yes, of course we will."

"What will they do with his body? They cannot take him back to Bethlehem. It is too far."

"Should he die, as you seem convinced; we will offer a burial tomb. It is one your grandfather prepared many years ago."

"I do not recall you mentioning it?"

"It is small, but adequate and located in a cave not far from the field."

"Thank you, Father. I hope they will accept your offer. Will you go see them in the morning?"

"No, I will go now. I want to ease any worry I can."

"Then there is a chance you can talk to Elimelech. He was still alive when I left."

"I must go quickly then. Dahlia, take Ruth home. Do not allow her to leave the house until I return."

Dahlia squeezed his hand. "Of course, Goad. Go quickly!"

He turned, running down the path toward the stables. They stood watching in the moonlight as he mounted a stallion and rode bareback past them toward the field.

Dahlia took Ruth by the hand. "Come."

"Please wait, Mother."

"Why?"

"I want to watch Father."

"That is the most ridiculous—" Dahlia's face filled with concern as she studied her. "You are not well? Goad!"

"No, Mother," she said, covering her mother's mouth. "Please let him go."

Ruth looked down the path, watching her father ride out of view.

"Just give me a few minutes, please?" Ruth said, sitting down.

Dahlia joined her. "I will, but please do not get sick again. I cannot bear to lose you."

Ruth's heart pounded and her body shook as they entered the house. Stumbling over the threshold, her mother reached out her hand, steadying her.

"Come, Ruth, the servants have prepared you something to eat."

The smell of smoked fowl lingered. "Oh, Mother," she said, holding her nose. "I cannot."

"But you must keep up your strength."

"If I tried, it would not stay down." A wave of nausea gripped her and she doubled over in pain.

"That is understandable. Come and sit."

Walking to the corner, Ruth lay on the rug, turning on her side. Dahlia knelt, pulling her head covering free as she stroked her hair.

"Do not worry, Mother. I am better now, I promise."

"Do you want to tell me what happened?"

Closing her eyes, she remembered the look on Elimelech's face. "As I arrived at the wheat field, I considered going home."

"Why?"

"I was not sure Elimelech would want to see me. I almost convinced myself to leave when I heard him call my name. He stood there with his arms extended, waiting for me. And then he fell. Oh, Mother!"

"I am sorry for you, Ruth. I am sure it was very difficult for you to see him in such a state. Was he able to speak?"

"Barely. He lay there, clutching his chest, groaning."

"It sounds as if his heart was failing."

"But even in that moment he was more worried for Naomi than himself. I saw it as he took her hand, telling her he loved her. And now they will never know . . ."

"Know what, dear?"

"It does not matter."

"Of course it does. Tell me."

"I wanted to continue helping Naomi."

"Perhaps you still can."

"Not if they return to Bethlehem."

"But how can they go back? The famine is too severe. They would not survive."

Ruth lay silent. Dahlia rose and left the room. Returning a short time later, she tucked a pillow beneath her head and covered her with a soft, woven sheet.

"Are you feeling better?"

"Yes," she said, allowing her body to relax under the security of the linen.

"Do not worry. Your father will do all he can to help them."

"I know he will try. I hope they will accept his offer."

"I am sure they will. Now, try to sleep."

"Thank you, Mother."

Dahlia walked along the walls, extinguishing the lamps. Ruth's eyes adjusted to the moonlight as she looked at the stars through the open window.

Alone, she remembered Elimelech's words, repeating them softly, burning them into her memory:

"*. . . I shall see for myself,*

And my eyes shall behold, and not another.

How my heart yearns within me!" (Job 19:27).

And then Ruth prayed. "Thank you, Adonai, that Elimelech knows You and will behold You with his own eyes on this very night. His mother named him well. You truly are his God and King. But what about his family? What will happen to them? Oh, Adonai, please comfort Naomi as she faces life without Elimelech. And please help Mahlon understand how very sorry I am. He wanted me to come sooner, but I refused.

"I love Mahlon, Adonai, but You already know, do you not? You see into the hearts of all mankind, for we are the work of Your hands. Thank you for allowing a Moabite to hear Your voice. I will forever treasure the sound of it. Thank you for allowing Elimelech to come to our land. My life will never be the same because of him. When he stands in Your presence, will You tell him for me?"

At last, she fell into a deep, restful sleep.

✡   ✡   ✡

"Ruth," Goad said, nudging her. "Ruth, wake up."

The mid-morning sun shone brightly through the window as she struggled to open her eyes. She sat up, remembering the sorrowful events of the previous evening.

He knelt at her side and touched her forehead. "Are you feeling ill? Your mother has been frantic with worry."

"I feel much stronger this morning. How long have you been home?"

"Not long. I knew you would want me to awaken you."

"You stayed through the night with Mahlon and his family?"

"Yes, I did."

"Is Elimelech still alive?" she asked, her chin quivering.

Goad brushed a tear from her cheek. "No, Daughter. I am very sorry, but he died a few hours ago."

Lowering her head, she stared at her hands as tears dripped on her tunic. "Were you able to speak to him?"

"Yes. He was in and out of consciousness, but thankfully each time he woke, he asked for us."

"I am grateful," she said, lifting her gaze. "What did you say to him?"

"I assured him that his family would be taken care of and if they

159

desired, I would help them return to Bethlehem."

She slipped her arms around his waist. "Thank you for your kindness to them, Father."

"Elimelech has been a diligent and trustworthy supervisor. He has also been good to you, my sweet daughter. It was the least I could do."

"What did Elimelech decide? Is he sending his family back to Bethlehem?"

"He told me Mahlon was now head of the family and those decisions would be his to make."

"But he is so young."

"No younger than I was when I ventured out on my own. He is very mature and I believe he is more than able to oversee the field, if he decides to do so."

"Supervisor! You told Mahlon he could supervise the field?"

"Yes."

"You trust him with such a huge responsibility?"

"Yes, I do. I have observed him in the field with the servants and I know they have great respect for him."

"What did Mahlon say?"

"He expressed his gratitude, but said he needs time to decide what is best for his family. He requested I give them two weeks to mourn his father's passing and allow his mother and brother time to express their desires."

"Oh, Father, the thought that they might stay!"

"Yes, I know. I hope they will too."

"And what about Elimelech? Will they accept your offer of the burial tomb?"

"Yes. Naomi wept when I told Mahlon."

"Should I go to them, Father?"

"No, Naomi specifically asked that you not come for two weeks."

"Two weeks! But why—"

"She is concerned for you. We all are. The stress of Elimelech's passing and burial will likely be too much for you to bear in your weakened state."

"But, Father, I feel fine."

"That is what you told me the day you collapsed. And you were not fine last night. You gave your mother quite a scare after I left. She was afraid you were going to faint."

Ruth shrugged, realizing his mind was made up. "I hope Naomi knows how much I want to come."

"Have no doubt, Daughter; she knows you care deeply for them."

"Did she mention any desire to stay?"

"No. Without question, she longs for her homeland."

"She said so?"

"Would you expect otherwise?"

"No." She looked away. Of course Naomi would want to leave. *What is there in Moab for me now, Adonai?*

✡ ✡ ✡

"Be patient, Ruth, we will know Mahlon's decision in two weeks. In the meantime, I am sending Orpah's father to supervise the field."

"Did he agree?"

"I have not spoken with him yet, but I sent Orpah to prepare him for my visit. I told her to tell him everything that has happened. I will leave here shortly to go and speak to him."

"What about Mahlon and Chilion? Were they agreeable to Orpah's father coming to supervise?"

"Yes. They wanted to stay close to their mother as they are concerned she will mourn so deeply she may fall ill."

"I know grieving can weaken one's spirit," Ruth said as Goad pulled her up from the floor.

"I will ask the servants to prepare you a special meal. Promise me you will eat, for your mother's sake."

"Thank you, Father. I will. I promise."

"And a leisurely walk through the garden will do you good. But do not go any further."

"I will obey your request, Father," she said, looking about the room. "By the way, where is Mother?"

Goad hesitated.

"Are you keeping something from me?"

"No, of course not." He sighed. "I hoped to share the news with you after you had eaten."

"What news? Where is Mother?"

"She has gone to stay with Mahlon's family—at Naomi's request."

"Why would she ask for Mother?"

"I do not know, but she did and your mother dropped everything and left immediately when I told her."

"She went alone—without the servants to attend her?"

"Surprisingly, yes."

"What has gotten in to her?"

Goad laughed. "I have begun to wonder the same."

"When will she return?"

"In two weeks."

"Two weeks!" Ruth crossed her arms and scowled.

"That is all I know, Ruth." Goad raised his hand. "No more questions," he said as he called for the servants.

She watched him walk from the room, shaking her head in confusion. Her mother had gone to Naomi's alone and without a single servant to attend her! Where would she sleep? On a bed of hay?

Ruth walked to the chair where her mother sat sewing the previous day. Searching the basket, she removed the small hand cloth, examining her mother's design. Grasping the needle, she pushed it through the fabric. What would she do for the next two weeks without Naomi or her mother? Likely all their tunics would have purple stitching on them before her mother returned!

Chapter 18

THE REUNION

Ruth sat on her bed, pulling a section of thread from the basket. Raising the needle, she peered through the eye, making several attempts to push the thread through before succeeding.

"Finally!" she said looking at the old woman with a broad smile.

Lilia smirked. "Need I remind you, the thread will slip through the eye easily if you lick it first?"

Ruth laughed. "I am quite sure Mother would deem licking thread unbecoming a maiden."

Lilia bit her lip in a futile attempt to restrain a smile. "I would agree," she said. Standing, the woman stretched and then leaned backward. "Getting old is not for the faint of heart, Miss Ruth. Now, if I have completed my duties here, I will prepare your evening meal."

"Will you join me?"

"Now, Miss Ruth, you know your mother will not allow that."

"I know, but I tire of eating alone."

"Maybe your father will make it home in time."

"He has not for the past ten days. He seems more interested in supervising his supervisors than in spending time with me."

"Perhaps it is your endless questions that keep him away, Miss Ruth."

"Perhaps." Ruth said, smiling at Lilia as she pulled the needle through the linen.

"Ruth!" Goad called.

Dropping the needle in the basket, she listened intently as he called her a second time.

"What is it, Father," she yelled, poking her head out the window.

"We have been invited to Naomi's for dinner."

"Dinner? But it has only been ten days."

"And you want to quibble?"

"No, Father!"

"Now hurry, Daughter, and get dressed. I will meet you by the well."

"But I am already dressed."

"Well, put on something colorful."

"My finest?"

"No, but not your harvest clothing, either, dear."

"Of course not, Father."

"And Ruth."

"Yes, Father?" She turned back, eyeing him.

"This needs to be a time of joy and laughter, not sorrow."

She frowned. Was he attempting to prepare her for Mahlon's decision?

"But I will not be happy, Father, if they leave Moab."

"True, but you want what is best for them, do you not?"

"I suppose so."

Turning, Ruth studied the old woman as she held a robe and colorful tunic.

"This one will do," she said.

"One with my stitching?"

"Yes," she replied, running her hand along the thread. "Your designs are as intricate as any I have ever seen."

Ruth kissed her cheek as she helped her slip into the garments.

Twisting her hair about her head, the servant inserted a comb and then pulled several locks free to fall about her face.

"My, but you are a beauty," she said, bowing as she left the room.

✡   ✡   ✡

Goad stood as Ruth approached the well.

"You look breathtaking this evening, Daughter."

"Too elaborate?"

"Not at all."

"How is Naomi?"

"Quite well, considering."

"And Mother?"

"Changed for the better, I would say. But then you will have to determine that for yourself."

"Has being around Naomi changed her belief in Chemosh?"

"No, Daughter, but she loves their family just the same."

"I am grateful."

"As I am." Goad looked into the distance, as though deep in thought.

"Is there something bothering you, Father?"

"Bothering me? No. I was just thinking what a wonderful daughter you have been to me."

"You are sounding rather sentimental."

He sighed. "You look very grown up tonight."

She smiled. "But I will always be your little girl."

Goad squeezed her hand as they continued in silence. Nearing the field, Ruth stopped, staring at the house.

"What is it?" he asked.

"I thought I was ready to see them, but now I am not so sure."

"They need you, Ruth. Whatever Mahlon's decision, I am sure you will accept with grace."

Accept his decision with grace? Could she? Though she reasoned her father was right; her heart rebelled. It was perplexing how she determined to do the right thing—but now faced with the reality of their leaving, was equally tempted to do the wrong. Sometimes she felt like a meandering stream, flowing at the mercy of its banks. And yet, it was remarkable how the God of the Israelites had forever changed her. Somewhere along the way, Naomi and her sons' security had become more important than her own.

She glanced sideways at her father as they neared the door. With a timid smile she tilted her head around the frame.

Mahlon laughed. "You know we can see you!"

"Oh," she said, flushing. "I should have known."

"You look very pretty tonight, Ruth," Mahlon said as she stepped inside. "I have missed you."

Ruth looked at Naomi. Missed her! Surely she would find Mahlon's greeting rather forward. But apparently not!

"And I have missed all of you," Ruth said, looking in his direction.

Mahlon smiled his usual captivating smile. Her heart sank. Perhaps he was acting strangely because this would be the last night she would ever see him!

Approaching Naomi, Ruth took her hands. "I pray you are well."

"I am," Naomi said. "We could not wait another day to see you. Nor could your mother."

Ruth faced her mother. "The house has truly been lonely without you."

"Thank you, Daughter." Dahlia crossed the room. Inspecting Ruth's tunic, she turned her this way and that. "My, what beautiful handiwork. I do not recall ever having seen this garment."

"I agree," Mahlon said. "You have never looked more lovely."

Ruth blushed. "Thank you. The stitching is my own."

"Really," Chilion said, feigning shock.

"Enough, Son." Naomi motioned toward the table.

"I thought you asked me to dinner, not a feast!" Ruth said, scanning the abundance of food. "And roasted lamb—my favorite!"

"We heard," Mahlon said.

Goad chuckled and then winked at Ruth. She did her best to ignore him.

"It smells wonderful."

"I am glad to see you have an appetite. You look as though you have lost weight. Are you well?" Mahlon asked.

Ruth looked at her father and frowned.

"Perhaps we should eat," Naomi said before Ruth could answer.

Mahlon pulled the side bench away, motioning for Goad and Dahlia, then pointed to the opposite end of the table. Chilion nodded, pulling the chair beside his away for his mother. One chair remained next to Mahlon. He held Ruth's gaze as he stood—waiting.

She hesitated and then reluctantly moved to the chair.

"Thank you," she said.

Mahlon scooted her close to the table and then took his place beside her. Looking intent, he extended his hand to her. With raised brows she sat—frozen. Turning, he grasped Dahlia's hand instead. The table followed suit.

Ruth's heart raced as she laid her hand in his. Mahlon's eyes, soft and unmoving, held hers as he bowed his head.

The words of his prayer ran together as he moved his thumb along the top of her hand. Her heart pounded erratically. What had gotten in to him? She felt Mahlon gently squeeze her hand and then release it as he stood and then began slicing the lamb.

"I will never forget the first time I saw you, Ruth," he said.

"Oh, no, please do not remind me!"

Goad chuckled.

"Now Father, you act as though you have already heard this story."

"Indeed. I have heard a lot about you these past ten days."

"Is that so?" Ruth looked at her mother.

Dahlia nodded.

"Perhaps it was not such a good idea to keep me away."

The table erupted in laughter.

Outnumbered, she giggled—then continued eating, contemplating the conversations bantering about. Her parents laughed and talked as though they had known these Israelites all their lives.

At last, Naomi and Dahlia stood. Ruth attempted to join them, but Naomi squeezed her shoulder. "Your mother and I will clean up."

"Fair enough, if you insist."

Her father continued on with the story of how he came to own the field Elimelech had supervised. When all the dishes and food were removed, Goad and Chilion rose.

As Ruth scooted her chair back, Mahlon reached for her.

"Please stay," he said. "There is something I must explain."

Ruth sank back into the chair. The moment had come. How could she bear to listen to what he had to say? But how could she not?

"I want to hear your decision, but do you mind if I take just a moment?"

Mahlon's face seemed filled with worry as he looked at her father.

Goad nodded. "Allowing Ruth a bit of fresh air after such a wonderful meal will do her good."

"Of course," Mahlon said, turning to Ruth. "Take all the time you need."

Ruth hugged her parents and Naomi. Leaving the house, she removed her sandals and walked into the field. Finding a suitable spot, she sat, looking up into the heavens as she dug her toes into the dirt. The moon, full and orange, seemed to stare down at her with a smile carved on its surface. If only she felt the way it looked.

"Help me, Adonai," she prayed, "to trust like Abraham. Even if I never see them after this night, help me accept their decision with grace."

Finishing her prayer, she stood, studying the stars. Suddenly, she felt a hand on her shoulder. Turning, she saw her father.

"Are you ready, Daughter?"

She nodded. "Thank you for understanding me so well."

"You are sounding rather sentimental this evening."

She giggled. "I guess I am. Do you mind going on ahead of me? I would like to walk to the house alone."

He kissed her forehead. "Not at all," he said, walking away.

Chapter 19

THE DECISION

Ruth studied Mahlon from the darkened field. He sat at the table, his frame illuminated by lamplight; his head bowed. Her heart ached for him. Not only had he lost his beloved father, he was now head of the family. Would he choose to stay in Moab or return to Judah? Given Naomi's longing for Bethlehem, Ruth felt certain they would leave.

Stooping, she grabbed a handful of earth, grinding it in her palm and letting it fall. Moab was the only home she had ever known, but it did not hold her heart the way Judah held Naomi's. She gazed into the distance; pondering the gray mountainous terrain separating their homelands. Dusting her hand against her tunic, she strengthened her resolve.

Retrieving her sandals, she began walking barefoot to the house, determining to do all she could to assure Mahlon life would continue without them. Perhaps one day she would journey to Bethlehem to visit his family. Likely, he would be married with a wife and children of his own by then. The thought pained her. There were many outcomes Ruth knew she could endure, but that would not be one of them.

Taking a deep breath, she stepped over the threshold, dropping her sandals by the door.

Mahlon rose. She smiled timidly as she approached, feeling the rough stone floor against her feet. He pulled a chair from the table.

"Thank you, Mahlon," she said, taking her place beside him. Glancing over her shoulder, she acknowledged Naomi, Chilion and her parents as they stood directly behind him.

"Are you ready?" he asked.

"I am."

"Mother, there is a leather pouch on Father's table. Would you bring it to me, please?"

"Yes, Son."

Naomi walked to the corner of the room. As she retrieved the pouch, Ruth noticed two large woolen packs lying nearby. Could it be they were already preparing to return to Bethlehem?

Naomi laid the pouch on the table. Mahlon pushed it in front of Ruth. Picking it up, she felt the worn leather, then held it against her cheek. It had been Elimelech's. She smelled the musky fragrance, remembering the Scriptures he stored there. Lifting the flap, she studied the scroll tucked inside.

"Ruth, I have something very important to share with you," Mahlon said. "I hope you will find it in your heart to have an open mind—and please do not run."

"I will not run." She eyed the rest of their families, standing behind him.

"Thank you."

Ruth removed the scroll, moving her fingers over the smooth parchment. "What is written inside?" she asked as she touched the twine tied around it.

"It has to do with a question you asked me."

Ruth dropped the scroll. Staring wide-eyed, she pulled her hands into her lap, clasping them tightly.

"Do you remember, Ruth?"

She looked at Naomi. "Yes, I remember. I asked if your God would accept me."

"The answer to your question is written inside the parchment," Mahlon said, drawing her attention.

"But where did it come from?"

"My father."

"Elimelech? But how?"

"I asked him the night he died."

"The night he died? And he was able to answer?"

"Yes. And he told me to write all he shared inside this parchment."

Her heart quickened. *Oh, Mahlon, please do not leave me.* Leaning back, she searched all their faces. It was odd how they held no hint of emotion; no joy, no sorrow.

Lifting the scroll, she ran the chord between her fingers and tugged it free.

"It is written in Hebrew," Mahlon said.

She carefully unrolled the parchment, studying the symbols inked within.

"Father asked me to start by telling you the story of a very special Canaanite woman. Her name was Rahab. At the time her story begins, the children of Israel left the wilderness and entered the Promised Land in order to take possession of it. Are you ready to hear her story?"

"Yes. I am."

Mahlon nodded in his brother's direction. Chilion began reciting from memory:

Now Joshua the son of Nun sent out two men from Acacia Grove to spy secretly, saying, "Go, view the land, especially Jericho." So they went, and came to the house of a prostitute named Rahab, and lodged there. And it was told the king of Jericho, saying, "Behold, men have come here tonight from the children of Israel to search out the country." (Joshua 2:1-2).

Ruth raised her hand, interrupting him. "Who was Joshua?"

"He was the man God appointed to lead the people out of the wilderness and into the land God promised."

"I see," Ruth said as Mahlon continued:

So the king of Jericho sent to Rahab, saying, "Bring out the men who have come to you, who have entered your house, for they have come to search out all the country."

Then the woman took the two men and hid them. So she said, "Yes, the men came to me, but I did not know where they were from. And it happened as the gate was being shut, when it was dark, that the men went out. Where the men went I do not know; pursue them quickly, for you may overtake them. (But she had brought them up to the roof and hidden them with the stalks of flax, which she had laid in order on the roof.)" (Joshua 2:3-6).

"Why did she lie to the king?"

"Because she believed the God of the Israelites was The One True God. She feared Him more than the king of Jericho."

"What did Rahab do after the king's men left in search of the spies?"

Naomi sat, wrapping her arm around Ruth's shoulder. "She went to the roof and spoke to the Israelites." Closing her eyes, she quoted Rahab saying:

"I know that the LORD has given you the land, that the terror of you has fallen on us, and that all the inhabitants of the land are fainthearted because of you. For we have heard how the LORD dried up the water of the Red Sea for you when you came out of Egypt, and what you did to the two kings of the Amorites who were on the other side of the Jordan . . . whom you utterly destroyed. And as soon as we heard these things, our hearts melted; neither did there remain any more courage in anyone because of you, for the LORD your God, He is God in heaven above and on earth beneath." (Joshua 2:9-11).

"She believed in Adonai, as I do!"

"Yes, she did!" Naomi laughed.

"What happened to her?"

"She asked them to have mercy on her family, saying:

"Now therefore, I beg you, swear to me by the LORD, *since I have shown you kindness, that you also will show kindness to my father's house, and give me a true token, and spare my father, my mother, my brothers, my sisters, and all that they have, and deliver our lives from death." (Joshua 2:12-13).*

"Did Adonai spare her?"

"Yes," Mahlon responded. "Because she believed He was The One True God—He not only spared her, but allowed her to live with His chosen people."

"A foreigner! He allowed a foreigner to live with them?" She frowned. "But I am a Moabite, Mahlon. God said He would never allow a Moabite in His assembly."

Mahlon unrolled the scroll. His eyes moved until settling near the bottom of the parchment. He took a deep breath and looked at his mother.

She nodded. "Go ahead, Son."

Looking at Goad, he shifted nervously. "It will be easier for me, Ruth, if I read Father's words."

"Of course." Bracing herself, she grasped the seat's rough edge and waited.

Fixing his eyes on the parchment, Mahlon began reading his father's words; "'Ruth, I believe Adonai brought me to the land of the Moabites because He saw your heart as you searched for The One True God. He brought us here for you.'" Mahlon paused, looking at her.

"For me!" she gasped.

He lowered his head and continued, "When Mahlon shared the vision you had as you lay near death; it was a confirmation for me as well. I saw your father's field in a dream. I heard Adonai's voice as He told me He had prepared a place for us here. I trusted Him, just as Abraham did."

Ruth laid her palms on the table and closed her eyes.

"'You also heard His voice, Ruth—for I AM THAT I AM told you, *fear* not for He had heard your plea. Now, the final decision is yours to make. Like Rahab, will you trust that He has accepted you as one of His chosen people?'"

Tears streamed down her face as she opened her eyes, looking at Mahlon. "Thank you for finding the courage to ask your father. Yes, I trust that He loves me. I trust it was His voice I heard in the wind calling out to me and saying, *'If you search for Me with your whole heart, you will find Me.'* Thank you, Adonai!"

Standing, Mahlon hugged his mother. She kissed his forehead and looked in Chilion's direction.

Walking to the table, Chilion retrieved a goblet and wine skin and placed them in front of Mahlon.

"What is this about?" Ruth puzzled.

"You will know soon enough," Mahlon said as he nervously poured wine from the skin into the goblet and continued reading, "'Because you have confessed your trust in Adonai, I now give my blessing to Mahlon to do what I believe Adonai has called him to do.'"

Mahlon took Ruth's hands in his. His palms were sweaty; his hands trembling. Was he afraid? She braced her back against the chair.

"We have a tradition among our people. It is a way of sealing a promise. It is known as a covenant. My father has given me permission to offer you a new covenant. If you accept, drink from the wine placed before you. If you do not, simply refuse the wine and I will never ask you again."

"Ask me what, Mahlon?"

"To be my wife."

"Your wife—"

Pulling her hands free, she covered her eyes. "But how can this be? You must marry from among your own people?"

"Now you *are* one of our people, Ruth. And just as Rahab married an Israelite, so you may also, if you so choose." He touched her cheek,

176

wiping the tears away.

"Rahab married an Israelite?"

"Yes, my love, and I offer you the same. Will you accept my covenant of marriage?"

Standing, Ruth paced the room—then stopped abruptly; glancing at Naomi. She was smiling!

Looking back at Mahlon, she held his gaze. "This day, I am thankful to know that my God and King has found me acceptable and has allowed me to marry the man I love with all my heart!"

"Yes! Then drink the wine," Mahlon said, "please!"

Grasping the goblet, she pulled it to her mouth as she kept her eyes on his. Finally, she felt the wine touch her lips and swallowed.

The room erupted in laughter as Mahlon pulled her in his arms, swinging her around.

"You will be my wife!"

"And you will be my husband!"

"Put her down," Naomi said. "I want to hug her, too!"

Naomi laughed, embracing her children.

"When will we marry?"

"That you cannot know," Dahlia said.

"Mother, are you happy for me?"

"Of course, my daughter! I have known since the day you almost died that your happiness lay with Mahlon."

"When will we marry?"

Goad chuckled. "After Mahlon has prepared a suitable home for you."

"But I do not want to leave Naomi!"

"We will not be moving away from Mother. We will repair the two rooms sealed off from this home, to make room for you *and* Orpah."

"Orpah? Orpah will live here, too?"

"Hopefully!" Chilion said, grinning.

"What do you mean?"

"If she accepts Adonai as her God, then Father has given his blessing for me to marry also."

"You will marry Orpah?"

"I hope to. I cannot assume she will say yes, as I have not yet asked her."

"Why have you not asked?"

"Mahlon and I must go to her father and tell him the conditions of the covenant. If he agrees, then I will ask Orpah. I waited because Mahlon is the oldest. Father's desire was for him to ask you first," Chilion added, squeezing his brother's shoulder. "A lot has happened since we saw you last!"

"It certainly has!" Ruth looked at her father with a mischievous grin. "So, am I right to assume that if Mahlon and Chilion will ask Orpah's father for permission to marry, that Mahlon did the same?"

"He did," Goad said. Reaching for Mahlon, he shook his hand.

"And when did that happen, Father?"

"The night I went to see Elimelech, he shared with me his desire for you to marry Mahlon. He asked me to consider it and I told him I would."

"It was also on that night I asked Dahlia to come and stay with me," Naomi said. "I wanted time alone with her to see if she would consider allowing you to marry Mahlon."

"You considered Mother's wishes?"

"Yes. Mahlon would not have taken it further, had either of your parents objected. This morning your mother said she could not wait another moment to see you and Mahlon together."

"Everyone seemed certain you would accept my proposal, but me. When you left the house and walked into the field, I was certain of your answer."

"You thought I might refuse?"

"I did. I asked your father to check on you—to see if he thought you might run."

Dahlia giggled. "I knew she would not run from you, Mahlon."

Ruth blushed. "What happened the night Father came to see Elimelech?"

Goad rested his hand on Mahlon's shoulder. "It was a very difficult time for all of us, as we knew Elimelech was dying. But I know he took comfort and even joy in discussing with Mahlon what he wanted to share with you."

Naomi wiped tears from her eyes. "After that night, your mother and I spent ten bittersweet days together sharing and growing to love each other. It was a very special time of healing for me."

"I am thankful you and Mother had time alone together." Turning, she crossed her arms in mocked annoyance. "Father, when I asked you why Naomi requested Mother come, you did not tell the truth."

Mahlon leaned back, laughing. "Ruth, you can be very frustrating at times."

"I would agree with Mahlon," Goad said.

"Well, Father, I forgive you, anyway. But please do not make a habit of hiding things from me."

"Only when necessary!"

"So we are going to live here?"

"Yes," Mahlon said. "There is still a famine in the land of Judah and Goad has graciously allowed me to continue supervising his field."

"You will make a fine supervisor," Goad said. "I am thankful for your willingness to continue harvesting the land."

"I am too! I could not bear the thought of your leaving *or* marrying another," Ruth said.

"Is that so," Mahlon said. "So you did not tell the truth either, the day we were at the stream."

"I guess not," Ruth replied with a coy smile. "How long will it take you to prepare our home?"

"That you will not know," Goad said. "I will explain everything tomorrow. Now, it is time for us to leave. You will not see Mahlon again until he comes for you on your wedding day."

"What?" Ruth frowned.

Mahlon nodded. Ruth knew better than to argue with these two strong men. It would do no good.

"Naomi, I hope I will see you soon. Please tell Mahlon to work hard and get the job done quickly."

"I do not think you need worry about that! He has pined for you from the first day he laid eyes on you."

Ruth raised her brows as she cut her eyes in Mahlon's direction.

He looked at her with a bold, broad smile.

"Some things cannot be hidden from a parent no matter how one might try," Naomi said.

Mahlon pulled Ruth into his arms. She could feel the beating of his heart. "You can rest assured I will come for you as soon as I can," he said, glancing at Goad.

"Of that I am certain," Goad chuckled as he walked to the corner of the room and retrieved the packs.

"Are those ours?" Ruth asked.

"Yes," Dahlia said. "Well, actually they are yours."

"Mine?"

"Yes." Mahlon said, "They contain the material for your wedding gown."

"Is that so? You must have been confident of my answer."

"No, my love. It was your father who was convinced."

"Yes, he knows me well."

"Thank you, Mahlon," Goad said, shaking his hand. "I will see you soon."

"Yes, sir," Mahlon responded. "We can discuss the wheat harvest when you return."

Stepping outside, Ruth waved at Mahlon. Joy filled her heart, but also sorrow. How both emotions could reside there at the same time she did not know.

"Father, one day Mahlon will likely return to the land of Judah. And when he does, I will go with him."

"We know, Ruth," Goad said, taking her hand.

"What will happen to you and Mother? I am your only heir?"

"Every parent desires the happiness of their child more than their own," Dahlia said. "We want all the happiness life can bring to you and Mahlon."

Stepping between her parents, she grasped their hands. Praying silently, she asked Adonai to bless her father and mother, just as Rahab had done for her family.

As they neared their home, Ruth sighed. Her joy was complete. "I will be a wife! I will be the mother of Mahlon's children and a daughter to Naomi!"

"That is all true," Goad said.

"Now I know that Adonai is a God of judgment but also love and mercy."

It was true! Adonai loved her—accepted her. She could not explain how she knew, but somewhere deep down in her soul, she did. And yet, an unexplained measure of foreboding also resided here, making her uneasy. What could it mean? She pushed the gloomy thoughts away.

"We have wedding robes to make," she said, looking at her mother.

"Yes, we do!" Dahlia said as they arrived home.

Chapter 20

THE TRUMPET BLAST

"How many months must I wait, Adonai?" Ruth yawned, stretching as she looked out her chamber window at the half-full moon. Her thoughts drifted to the evening of Mahlon's proposal, recalling with delight each detail. Since that night, she had not slept well. And who could blame her? She was now fifteen years old and the wheat harvest had long been completed. Still Mahlon had not come for her!

Lying back on the bed, she glanced at the lamp, observing its small, flickering flame as the smell of olive oil permeated the room. *Remind her to keep her lamp filled*, Mahlon had told her father. *She must be ready at a moment's notice.* She did her best to comply, trimming the wick and replenishing the oil every evening before retiring.

She closed the window's shutter and removed her nightgown. Dipping her hands into a bowl of perfumed ointment, she massaged the creamy mixture into her fair skin. The sweet aromas of lavender and myrrh calmed her anxious nerves. Her mother had instructed her to bathe and apply the fragrances daily in preparation of her wedding night. She moved her fingers over her arms and legs; satisfied with their silky smooth texture.

Slipping into her nightgown, she finally drifted to sleep, dreaming of trumpet blasts.

Trumpet blasts! She sprang from bed, listening intently. *Who would be sounding a trumpet at this hour?*

Tiptoeing out the front door and through the courtyard, she paused, squinting down the path. The landscape lay before her in muted shades of blue and gray beneath an opaque sky. She held her breath, straining to hear the music as it mingled with the sounds of rustling trees.

"Mother, Father!" she yelled as specks of light appeared in the distance.

"What is all the commotion?" Goad called, his voice hoarse as he roused from sleep.

"Come quickly!"

Within moments, he was standing in the doorway, barefooted and rubbing his eyes. "What is it?" he asked, sounding groggy.

"Look! There are lamps. Do you see them, Father?"

He hurried to join her. "I do, Daughter."

"Today is the day!" Dahlia shouted. "We must get your wedding gown on!"

"But why is he coming when the sun has not yet risen? Did he not know I would be sleeping at this hour?"

"Mahlon determined neither the day, nor time, but he will explain. Now, make haste, Daughter!"

Ruth rushed past Dahlia, entering the main living area. Suddenly, she stopped. The melodic sounds of tinkling bells and whistling flutes fluttered through the windows. She twirled in a circle, dancing about.

"Ruth, hold still!" Dahlia said, reaching for her.

"Lilia! Where is Lilia?" Ruth asked as the old woman hobbled into the room.

"I declare, Miss Ruth, I was on my way! Who could sleep through all this commotion?"

"He is coming, Lilia!"

"I do believe every inhabitant in the plain knows he is coming, dear."

"Wait, Mother!" She froze; hearing another trumpet blast. Retrieving her lamp, she skipped to the path. Holding it above her head, she swung it back and forth.

A single lamp mimicked hers. "Oh, Mother, it is Mahlon! He is coming for me! Finally, he is coming!"

"Yes, he is," Dahlia said, waving from the doorway. "Do you want him to find you in your nightgown?"

"Give me a moment, please, Mother."

Running past Lilia, Ruth slammed her chamber door. Removing her nightgown, she tossed it aside. As she stood bare from head to toe, her heart quickened. She and Mahlon would belong to each other—body and soul, before the day was through. *Thank you, Adonai, for allowing me to marry such a wonderful man.*

Scurrying across the room, she retrieved her undergarments and slipped them on just as Dahlia rapped on the door.

"Ruth! We are coming in!"

"Very well, Mother! I am ready."

Dahlia opened the door. Lilia was at her side; the wedding gown draped neatly over her shoulder. It was white as snow with lacey patterns of gold stitching.

"This is no time for modesty, Miss Ruth," Lilia said, tugging the gown over Ruth's head.

The light, airy fabric felt soft against her skin; flowing over her young curves and resting atop her ankles.

"Turn around, please," Dahlia said, tying a gold sash just beneath her breasts.

Lilia braided her hair and then arranged an intricate headdress over her brow. It was fashioned from gold with tiny strands of pearls.

Dahlia grasped long locks of hair, entwining them around her finger and laying them about her face. Ruth touched her hand. "Thank you,

Mother, for accepting Mahlon."

"He is a good man, Ruth. Your father and I both agree." She kissed her cheek. "And look at you! You look gorgeous!"

"Thank you, Mother!"

Lilia knelt at Ruth's feet. "No more time for sentiments, dear," she said, guiding several intricate, gold anklets into place.

"Thank you for being here with me this morning, Lilia, and for being my friend."

Raising her head, Lilia looked at Ruth. Her countenance was filled with love, but she spoke not a word. Ruth smiled, stepping into her sandals as she started for the door.

"Wait!" Dahlia grasped the linen train, laying it over Ruth's arm. "Go, my child."

Ruth hurried from the house. As she stood at the edge of the courtyard, Mahlon came into view. The lamps illuminated his tall, slender frame and broad shoulders. She stopped a short distance from him; admiring his crisp new tunic. It hung to his knees and was gathered snug at his waist with a purple sash.

Four long months had passed since she last saw him. He looked older with his dark, wavy hair pulled at the nape of his neck. He set his lamp on the ground. Dropping the donkey's reins, he motioned for her to come. She approached him shyly until she was standing before him, looking up into his dark, brown eyes.

"Oh, Mahlon, I thought this day would never come!"

He wrapped his arms around her tiny waist and held her close. "The wait has been almost unbearable, I can assure you," he said in a hushed voice. "As I left the house to come for you, I thanked Adonai."

"For what?" she asked, coyly.

"That tonight you will be my wife."

His smile was full and captivating. She rested her head on his chest. "What took you so long?"

"Only my father knew the day of our wedding. It is our custom."

"But how could that be?"

"Father wrote the date on parchment and asked Mother to seal it in a pouch. She brought it to me yesterday. He requested that I come for you, just before the rising of the sun. It took us well into the night to finish preparing the feast . . . Goad!" Mahlon called, acknowledging him as he approached.

"Son," Goad responded, shaking his hand. "Dahlia and I are thankful you did not have to wait another day. Ruth's restlessness has been difficult to bear."

"Have you had trouble sleeping too, Father?"

Goad sighed. "I will not bore you with the details, sweet Daughter."

"Ruth!" Naomi said, embracing her. "I hope you were not startled by our early arrival."

"Not to worry, Naomi. I am so happy! Adonai has blessed me!"

The servants circled around, holding their lamps in the air. Mahlon stepped backward, admiring Ruth's gown as the lamplight caught the flecks of gold stitching. "You look stunning!"

Cheers erupted and the servants swung their lamps in unison as Mahlon hoisted Ruth onto the donkey.

"I can walk, Mahlon!"

"Perhaps. But not on *our* wedding day."

Chilion skidded to a halt beside Ruth. "Who can keep up with this Israelite!" he said, panting. "You would think he was late for his own wedding."

Ruth giggled as she leaned from the donkey's side to hug him. "Where is Orpah?"

"At her parents', waiting for our wedding day."

"She accepted your covenant?"

"She did."

"But she will miss our celebration?"

"Yes," Mahlon said. "But I am sure she understands. Chilion cannot see her until the day they marry."

"And she will not know the day, just as I did not. Did you remind her to keep her lamp filled?"

Chilion nodded. "I did. And, by the way, welcome to our family!"

"Thank you, Brother."

"You look beautiful, Ruth."

"That she does," Mahlon said as he handed the reins to Chilion. "Ruth, I have a confession to make."

"And what would that be?"

"I have loved you from the moment I first saw you on The King's Highway, studying me shyly."

"You knew I liked you?"

"Of course! It was written all over your face."

"Mahlon, it was not!"

Chilion chuckled. "Oh, yes, it was."

"Well, if we are confessing, I admit I found you attractive, but also irritating."

Mahlon smiled, keeping his gaze steady. There was something in the way his eyes met hers that made her blush. *Calm my heart, Adonai!*

The sun's rays crept over the horizon as the servants began extinguishing their lamps. The sky was clear and blue as a gentle wind drifted across the plain, lifting the pearl fringe from Ruth's brow.

Chilion jerked the donkey's reins. "On any other day she would cooperate."

"Do not worry, Son, we have the whole day ahead of us," Naomi said.

Ruth reached for Naomi's hand. "Thank you for welcoming me into your family."

"It is our blessing, Ruth. I love you as my own daughter."

"Stubborn animal!" Chilion chided, yanking the long leather straps.

"This donkey is going to an early grave if I have anything to do with it."

"You have done your duty," Mahlon said, sounding amused. "You and Mother should go on ahead."

Chilion dropped the harness. "Thank you, Brother," he said as he and Naomi walked toward the house.

Mahlon chuckled. Laying the leather straps over the donkey's neck, he made a clicking noise as he stepped next to Ruth. The donkey immediately began lumbering down the path of its own volition.

"Mahlon!"

He laughed. "Bess is actually very cooperative. You just have to know how to handle her. My teasing Chilion was all in jest, my love. And trust me, it was owed him."

"Well, never mind then." She smiled. "Will anyone from your homeland be at the wedding?"

"Your father located a few musicians from the land of Judah who are living in a village not far from here."

"The ones I heard this morning?"

"Yes. Mother was overjoyed when Goad surprised her with the news."

"But none of your near kinsmen from Bethlehem could come?"

"No. Most were forced to leave the land before we did. Only the wealthiest of landowners stayed. They were able to grow enough food for their immediate household and servants, but no more."

"And what happened to your father's field?"

"It did not produce enough food for us, let alone our servants. When Goad invited my father to sojourn to Moab, he bartered our field to acquire the supplies needed for our journey."

"I am thankful you came for me."

Mahlon motioned for Ruth's parents to join them. "The journey has been difficult, but worth it to find you."

Ruth looked down the path, seeing the field in the distance. People were milling about a large tent. She could hear musical instruments tuning. Taking a deep breath, she smelled the varied aromas of freshly baked foods drifting across the field.

"The day has finally arrived," Goad said.

"Yes, now may I please walk the rest of the way, Mahlon?"

He lifted her from the donkey as Dahlia moved around her, straightening her gown. "Our joy is now complete," Dahlia said.

"Thank you, Mother. But I worry for Father."

"Why?"

"Because I am his only heir and Mahlon and I will likely return to the land of Judah one day."

"Well—" Dahlia said, looking at Goad.

"Father, what is going on? No more secrets!"

"It is not a secret, Daughter. We planned to share the news with you after the wedding."

"What news?"

"Your mother is with child."

"Father!"

"What?"

"When did *that* happen?"

Mahlon laughed and Ruth giggled. "I meant to say, how long have you known?"

"About three months, Daughter."

Ruth looked to the horizon, remembering her prayer the night Mahlon proposed.

"Adonai answered my prayer! I asked Him to bless you as He blessed Rahab's family."

"What do you mean?" Dahlia asked, looking confused.

"Do you not understand, Mother? I asked Adonai to bless you and Father because you gave up your only daughter, and now you are with child."

"Thank you," Goad said. "I know your mother appreciates your prayers."

Dahlia shook her head, looking bewildered. "Why, yes, Goad, of course I do."

"And now it is time for our daughter to marry!" Goad kissed Ruth, and then waved as he and Dahlia walked toward the tent.

"Do you believe Adonai answered my prayer, Mahlon?"

"Yes, I do."

"Why does Mother not believe?"

"I do not know, but perhaps one day she will understand. Come, Ruth, we have much to celebrate!"

Mahlon held Ruth's hand as they walked across the field. Closing her eyes, she delighted at his touch.

Hearing him chuckle, she looked at him.

"Soon you will be my husband."

"I will, my sweet Ruth. I love you," he said and then pointed at the tent. "Does it meet with your approval?"

She studied the tent's features, admiring the sheer, linen sheets draped along the sides. Some sections of material hung free, waving in the breeze; others were secured to poles cut from acacia wood and entwined with colorful cords. Large earthen vases filled with flowers of every size and color sat at the base of each pole.

"It looks exquisite *and* familiar! Is it my mother's design?"

"It is."

Entering the tent, Ruth walked beside the tables lining the linen walls. They were filled with every food imaginable. She took a deep breath, smelling the roasted lamb and fresh bread.

Naomi handed a goblet to Mahlon as she cleared her voice, drawing everyone's attention.

Taking a parchment, Chilion began to read:

And the LORD *God formed man of the dust of the ground, and breathed into his nostrils the breath of life; and man became a living being. (Genesis*

191

2:7).

Chilion handed the parchment to Mahlon, and he continued reading:

And the LORD God said, "It is not good that man should be alone; I will make him a helper comparable to him."

And the LORD God caused a deep sleep to fall on Adam, and he slept; and He took one of his ribs and closed up the flesh in its place. Then the rib which the LORD God had taken from man He made into a woman, and He brought her to the man.

And Adam said:

"This is now bone of my bones

And flesh of my flesh;

She shall be called Woman,

Because she was taken out of Man." (Genesis 2:18; 21-23).

Mahlon grasped Ruth's hand. "Ruth, I covenant with you from this day forward—you will be bone of my bones and flesh of my flesh."

Naomi raised her goblet and said:

Therefore a man shall leave his father and mother and be joined to his wife, and they shall become one flesh. (Genesis 2:24).

Mahlon lowered his goblet to Ruth. Lifting her eyes to his, she tasted the sweet wine against her lips and swallowed. The crowd cheered as Mahlon drank, motioning for them to join him.

Several musicians began plucking harps as the other instruments joined in the upbeat melody. The skillfully played sounds of flutes, bells and various stringed instruments resounded as Naomi guided Ruth to an open area. Raising her hands above her head, Naomi clapped and began to dance.

Her movements were captivating as Ruth watched in awe. The years seemed to melt from Naomi's petite frame as she moved gracefully to the music.

"Come!" Mahlon said. "Mother will teach you."

Moving beside Naomi, Ruth raised her hands, imitating Naomi's steps.

"Who taught you to dance so beautifully?" Ruth asked.

"My mother. And now I will teach you."

The tent filled with laughter as Dahlia invited the servants to eat and join in the festivities.

✡   ✡   ✡

The moon shone brightly overhead as the servants began lighting their lamps.

Mahlon approached his mother, kissing her cheek.

"Dahlia and Goad have graciously invited Chilion and me to spend several days with them at their home," Naomi said.

"Thank you, sir," Mahlon responded, shaking Goad's hand.

"You are most welcome, Son."

Mahlon waved at the crowd. "Thank you for celebrating with us," he shouted, lifting Ruth into his arms. The servants' clapping and chatter faded as Mahlon carried Ruth across the field toward the house. Feeling suddenly awkward, she leaned her head against his shoulder.

"Did you enjoy the celebration, sweet wife?"

She spoke not a word, but nuzzled her head gently in the crook of his neck.

Carrying her over the threshold, he lowered her to the ground and bent to remove her sandals. Tossing them to the side, he took her hand as they walked across the main living area toward two doors.

"The one on the right is ours," he said, swinging the newly hewn door open.

Ruth glanced at him shyly as they stepped inside. Candles flickered and the sweet fragrance of freshly cut flowers filled the small room. She looked from the new ceiling beams to the large window facing the hills east of the house. "Our room is perfect, Mahlon," she said admiring the craftsmanship of the table and chair in the corner of the room. "Now I understand what took so long."

"I made each piece of furniture for you, Ruth. I hope you like them."

"I love them," she said.

Approaching the bed, she touched the blankets folded neatly on top. "They are soft . . ." she said, keeping her back to him, "and colorful."

Her heart quickened as she felt his lips against her neck. Turning, she faced him, lifting her gaze to his.

"Mother made them for us," he said, holding her close. "Do not be afraid, Ruth, of what lies ahead for us on this night."

"You knew what I was feeling?"

"I have always known what you were feeling." He moved his fingers down her arm. "We did not finish the Scripture at the tent. I saved a very special verse for us to share alone."

"What does it say?"

"It says:

And they were both naked, the man and his wife, and were not ashamed. (Genesis 2:25).

Her body trembled as she closed her eyes feeling his lips against hers.

✡   ✡   ✡

As the sun rose, Ruth laid her head on Mahlon's chest, listening to his steady breathing. He had loved her on their wedding night the way Adonai intended and they were one flesh. Her heart was full of joy beyond measure.

What is it, Adonai? What lies ahead for us? she asked, feeling the same uneasiness she felt the night Mahlon proposed. I choose to trust You, Adonai, just as Abraham trusted when he did not withhold his only son from You.

She kissed Mahlon's forehead and nestled against his side, waiting for him to awaken.

Chapter 21

LIOR

Ruth secured the latch to the animal pen and began making her way up the hill. Reaching the crest, she observed Mahlon as he knelt, inspecting the newly sown barley. The delicate shoots blanketed the plain in hues of green. She paused, her thoughts wandering to Adonai. Even as a child, she knew He existed. Adonai had drawn her heart, accepting her long before she realized the truth.

A tiny lizard darted along the field's boundary. It froze for a moment; the rhythmic pattern on its body capturing her attention. *Thank you, Adonai, that Your handiwork declares Your glory.*

Focusing her attention on Mahlon, she admired his strong, lean frame as he dug his fingers into the rich soil. It seemed only yesterday they married. She was blissfully happy! He was everything she dreamed of and more. Not only was he handsome, he adored her. He reminded her of her father—strong of heart and kind in spirit.

Suddenly, he stood. "Ruth!" he called, pointing down the path.

"Yes, Mahlon, what is it?"

"Your mother is coming," he said, waving.

Ruth smiled, observing Dahlia waddling in their direction. The sun's late afternoon rays glistened on the ornate silver combs fashioned in her long, straight hair, her robes hanging like a tent over her protruding belly. She laughed, running down the path to meet her.

"Mother!" she called. "Should you be out walking in your condition?"

Dahlia stopped, waiting as she moved her hand over her abdomen. "Actually, I feel wonderful."

"But your feet and hands are swollen. Are you certain you are feeling well?"

"You sound like your father. I am fine," she said, waving at Mahlon. "Enough about me. I want to hear about you. Any news to share?"

"Mother, if you are asking if I am with child—the answer is no."

"Oh, well, it will happen."

"I hope so, but sometimes I wonder if I will be like Sarah."

"Who is Sarah? I do not believe I know her."

"She was a past relative of Mahlon's. She lived a long time ago."

"I see. But why do you wonder if you will be like her?"

"She did not conceive until she was very old."

"That will not happen to you!" Dahlia reached for Ruth's hand, laying it on her belly. "I was younger than you when I had your elder brother and now look at me! After fifteen years, I am with child again!"

Ruth felt the baby kick and pulled her hand away.

Dahlia laughed. "It is an odd feeling, Daughter. But you will learn for yourself when you have a baby of your own. By the way, how is Orpah?"

"She is not expecting either! She has scarcely been married long enough."

"You would be surprised what can happen in three months."

"Mother! Your bluntness is shocking!" Ruth giggled.

"Someday when your children marry, you will understand."

"We will see. Now come, you are just in time for dinner and stories."

"Stories?"

"Yes! It is my favorite time of day. After our evening meal, the five of us sit for hours and listen to stories about the people of Israel."

"Sounds like the perfect way to fall asleep."

"Mother! You will love them, too. I am sure of it. Tonight Mahlon will tell us the story of Joseph."

"Dare I ask who he was?"

"Well, Abraham had a son named Isaac and Isaac had a son named Jacob. Jacob had twelve sons. One of them was named—"

"Stop, Daughter!" Dahlia sighed. "I will join you, but only because your father went to visit his brother this morning and I am lonely for your company."

"Good enough!" Ruth said as they slowly made their way into the house.

"It is good to see you, Dahlia!" Naomi said, placing an extra plate on the table.

"Thank you, but I think I should have asked the servants to bring me. I do not recall the walk from my home taking so long."

Naomi reached for Dahlia, examining her mid-section and swollen feet. "Where is Goad?"

"He went to visit his brother."

"He allowed you to walk here alone?"

"I had not planned to, but it was such a beautiful day, I decided the fresh air would do me good."

"I hope Goad's brother lives nearby."

"He does. I convinced him to spend the night, in fact. He does not get many opportunities to see his brother's family and considering the situation—"

"Is Uncle ill?" Ruth asked.

"No, but some of his goats stopped producing. He wanted to know if your father could stop by to assess them. Goad finally agreed when I told him of my plan to visit you."

"Do you think he may come home this evening, despite your request?" Naomi asked.

"Why? Is something wrong?" Ruth asked, noting the odd expression on Naomi's face.

"I think the baby could come anytime," Naomi said as she grasped Dahlia's hand. "Orpah, would you and Ruth please finish preparing the meal?"

"Yes, Mother, but—"

"Please excuse us," Naomi said as she led Dahlia into her room and closed the door.

The four remained still. Mahlon looked at Ruth, his eyes filled with understanding. "Would you like Chilion and me to help you finish preparing the meal?"

"Yes, thank you," Ruth said, taking a deep breath as she attempted to slow the rapid beating of her heart.

"Is something wrong with Dahlia?" Orpah asked.

"I am sure she will be fine," Chilion said, patting Ruth's shoulder.

The four fell silent, moving about the room as they finished preparing the meal and setting the table.

The sun was setting and Mahlon was lighting the lamps as Dahlia emerged from the room. Naomi followed close behind.

"What is wrong?" Ruth asked, observing the worry lines etched on her mother's brow.

"It seems my baby is breech."

"Breech? What does that mean?"

"It means the baby's body is in the wrong position. It should be head down, but is sitting up."

Mahlon wrapped his arm around Ruth. "Do not worry, Mother knows what to do to turn the baby."

"Chilion, do you know where Goad's brother lives?" Naomi asked.

"Yes, I went with Mahlon and Ruth there to visit him shortly after their wedding."

"Then go quickly and tell him to come."

"I will leave immediately."

"I am going with you!" Orpah said.

"I am sorry, Orpah, but Chilion must make haste."

"Then he should take Father's stallion." Ruth said, looking at Mahlon.

"Yes, I agree. Run to Goad's house and ride his stallion on to his brother's."

"But what am I to do?" Orpah asked in a plaintive voice. "I do not want to stay here."

"Orpah could go to Mother's house and bring Lilia back here," Ruth said.

Naomi touched Orpah's shoulder. "Yes, Daughter, I need Lilia. Please go to the servants' quarters and ask Gardish to accompany you. Tell him to bring the cart. Lilia is too old and frail to walk."

"Yes, Mother," she said, turning to Chilion. "Please be careful. That stallion is strong-willed and may attempt to run away with you."

"I will. Dahlia, do not worry, we will have Goad here before you know it."

"Please hurry. He will be upset with me for sending him away when he hears the news."

"Any worry he feels will be short-lived as soon as he sees you holding his newborn baby," Mahlon said.

Chilion took Orpah's hand as they ran from the house. Naomi turned to Mahlon. "Son, please take Ruth to the garden—"

"But, Naomi, I—"

"Do as I say, Ruth. I will call for you when it is time."

Ruth searched Naomi's face, hoping for reassurance, but found none. Turning, she gently cupped her mother's panic-stricken face in her hands. "Naomi will do all she can to move the baby into the right position for birth."

Dahlia nodded, but Ruth recognized the fear in her eyes. She must be strong for her mother, but how could she when she felt fear rise in her own heart? *Oh, Adonai, please protect my mother and the baby and guide Naomi's hands.*

As Mahlon and Ruth stepped from the house, Chilion was running toward them down the darkened path.

"I will return as quickly as possible!" he yelled, hurrying past them.

"God be with you, Brother!"

"We are on our way, Miss Ruth," Gardish said as they approached with Bess, pulling a small cart.

"Thank you, Gardish, for your help. Please take your time with Lilia. She is very old and frail."

"Rest assured, Miss, I will bring her here safely."

"Thank you, Sister, for going with Gardish."

"I will try to be brave," Orpah said.

"I know you will," Ruth said, kissing her cheek. As Gardish made a clicking sound, Bess began lumbering down the path.

Mahlon took Ruth by the hand. Leading her to an open spot in the garden, he spread a blanket on the ground. They lay down, observing the stars as they flickered like candles in the cloudless sky.

"It is a perfect night for storytelling. Would you like to hear the story of Joseph?"

"No, not now. I am too worried about Mother."

"I understand, but may I ask a question?"

"Of course you may."

"Do you remember your prayer to Adonai the night I asked you to be my wife?"

"Yes. I asked Him to bless my parents for allowing me to marry you."

"And do you still believe Adonai answered your prayer by opening your mother's womb?"

"The moment Father told me, I knew the baby was a gift from Him."

Mahlon turned on his side. "Your mother will need you to be strong tonight, Ruth. She may test your trust, but you must remember what you asked of Adonai and His answer. Do you recall Abraham's response to Adonai when He tested him concerning Isaac, his son?"

"He trusted Him with his son's life, even to the point of death."

"Yes, my love. We will be strong in the LORD and trust Him with your mother and the baby." His kiss was tender as he gently placed his lips on hers. "Do you remember the Scripture I taught you?"

Ruth nodded and closed her eyes.

"Have I not commanded you? Be strong and of good courage; do not be afraid, nor be dismayed, for the LORD your God is with you wherever you go." (Joshua 1:9).

"He is with us, Ruth. Even here in Moab, He watches over us. What He determines will come to pass."

"I know. Thank you for reminding me." Ruth sighed as she observed a shooting star streak across the sky. Did she and Mahlon appear the same to Adonai as He looked upon them from the height of the heavens; as a momentary light in a world filled with darkness? *Thank you, Adonai, for determining our days and directing our steps.* As Ruth relaxed in Mahlon's comforting arms, she drifted to sleep.

✡   ✡   ✡

"Mahlon, Ruth!" Naomi screamed, her voice slicing through the darkness. Ruth gasped, staring toward the house. "Come quickly!" Naomi waved, standing in the dimly lit doorway.

Ruth felt lightheaded as Mahlon pulled her from the blanket.

"Be strong, Ruth!"

"I will," she said.

Taking his hand, they ran to the house. As they hurried through the doorway, Naomi grabbed Ruth's arm, stopping her midstride.

"Chemosh! No! Please do not take my baby!" Dahlia screamed from the adjacent room.

"Please let me go to her," Ruth said, wiping tears from her cheeks.

"Of course you may, my daughter. But know this, I was able to reposition the baby, but in the process Dahlia has gone into labor. The baby is in the birthing position, but Dahlia is unable to push."

"Why?"

"She is filled with fear and talking out of her head. You must try to calm her, or we risk losing both of them."

Ruth squeezed her hand. "I understand."

Entering the room, Ruth observed her mother lying on the bed. She was covered in perspiration. Her face was ashen, her breathing labored.

As Ruth approached, Dahlia clutched the side of the bed; her knuckles white, her teeth bared. Ruth touched her arm. Dahlia began to toss her head back and forth—chanting.

"Mother, stop!" Ruth knelt, feeling her forehead.

"Chemosh?" Dahlia growled, opening her eyes. They were dark and empty as she stared past her.

"No, Mother, it is Ruth."

"Chemosh!" Dahlia shrieked, turning her head toward the wall as she pushed Ruth's hand away.

Ruth's heart raced at the guttural sounds. Looking toward the doorway, she saw Mahlon. He stood silent; his countenance filled with love and understanding. She nodded, turning back to her mother.

"No! Do not take my baby!" Dahlia cried. Rolling on her side, her body began to jerk.

"Mother, it is Ruth. Do you hear me?"

Dahlia covered her eyes. "Run, Ruth, or he will take you from me, too!"

"I am not afraid of Chemosh nor do I serve him."

"You took my son, Chemosh! Please, not this baby too! No! Please, Chemosh!"

Ruth pulled her hands away. "Look at me, Mother!"

She did not respond.

"Mother! Chemosh has no power over Adonai! None! Do you understand?"

Dahlia continued to toss her head back and forth.

"Chemosh is angry with me!"

"No! Remember what I told you the day Father said you were with child?" Ruth grasped her hand holding it against her cheek. "Please listen to me, Mother. Adonai allowed you to conceive this baby, not Chemosh."

Dahlia turned her head to Ruth. "Daughter? Is that you?" she asked as her eyes began to focus.

"Yes, Mother, I am here."

The look of terror was suddenly gone. "Do not leave me, Ruth!"

"I will not leave you."

"Chemosh will kill my baby." Dahlia began to weep. "Goad will never forgive me."

"This baby will not die."

"But how do you know?"

"I trust Adonai will not allow any lesser power to undo what He determines."

Dahlia took a deep breath, releasing it slowly. "It hurts! Worse than I remember."

"Do you feel birthing pains?"

Naomi entered the room, closing the door. Approaching the foot of the bed, she assessed Dahlia. Suddenly she shouted, "Praise Adonai! Dahlia, it is time to birth this baby! Push!"

As Dahlia felt another birth pain she grimaced and screamed. "No! I cannot."

"You can, Dahlia! I command you to push!"

"Goad! I need Goad!" she screamed, pushing.

"Praise Adonai! I can see the baby's head! Now push!"

Ruth watched in wonder as the baby's head crowned; its dark hair covered in a slippery film of red and white. Dahlia groaned and gritted her teeth as she pushed.

As Ruth watched in amazement, the baby's head slipped from the canal.

"The baby is almost here!" Ruth cried. Just then she heard a rooster crow.

"A new day is dawning!" Naomi shouted. "One more push, Dahlia! Push!"

"I *am* pushing!" Dahlia groaned as Naomi lifted the baby.

"It is a boy, Mother!" Ruth said as the baby let out a robust cry.

Dahlia began to weep. "Thank you, Naomi."

"Praise The Giver of Life!" Mahlon yelled from the main living area. "Is he healthy?"

"Yes!" Naomi said. "Praise Him! Now go and meet Goad. I am sure he is on his way here by now and frantic with worry."

"Wait!" Ruth said, running from the room and into Mahlon's arms.

Lifting her, he spun her around and then they rushed from the house, running down the path. Nearing the well, they stopped; hearing hoof beats. Suddenly, Goad appeared from around the bend.

"Father!" Ruth cried as he raced toward them on the stallion. Nearing, he pulled the horse's long mane. Tossing its head back and forth, it rose on its hindquarters, snorting; its body lathered with sweat.

"Dahlia!" he yelled.

Ruth laughed. "She is fine, Father."

"And the baby?"

"Congratulations, sir! It is a boy," Mahlon said.

"Thank you," Goad said, lowering his hand to Ruth. Pulling her up, Goad smiled. "We will see you at the house, Son."

"Yes, sir," Mahlon said as the stallion raced away.

As they arrived, Goad held the stallion steady as Ruth dismounted. Goad slid from the stallion. "Home!" he yelled, slapping its rump. The stallion bolted, snorting and kicking its hind legs as it galloped out of sight.

They hurried into the room. Naomi had already swaddled the baby in a blanket and he was safely nestled in Dahlia's arms. Dahlia pushed strands of sweat-laden hair from her face, her combs askew.

Naomi sighed, plopping into a chair near Dahlia. "I am thankful you have finally arrived, Goad!"

He laughed as Dahlia looked up from the baby.

"How are you and the baby?" Goad asked as he bent down and kissed Dahlia, pulling the linens away from the baby's face.

"We survived!"

"I am thankful!"

"He is perfect, is he not?"

"He is indeed," he said, touching his son's tiny hand and studying his fingers.

"I am so sorry, Goad. I did a foolish thing walking here by foot. Will you forgive me?"

"Yes, love," he said, carefully lifting his son into his arms. Turning, he faced Naomi.

"Thank you, Naomi," he said. "I fear the outcome, had Dahlia not been here."

"You are not angry with me?" Dahlia asked.

"No, my love, I am not upset in the least."

"Thank you, Adonai," Naomi said as they heard Chilion and Mahlon calling from some distance away.

Ruth ran from the house and down the path to meet them.

"Did Mahlon tell you, it's a boy and Mother and baby are fine!" Ruth yelled.

"Yes! Praise Adonai!" he said. "By the way, I stopped by your house. Gardish is on his way with Lilia and Orpah."

✡   ✡   ✡

"Welcome to this world, Lior." Goad said. "Naomi, do you mind if I leave

205

Dahlia and Lior here with you for a few days? I do not think it wise to take them home now."

"Of course not, Goad. I would not allow you to take them home today, even if you insisted."

"Lilia will be here soon, Mother," Ruth added.

"I would like Lilia to stay with us a few days also, if you are agreeable, Goad," Naomi said.

"Of course she may. Thank you for your kindness, Naomi."

"It was a great joy and blessing to deliver your son. It has been a long time since I have heard a baby's first cry."

At her words, Ruth's heart was filled with sadness. How could she feel such happiness at the birth of her brother and yet sorrow at the same time? Would Adonai open her womb as he had done for her mother?

Adonai, please bless Mahlon with an heir. But even as she prayed, her heart ached.

Mahlon pulled her close. Lifting her chin, he wiped a tear away and then kissed her. "Do not worry, Ruth, we will continue to trust Adonai no matter what the future holds."

"We will," she said as they walked arm-in-arm from the room.

Chapter 22

THE PASSOVER

Ruth yawned and stretched as the sun's rays peeked through their bedroom window, warming her skin. *It is a beautiful morning You have created, Adonai, and I know I should be happy. Please forgive my ungrateful heart.* Turning toward Mahlon, she eyed his disheveled hair and then snuggled into his chest, smelling traces of lavender lingering on his nightclothes. *Perhaps if You had not fashioned Mahlon so irresistibly, I would not mind his leaving.*

Holding her breath, she counted the strong, rhythmic beatings of his heart as her thoughts wandered to the night Lior was born. It was hard to believe nine years had passed since that night. Closing her eyes she recalled the details of her brother's birth, thankful her mother and brother survived the difficult delivery. But as Mahlon reminded her— what Adonai determines will come to pass.

Looking out the window, she saw a colorful warbler land on a tree branch near their window, whistling loudly. Any other day, she would welcome the tiny bird's declaration of a new dawn, but not this morning. When Mahlon awakened, he and Chilion would begin their journey to the land of Judah. They were going to celebrate The Passover in memory of Adonai bringing His people out of Egypt and into the Promised Land.

They would not return for four long weeks.

"Must you go to Judah this year?" Ruth whispered, holding Mahlon's hand against her cheek.

"Yes, my love," he said, rousing. "Adonai's command requires us to celebrate The Passover in Jerusalem."

"Tell me the story again."

"I am sorry, but there is not time. I must be dressed and out the door before Mother reminds me of the importance of this day."

"Please? I need to know the story well so I can recite it to our children." Mahlon chuckled as Ruth cupped her hand over his mouth. "Shhh, your mother will hear you!"

"*Our children?*" he teased. "Is there something you have not told me?"

She did not attempt to hide her sorrow. "No, Mahlon. I am not with child. I am sorry, I–"

"Please do not worry, Ruth. We will have children in God's timing, just as Sarah did. The same is true for Chilion and Orpah."

"I know you are right. Still–"

"Mahlon!" Naomi called. "It is time to go. Chilion is waiting!"

"I told you!" Mahlon said, brushing his lips against her forehead as he sprang from bed. Hurrying across the room, he removed his nightclothes. She admired his masculine frame as he pulled his robe and tunic over his head and stepped into his sandals.

Standing on her tiptoes, Ruth brushed his thick, wavy hair; tying it at the base of his neck with twine. "Much better!" she said, arranging his head covering and tying a cord at his brow. "Please be sure to keep your face protected from the sun."

"Yes, love."

"It will be lonely here without you."

"I am sure the time will pass quickly enough. Mother and Orpah will keep you busy and you can share stories with them in the evenings."

"I suppose so. I am thankful Naomi agreed to stay."

"Yes. The trip would be too long and arduous for her to make on foot."

"I will pray for your safety and already long for the day I see you and Chilion returning on the path."

"And I will imagine you standing at the edge of The Highway with your curious face and shy smile, just as the first time I laid eyes on you almost ten years ago. I love you, my sweet Ruth." Her heart raced as he held her gaze and then brought his lips to hers. *Adonai, thank you for blessing me with such a wonderful husband!*

Naomi tapped on the door. Mahlon winked at Ruth as he pulled it open. Sweeping his mother off her feet, he carried her outside the house.

"Mahlon! Put me down!" Naomi laughed. "I am not a child."

He swung her full circle. "True," he said, resting her feet on the ground, "but as long as you are light enough to carry, I will continue to do so. Especially when I must leave you to go on such a long journey."

"Enough," Naomi said, pointing toward Chilion as he waited with Bess some distance down the path. "It is time for you to go."

"Shalom, Mother," he said, kissing her cheek.

"And what about me?" Orpah asked, poking her head out the window.

"Shalom, Orpah. Take care of Mother and Ruth."

"Of course I will! And they will take care of me," Orpah said, handing him a cloth filled with bread and dates. "Your mother said you could eat your morning meal as you walk to The Highway since you chose to rise so late."

"Is that so!" Mahlon chuckled as he tucked the cloth into his pack and walked away.

When he reached Chilion, the two turned and waved. "See you after Passover!" they called in unison, continuing down the path.

Ruth observed Mahlon as he slapped Chilion's shoulder; savoring the sound of their deep, mellow voices.

"Have they always been close, Naomi?" Orpah asked.

"Always. They certainly never tire of each other's company."

With each step the brothers took, Ruth's heart grew heavier and loneliness filled her. Reaching the bend, they disappeared from sight.

"Ruth, come to the house," Naomi said.

"Do you mind if I take a walk?"

"No, not at all, but please come back before too long. We will miss you."

"I will."

Strolling down the path, she realized she felt no different than when she first saw Mahlon and his family approaching on The Highway ten years previous.

The moment I first saw Mahlon is still etched in my memory, Adonai. His eyes and brows were strong like his father's, but it was his smile that stole my heart. I did not realize Your plan the day of our first meeting, but looking back, it is so clear. Thank you, Adonai.

Reaching The Highway she turned and eyed the grove, remembering the day she waited beneath the tall palm for their arrival. She ambled to the tree and sat, scooting her back against the trunk.

You have been good to us, Adonai. Please bring Mahlon and Chilion home safely, and please let this be the year You bless us with a child.

Closing her eyes, she recalled the story of The Passover, reviewing each detail until she reached the last bit of Scripture Mahlon taught her. Looking through the palm branches, she began to recite:

"Now the blood shall be a sign for you on the houses where you are. And when I see the blood, I will pass over you; and the plague shall not be on you to destroy you when I strike the land of Egypt.

'So this day shall be to you a memorial; and you shall keep it as a feast to the LORD throughout your generations . . .'" (Exodus 12:13-14).

"Adonai, thank you for delivering the children of Israel out of the bondage of Egypt and into the Promised Land. Please allow me to share these special stories with our own children someday."

"Ruth!" Orpah yelled.

"I am here!" she said, standing. "What is wrong?"

"Naomi is worried about you."

"I am sorry," Ruth said, running to her.

They held hands swinging them to and fro as they scurried down the path. Approaching the house, they saw Naomi standing in the doorway.

"I am so sorry, Naomi! I was thinking of The Passover, reciting the story from memory, and lost track of time."

"I should have known. I am just thankful you are home."

The three women entered the house, chattering about the events of the day as they began preparing their mid-day meal.

✡   ✡   ✡

Each evening Ruth lay in bed alone, struggling to sleep. Each morning she put a mark on parchment, tracking the number of days until Mahlon and Chilion's return. They continued to busy themselves with cooking and cleaning; enjoying the evenings of fellowship and storytelling, but still Ruth longed for Mahlon.

Four weeks and two days passed, but still they had not returned. The following morning as the rooster crowed, Ruth hurried from the house and started down the path. The air was warm and a dry southerly wind whipped her robes about. She made her way slowly until she stood at the bend where she last saw them. Her gaze remained transfixed for almost an hour.

Where are they, Adonai? Something is wrong.

Choking back tears, she returned to the house.

As they finished their evening meal, Ruth watched Orpah retreat to a chair in the corner of the room. The house felt strangely silent. Naomi made no attempt to visit or share stories. Finally, Ruth stood. Approaching the table, she retrieved a pouch. Removing the parchment, she counted the marks and then placed the scroll back on the table.

Orpah motioned for Ruth to come.

"What is it, Orpah?" Ruth asked, kneeling beside her.

"It usually takes them four weeks to make The Passover journey," Orpah said softly, looking at Naomi as she spoke.

"I know."

Orpah dropped her head.

Naomi turned toward them. Placing the blanket she was mending in her lap, she continued to stare at Orpah.

Ruth stood. "Orpah was asking me about Mahlon and Chilion," she said clasping her hands in front of her. "It seems to be taking them longer than in years past."

Observing the worry lines creep across Naomi's brow, she approached, placing her hand on Naomi's shoulder.

"It is taking longer," Naomi said. "But perhaps something came up while they were there that has delayed their return."

"Perhaps," Ruth said, pacing about the room.

Naomi rose. "I am unusually tired this evening. Do you mind, my daughters, if I retire early?"

"Not at all," Ruth said as Naomi walked to her room and shut the door.

✡   ✡   ✡

Ruth lay in bed staring at the ceiling beams. She prayed for Mahlon and Chilion's safety, but her heart was filled with dread.

What can it be? What can be keeping them from us so long, Adonai? I cannot bear to wait any longer.

She tossed the bedding aside and crept to Orpah's room. Lifting the latch, she pushed the door open. The moonlight shone through the window, illuminating the small room. She saw Orpah sitting in the corner. Her arms were locked around her legs—her chin resting on her knees.

Approaching, she knelt next to her. Orpah lowered her legs, revealing a statue of Chemosh hidden in her lap.

"No, Orpah," Ruth said, pulling the small stone replica from her and laying it on the floor.

"They are not coming back!" Orpah sobbed as the moonlight glistened through the tears streaming down her face.

"Shhh," Ruth said, holding her hand over Orpah's mouth. "I am going to find them."

"You cannot go! Naomi will not allow it."

"I am not going to ask her. I am leaving now."

"In the dead of night?"

"Yes. Please listen, Orpah. When she awakens, tell her not to worry. I will take several of the servants with me. I will not come back until I find them."

Orpah hugged her tightly. "You have always been the brave one. I wish I were more like you."

"My strength is not my own. It comes from Adonai. He will sustain me."

"What am I to do?" Orpah asked, sniffling.

"I will come back to you, Orpah, and Mahlon and Chilion will be with me when I do."

Ruth squeezed Orpah's hand as she stood. Looking at the statue, Ruth wondered how long Orpah had hidden it from Chilion and if she should attempt to remove it from the room.

Suddenly, Orpah snatched the figure from the floor, tucking it under her pillow.

"I am sorry, Ruth," she said.

Ruth nodded as she left the room, closing the door behind her. Tiptoeing to her room, Ruth changed into her harvest clothing. Taking a pack, she added several additional items and then slipped from the house. Once out of Naomi's hearing, she ran down the hill. Her sandals skidded along the gravel as she came to a halt just outside the servants' quarters. Taking a deep breath, she rapped her fist on the door.

"Haron, Gardish?"

Moments passed.

"Yes." Gardish replied, his deep voice sounding raspy.

"Please prepare food for two week's travel. We are going out toward Jerusalem in the land of Judah to search for Mahlon and Chilion."

"Yes, ma'am," Haron said in a groggy voice.

"Please hurry!" she said, hearing them moving about their quarters.

Ruth stood on the path, looking at the stars. It was a beautiful, clear night and the air smelled of moistened earth from a recent rain. Suddenly a cool breeze lifted her tunic, sending chills through her. She tugged her shawl about her shoulders as her thoughts drifted to Elimelech. He trusted Adonai, even as his life on earth was nearing its end.

Oh, Adonai, thank you for sending Elimelech to Moab for me. Now I pray You will lead me to his sons—and bring them safely home.

"We are ready," Haron said as she turned to face him.

Gardish approached from behind with oxen pulling a large cart filled with food and other supplies.

"Do you have extra blankets in your quarters?" she asked.

"We do," Haron said. "Why?"

"We may need them. Please get as many as you can spare."

The men nodded as they went. Returning a short time later with the blankets, they loaded them on the cart and then followed Ruth down the path.

They continued on in silence through the remainder of the night. At daybreak they stopped and ate roasted grain and dates before continuing their journey.

About noon on the following day, Ruth's eyes were drawn to a well some distance back from the road. She stopped, her eyes transfixed on the stone structure.

"Is something bothering you?" Haron asked.

"How is our water supply?" she responded.

"We have plenty of water and there are several more wells located further down The Highway," Gardish said.

Ruth started down the road and then stopped again and stared in the direction of the well.

Listen to your heart, Ruth.

"Did you hear me, Miss Ruth? We have plenty of water," Gardish repeated as he tugged the oxen's reins.

Anguish gripped her.

"No," she said, shaking her head. "Mahlon? Chilion?" she screamed as she ran.

"Miss Ruth! Where are you going?" Haron yelled.

She stopped and listened as she took a deep breath. What was that putrid smell? "Mahlon?" she cried.

"Ruth?" he answered, his voice weak and broken.

Looking in the direction of Mahlon's voice, she saw him lying near the well. His once strong frame lay gaunt, his body contorted on the ground.

"Oh, Mahlon!" she cried, approaching. The stench of death was overwhelming. She grimaced, kneeling beside his emaciated body. "What happened?" she asked, taking his hand.

"The well water," he said hoarsely. "It has been poisoned."

She placed her palm on his forehead and felt his cheeks. They were dry and hot to the touch, his skin ashen.

"How long have you been here?" She cried, kissing his hands as the pungent smell of vomit and hyssop oil made her eyes water. She knew Mahlon carried the oil with him whenever he traveled; using it to settle his stomach.

"Three days . . . I think."

"Oh, Mahlon, I should have come sooner."

"No," he said, pointing to a tree. "Chilion . . . is he still alive?"

215

"Yes," Ruth said, hearing Chilion mumble Mahlon's name. Turning she saw him lying beneath a sycamore. She rose and hurried to where he lay as Haron and Gardish arrived with the cart. Kneeling beside him, she took his hand.

"I tried to check on Bess," Chilion said, weeping. The sound of his lament brought a lump in her throat. "I cannot make it much longer. Please get me home to Mother and Orpah."

Ruth winced as she searched the nearby brush, seeing Bess's dead carcass. Her stomach was bloated and flies swarmed about her lifeless, glazed eyes.

Squeezing his hand, she rose. "I am so sorry, Chilion. With Adonai's help, we will get you home."

Returning to Mahlon, she knelt. "Mark the well," he whispered.

"What?" she asked as she placed her ear close to his mouth.

"Mark the well," he said, "so other travelers will not drink from it."

Ruth turned to Gardish and repeated Mahlon's request. He nodded and began to gather stones, placing them in formation around the well, warning travelers to stay away.

"Haron, please keep only enough food and water for one day's travel. We must unload the cart to make room for Mahlon and Chilion."

"Yes, ma'am," he said, tossing provisions into the brush.

Gardish and Haron spread the blankets on the cart's floor, rolling them against the shallow walls and then carefully placed the brothers side by side. Haron offered them a skin of water, but they refused to drink. As the oxen dug their hooves into the ground, Mahlon reached for his brother's hand.

They traveled a few hours when Ruth heard Mahlon call her name.

"Yes, Mahlon," she said, motioning for the men to stop.

Stooping over his sickly body, she placed her ear near his mouth and waited.

"The famine—"

216

"What about the famine?"

"Adonai lifted it."

"There is bread in the land of Judah?"

"Yes. The fields are full of grain." He paused a moment as he took a shallow breath. "We were coming to tell Mother."

"Rest, Mahlon," she said. "I will tell your mother when the time is right."

He nodded his head and closed his eyes.

Ruth cried as they traveled along The Highway. She mourned and grieved and asked Adonai for a miracle. When they stopped to rest, Mahlon took her hand in his. His eyes were distant. It was the same look she remembered seeing on Elimelech's face the night he died.

"Oh, Mahlon, if only I had come sooner."

"It would not have mattered, my love," he struggled, his speech rough and slurred.

"You must get well. I cannot face life without you."

"You will, Ruth, because you know The Giver of Life."

She laid her head on his chest.

"With Adonai's help you will be home soon to see your mother."

Mahlon and Chilion coughed and choked as Ruth again attempted to give them fresh water.

"We must continue through the night," Ruth said to the men, realizing they were running out of time.

"I understand, Miss Ruth," Gardish said, his voice cracking. "We will not stop until we arrive home."

✡   ✡   ✡

As the sun rose, dark storm-filled clouds moved across the horizon and a strong westerly wind blew through the plain. Thunder sounded as their home came into view.

"We made it Mahlon! Your mother and Orpah are coming!" Ruth cried, seeing the women run from the house.

217

Mahlon reached for her. "Please do not leave my mother when I am gone."

"Do not worry, Mahlon, I will never leave her," she said, stepping away from the cart.

Naomi and Orpah dropped to their knees as dust from the path swirled around them.

"No!" Orpah sobbed laying her head on Chilion's chest. As Chilion attempted to comfort her, their words evolved into an indiscernible stream of sorrow.

"Why, Adonai?" Naomi wailed as she cradled Mahlon in her arms. "Not my beloved sons!"

"Mother, please do not cry," Mahlon moaned.

Naomi kissed his forehead and moved to Chilion. Orpah scooted away from the cart and dropped facedown on the path. When she lifted her head, it was covered in dust and streaked with tears.

Naomi hovered back and forth between her sons, kissing their hands and touching their faces. Ruth turned away, unable to bear the sight of Naomi's mourning.

"Miss Naomi," Haron said. "We need to get Mahlon and Chilion settled in the house."

"I know," Ruth said as Gardish slapped the oxen's hindquarter with his burly hand. As they continued to the house, Orpah walked on one side of the cart and Naomi on the other. Ruth followed behind. *Why Adonai? Why did You allow this to happen? Please help me understand.* Dropping her head, she wept bitterly.

As the men carried Mahlon and Chilion into the house, Naomi grabbed Ruth's arm.

"What happened?" she asked, her lips pursing.

"They stopped for the night at a well about two day's travel from home. When they drank from the well, they got sick, almost immediately."

"How long had they been there when you arrived?"

218

"Mahlon thought it had been three days."

"And Bess?"

"She was already dead when I found them."

Naomi clinched her fists and left the room.

Almost from the moment they arrived, Mahlon and Chilion began to slip away. As they did, Naomi grew distant and refused to speak.

As the sun began to set, Mahlon and Chilion took their last breaths. Haron and Gardish removed their bodies, placing them in one of the servants' vacant quarters.

Leaving the house, Ruth walked deep into the field. The night was dark, the stars hidden as thunder rumbled overhead. Kneeling, she lifted her eyes to the heavens as rain spattered on her face.

Remembering the words Elimelech shared the night he died, she prayed:

"For I know that my Redeemer lives, and He shall stand at last on the earth; and after my skin is destroyed, this I know, that in my flesh I shall see God, Whom I shall see for myself, and my eyes shall behold, and not another. How my heart yearns within me!" (Job 19:25-27).

Lying prostrate on the muddy ground, she humbled herself before Adonai and worshiped Him, knowing Mahlon was right. She would continue to face life, because The Giver of Life was with her. He would never leave her or forsake her. She did not know what the future held, but she knew the One who held it in His hand and she trusted Him.

Chapter 23

JUDAH—MY HOME

The house was dark and still as Ruth sat alone in her robes of mourning. The coarse weave of the woolen fabric made her body itch. She glided her fingertips over her chapped legs, feeling the angry rash. Giving in to the torment, she scratched. The momentary relief turned to burning. She reached for a slice of cucumber, rubbing the soft core across the bumps, sighing as the juices brought blessed relief.

Grasping a linen cloth, she wiped tears from her swollen eyes and blew her nose. How could their lives change so quickly?

Seven days had passed since Mahlon and Chilion were laid to rest in a cave near where Elimelech's body lay. The sweet smell of aloe and myrrh still lingered. Closing her eyes, she recalled the day she and Lilia soaked strips of linen in the spices, wrapping them about Mahlon and Chilion's bodies—as Naomi had instructed her.

She glanced at Orpah and Naomi's rooms. Her heart ached for the sounds of their joyous laughter and endless chatter. No longer did Naomi share stories in the evenings or even allow Ruth and Orpah to brush her hair, as had been their nightly routine.

Standing in the doorway, she looked down the moonlit path. Recalling the day of their burial, she covered her mouth, muffling her sobs. Her father had sent Haran and Gardish with the oxen drawn cart to transport the bodies to the cave. The three women followed behind. The agonizing sounds of Naomi's weeping still haunted her. Seven times Naomi dropped to the path, raising her hands to the heavens as she mumbled and moaned.

Since that day, Naomi remained secluded in her room, only emerging to relieve herself. Ruth left food and water at her door, but she barely touched them. With each passing day, Ruth grew more concerned.

Now is the time, Adonai. Please give me strength.

She walked to Naomi's door. Lifting the latch, she entered. The window was covered, the room dark. She felt her way along the rough, stone walls until she reached the bed. Pulling a chair next to it, she sat, weaving her fingers through long, tangled tresses of Naomi's hair. Its smooth texture and smells of lavender were gone.

"Naomi," she said softly, touching her shoulder.

"What is it?" Naomi replied, her voice monotone as she kept her back to Ruth.

"Mahlon told me to share something with you. I pray it brings you hope."

"Are you with child?"

Ruth jerked her hand away. *Why, Adonai? Why did you not bless Mahlon with an heir?* "I am sorry, no," she said, her voice quivering. "But there is bread in the land of Judah."

"Bread?"

"Yes. Mahlon told me Adonai lifted the famine. The fields are lush with barley."

"I am thankful he did not tell me," Naomi said, weeping.

"I knew you could not bear the news the day he died. But do you not see, now we can return to Bethlehem?"

"Yes, I must return there. I want to die among my people."

"Please do not say that, sweet Mother. You will not die, nor will you go alone. Orpah and I are going with you."

"No!" Naomi said, her voice trembling and filled with anger. "You and Orpah must stay here!"

"We *are* going with you," Ruth said, crossing her arms. "Father already made arrangements for us to travel in the morning. We leave at daylight."

"But—"

Ruth held up her hand. "My decision is final. Father is sending Haron and Gardish with us. Once we are settled, they will return to Moab."

Naomi buried her face into the bedding. Her body shook. Ruth sat waiting until she lay still and then left the room, returning with a lamp and goblet of water. Placing the lamp on the table, she pulled the linens back, scrutinizing Naomi's face under the flickering light. Her cheeks were sunken, her eyes red and puffy. Handing the goblet to Naomi, she waited. When Naomi finished drinking, Ruth extinguished the lamp. As the room grew dark, Ruth settled into the chair, determined to keep vigil through the night.

✡   ✡   ✡

Ruth awoke with a start. "Naomi!" she cried, searching the empty bed. Feeling her way along the darkened walls, she hurried into the main living area. A single candle flickered on the table. Naomi sat in her robes of mourning. The dark, roughly woven wool was wrinkled and unkempt. Her back was bent, her elbows resting on the table. A plate filled with nuts and dried fruit rested between her arms.

"I need strength if I am to travel," Naomi said.

Ruth wondered at her empty expression. *Please give me courage to face what lies ahead, Adonai. Naomi's life depends on mine and by Your grace; I will be strong enough for the both of us.*

"I am thankful your appetite returned," Ruth said, noticing several packs lying nearby. "How did you manage to gather your belongings without my knowing?"

Naomi ignored her question, continuing to eat. After several minutes, she looked up from her plate. "Have you and Orpah prepared for the journey?"

"Yes. We already loaded our belongings on the cart. The men prepared enough food and water for two weeks' travel."

"And your parents know you plan to go with me to Bethlehem?" Naomi's eyes met Ruth's—her expression hard and detached.

"Yes. They will be here at first light to say goodbye."

Naomi clinched her fists, pounding the table as several dried dates fell from the plate. "Why?" she asked, glaring. "Why would they allow you to leave Moab?"

"My parents know my life is with you, Naomi. Do you not see? I love you as my own mother?"

Rising, Naomi walked to her room and slammed the door.

Ruth sat at the table. Burying her head in her arms, she wept. *Adonai, why does Naomi not understand? You lifted the famine. There is no other place for me to go. Judah will be my new home.*

Tears slipped down her cheeks as she carried Naomi's packs to the cart. Returning to the house, she gathered additional items Naomi would need when they arrived in Bethlehem. Finally she sat, waiting for first light.

✡   ✡   ✡

Ruth and Orpah stood in the doorway, waiting for dawn. Orpah was dressed in black wool, her hair tied with a frayed sash. She spoke only when spoken to, her face anguished and brooding.

A dusty haze covered the plain and the sky billowed with lofty white clouds as they saw their parents and Lior in the distance, approaching together. Orpah began to weep as they rushed to meet them. As they drew near, Orpah collapsed on the ground. Her mother dropped to her knees beside her. "Come home!" her mother wailed. "There is nothing for you in that foreign land! Nothing!"

"But I must go!"

"Your mother is right. All that awaits you there is loneliness and heartache!" her father chided, his eyes glaring.

"But I gave Chilion my word!"

"Your word? It means nothing to a dead man! Let Ruth go, if she will, but both of you do not need to."

Ruth watched Lior as he ran through the field, attempting to capture a tiny field mouse darting along the ground. She studied him, imagining her father at his age. A lump formed in her throat. *How much more can I endure, Adonai? My beloved Mahlon is gone and I will likely never see my family again.*

Ruth looked at her father. His eyes were filled with sorrow. "Orpah, would you mind going on ahead?" he asked. "We would like a few moments alone with Ruth."

"Yes, Goad," she sniffled. Rising, the three walked away in heated conversation.

"So you are going?" Goad asked as he held out his arms to Ruth.

Tears streamed down her face as she embraced him. "Yes, I must go."

"We knew this day would come," Dahlia said. "But I thought Mahlon would be with you. What will become of you and Naomi without him by your side?" she asked, wiping her tears on a lacey linen hand cloth.

"Adonai will provide."

Goad kissed her forehead. "Hopefully, I will be able to visit you one day."

"It will be very difficult for Lior and me to come," Dahlia said.

"I know, Mother. Do not be sad. I will always love you with my whole heart." She turned, seeing Naomi standing in the doorway.

"I will be right back," Dahlia said as she hurried down the path to say goodbye.

Suddenly, Lior was at Ruth's side, his eyes filled with tears. "I am sorry," he said, his chin quivering. "I loved Mahlon."

"I know, Lior, and he loved you like a brother."

"Father said perhaps we would come to see you."

"I hope so, but if not, know I will never forget you."

Lior buried his head into her waist as Ruth and her father continued to visit.

A short time later Dahlia returned, her eyes red and swollen. "Life will not be the same without you and Naomi."

"I know, Mother, but Naomi must return to her people."

"I do understand. Go, sweet Daughter," Dahlia said, kissing her cheek as she pulled Lior into her arms.

As Ruth started to leave, her father suddenly embraced her, whispering into her ear, "May the God of your people watch over you, my daughter, and keep you safe all the days of your life."

Ruth kissed his calloused hands and wiped his tears. Stepping from him, she bowed her head and walked away.

Arriving at the house, Ruth's eyes rested on Orpah's as her parents slipped past them and down the path without speaking. Orpah lowered her head and walked to the cart. Naomi stood waiting.

"Are you ready?" Ruth asked.

Naomi nodded as they strolled to the cart in silence. Gardish and Haron pulled at the oxen's reins as they started down the path. Ruth could hear Orpah's mother wailing in the distance. As the mournful laments grew softer, Orpah began to sob. When they reached The Highway, Naomi turned, stepping away from them. Shaking her head, she held up her hand and said:

"Go, return each to her mother's house. The LORD deal kindly with you, as you have dealt with the dead and with me. The LORD grant that you may find rest, each in the house of her husband."

So she kissed them, and they lifted up their voices and wept. And they said to her, "Surely we will return with you to your people."

But Naomi said, "Turn back, my daughters; why will you go with me?

Are there still sons in my womb, that they may be your husbands? Turn back, my daughters, go–for I am too old to have a husband. If I should say I have hope, if I should have a husband tonight and should also bear sons, would you wait for them till they were grown? Would you restrain yourselves from having husbands? No, my daughters; for it grieves me very much for your sakes that the hand of the LORD has gone out against me!"

Then they lifted up their voices and wept again; and Orpah kissed her mother-in-law, but Ruth clung to her.

And she said, "Look, your sister-in-law has gone back to her people and to her gods; return after your sister-in-law." But Ruth said:

"Entreat me not to leave you,
Or to turn back from following after you;
For wherever you go, I will go;
And wherever you lodge, I will lodge;
Your people shall be my people,
And your God, my God.
Where you die, I will die,
And there will I be buried.
The LORD do so to me, and more also,
If anything but death parts you and me." (Ruth 1:8-17).

When Naomi saw Ruth was determined to go with her, she stopped speaking and began following the cart, which by this time was some distance down The Highway.

✡ ✡ ✡

After two days' travel, they reached the well where Ruth found Mahlon and Chilion. The stench of death still remained. As Naomi reached the well, she stood silent; eyeing what little was left of Bess's carcass. Ruth showed her where her sons had lain and she touched the ground.

As they walked away, Ruth looked back at the well for the last time.

After three days on the hot, dusty highway, Gardish was finally able to convince Naomi to ride on the cart. Ruth walked at her side, contemplating the magnificent and varied land.

They spent their nights sleeping on oxhide under the starlit heavens and began their days eating dried fruit, roasted nuts and stale bread.

As they continued their slow journey along The Highway, Ruth attempted to visit with the men about the beauty of the terrain, the magnitude of Adonai's provision and her excitement to see Bethlehem. Haron and Gardish seemed to tolerate her conversation, although she saw them rolling their eyes on occasion.

Various tradesmen passed them as they went. Ruth's heart raced with apprehension each time, remembering her father's warnings when she was a child. Thankfully, no one harmed them. Perhaps her father believed Haron and Gardish's tall, robust frames were imposing enough to ward off trouble. But somewhere deep inside Ruth knew Adonai would see them safely to Bethlehem. She sensed His presence on the road. *I will take courage, Adonai. I will face life as Mahlon said I would. Thank you for allowing me ten precious years with him.*

Although Ruth continued her attempts to engage Naomi in conversation, she remained withdrawn. After almost two weeks' travel, they neared the outskirts of town.

"Look, Naomi! Mahlon was right. There is bread in Bethlehem!"

Ruth examined the vast fields of barley stretching as far as her eyes could see. They were indeed white unto harvest. She watched in amazement as a breeze wafted through the stalks, moving them in gentle waves. She closed her eyes and breathed in the deep, rich aroma of earth and grain. For a moment, she felt as though she were back in the land of Moab.

As they saw Bethlehem in the distance, Ruth marveled at its features. The roads were fashioned from stone. They were long and narrow, twisting out of view. Tall stone structures towered on either side.

"Are those homes I see?" Ruth asked.

Naomi eyed the city before responding. "Yes, they are," she finally said, sighing. "Elimelech and I used to have many family and friends in Bethlehem living in those homes, but as the fields grew parched and barren, it became almost deserted."

As they continued into the city, women and children emerged, staring at them curiously. Ruth could hear the buzz of their high-pitched voices as they talked and giggled, hovering closer and closer. As they neared, Naomi stared at the road beneath her dusty feet. At last, one of the older women spoke:

"Is this Naomi?"

But she said to them, "Do not call me Naomi; call me Mara, for the Almighty has dealt very bitterly with me. I went out full, and the LORD has brought me home again empty. Why do you call me Naomi, since the LORD has testified against me, and the Almighty has afflicted me?" (Ruth 1:19-21).

An old woman stepped from the gaggle of chattering women. "Naomi," she said, embracing her. "I understand your sorrow. Word came yesterday from a tradesman that you were returning without your sons, but even so, only Adonai has authority to change your name." She looked at Ruth, her eyes curious as she continued, "Bethlehem is not yet fully populated and there are many rooms available. Look!" she said, motioning toward a door only a few feet from them. "This is one of our rooms. You will stay with us for now."

Naomi stared at the door in silence.

"Naomi!" Ruth said, inspecting the two small windows on either side of the tall, narrow door.

Naomi's shoulders trembled and she dropped her head. "Thank you for your kindness. How will I ever repay you?"

"No need! Your coming back to Bethlehem is payment enough! Do you not see, Naomi," the woman said, "The Giver of Life made a way for you?" Walking to the door, she lifted the latch. The door creaked as she pushed it open, inviting them to enter. "He has provided a roof over your head and will continue to provide all you need—of that I am certain."

As they entered the small, one-room living space, Ruth extended her hand to the woman. "My name is Ruth."

"My name is Elizabeth," she said. Pushing Ruth's hand away, she hugged her. "Welcome to Bethlehem!"

Ruth smiled as she pondered her robust features. She was short and round with gray crinkled hair. "Thank you! I am grateful to be here with Naomi."

"I am sorry I did not introduce you sooner," Naomi said as she walked the length of the dirt floor and then leaned against the old, wooden table.

"What it lacks in space is more than made up for in location!" Elizabeth chuckled as she sauntered about the room. "How many can boast a room in the heart of town and close to the market, mind you?"

"The market? What use will it be to us? My resources to barter for food are limited," Naomi said, plopping her body in a chair as it tipped precariously to one side. Laying her hands over her eyes, she moaned. "What am I to do now?"

Ruth knelt beside her.

"Do not worry," Ruth said. Grasping Naomi's hand, she held it against her cheek. "We have at least a month's provision that Father sent with us, and the barley is ready for harvest!" Ruth stood, pacing about the room. Her heart ached for Mahlon, but even so, she was filled with hope. She was standing among God's chosen people! Oh, that Mahlon had lived to see this day! The joy she felt was overwhelming.

"Your happiness will be short-lived," Naomi said, smirking, "when your stomach longs for the taste of grain."

Ruth giggled. "No, sweet Mother, we *will* have grain for I will go and glean in the field!"

"Well, there you have it, Ruth!" Elizabeth guffawed. Her plump belly seemed to echo her laugh as it shook. "I doubt Naomi ever dreamed of the day she would hear those words. Is it true, you are a Moabite?"

"I am."

"Then how do you know of our mitzvah of gleaning?"

"It was one of the first stories Naomi told me about your people. When I heard, I went to my father and asked if he would allow us to invite the poor into our fields to glean after the reapers. He said yes."

"Your father is a field owner?"

"Yes."

"He is wealthy then?"

"He is."

"I can see he raised you well."

Ruth smiled at Naomi. "But it was Elimelech's family who brought me the greatest treasure."

"What treasure do you speak of?"

"The knowledge of The One True God, Adonai!"

"Praise be to the LORD! You believe in our God?"

"I do. I believe in Him alone as The One True God."

"And you were willing to leave the land of your birth and travel to a foreign land because of your belief?"

"Yes."

"And give up a life of comfort and wealth to return to a life of—"

"It was not a difficult decision," Ruth said, taking Elizabeth's hand. "My life is with Naomi and with her people and my God!"

"But you lost Mahlon," Elizabeth said.

At the mention of his name Ruth's heart sank. "Mahlon was a kind and loving husband. But it is Naomi who has experienced the greatest of losses."

"I know," Elizabeth said, cupping Naomi's face in her chubby hands as she knelt beside her. "My sweet friend, you have lost all that was dear to your heart." She pulled Naomi against her chest. "I am so sorry."

Naomi nodded. "I lost my husband, my sons, even Orpah."

"Orpah?"

"She was Chilion's wife."

"Did she die?"

"No," Naomi said. "She chose to stay with her people in Moab."

"She did not want to come with you?"

"Her parents did not want her to leave and I do not think she wanted to either. I loved her as my own."

"I am sorry, but you still have much to be thankful for. Look at Ruth! She came with you and is willing to glean in the fields!"

Naomi nodded. "Yes, I still have Ruth."

"Ruth, you are Naomi's only family now," Elizabeth said. "I pray Adonai blesses you for the sacrifice you made in coming to Bethlehem." She patted Naomi's knee as she stood. "Well, I will leave you to settle into your new home. I will return tomorrow and bring you some fresh bread."

"Thank you, Elizabeth, for your kindness," Ruth said, following her into the street.

Haran and Gardish were waiting by the cart just outside the door. Elizabeth held out her chubby arms, pulling their heads together as she hugged them. "Thank you for bringing Naomi home safely!"

The men flushed looking at Ruth with wide eyes. She giggled at the sight of their panic-stricken faces.

"My husband has a stable just down the way," Elizabeth said, pointing down the street. "We will put you up for the night and give you food and water for your journey home."

"Thank you," Haran said.

"Will you wait for us while we unload the cart?" Gardish asked.

"Of course."

Haran and Gardish made several trips in and out of the room, until the last of the supplies lay neatly along the walls.

Gardish seemed nervous as he turned to Ruth. "I guess we are finished here," he said, hesitating.

Ruth and Naomi approached the men together. The four huddled in a circle, embracing.

"I pray Adonai watches over you as you travel to Moab," Ruth said. "Please tell my parents I am well and thankful to be in my new home."

"We will, Miss Ruth," Gardish said.

"And I will never forget you," Haron added, clearing his throat.

"It will certainly be a quiet trip home." Gardish smiled. Haron punched him in the shoulder as they exited the house, chuckling.

She waved as the men led the oxen down the street and out of view. Closing the door, Ruth saw Naomi standing in the corner.

"There is only one bed," Naomi said, standing beside a stone ledge. It was narrow and filled with hay.

"I think we will both fit," Ruth said, grinning. "You can sleep next to the wall and I will sleep with my head at your feet."

"You never cease to fill me with joy."

"Oh, Mother! Adonai brought us here safely and provided a roof over our heads! I hope to never sleep on oxhide again!"

"Agreed." Naomi said as she lay on the bed and closed her eyes. "Do you mind, Daughter, if I sleep?"

"Not at all."

Ruth inspected the small room, touching the hearth, brushing her hand against the wood grain of the table and poking her head through the windows. It felt good to be home. Stepping to the small pit where they would prepare their meals, she inspected the stone vent that exited the house by one of the windows. She sighed. They had all they needed and each day would be a new adventure.

As the room grew dark, she lit a lamp, trimming the flame to a flicker. Carrying the lamp to the opposite side of the room, she placed it on a small table and then closed the shutters, securing their latches and dropping the burlap tied above them. Filling a small basin with water, she removed her garments. As she swept the bar of soap over her weary body, she longed for the pleasures of home where water for washing was plentiful. Finishing, she dried her skin and then rubbed a light covering of olive oil on her face and arms. Dipping her hair in the basin, she did her best to wash the dust from her long, auburn locks. She would find a stream to bathe in when she could, but for now, this would have to do. She opened one of the packs and removed her nightgown, slipping it over her head.

Turning, she stared at the room. She was not looking forward to sleeping by lamplight. From the time she was a small child, the windows remained open so she could see the stars. Only when it rained had her parents convinced her to close them. Now they lived on a busy street in the heart of town and she knew it was a luxury they would have to forgo. Approaching the shutters, she lifted the burlap, securing them above the windows. At least some of the street could be seen through the slats.

Walking to the narrow ledge, she studied Naomi as she slept. There was something different about her. Was it peace she saw on her face?

She scooted to the opposite side of the bed and sat. Carefully she pulled her feet next to Naomi's shoulders. The bed was certainly smaller than it looked. Rolling on her side, she adjusted her body, hoping not to rouse Naomi. She listened to Naomi's rhythmic breathing as she closed her eyes.

Thank you, Adonai, for providing us a place to live. As I go to glean in the morning, I ask You to lead me—just as You did in my homeland when You brought Elimelech to my father's field.

Finally, she yawned as her body relaxed and she drifted off to sleep.

Chapter 24

BOAZ

Ruth awoke with a start as she felt her body teetering on the edge of the bed.

"Ruth?" Naomi asked, sitting up from the opposite end.

The lamp's small flame flickered, illuminating Naomi's wide-eyed stare.

"I am so sorry to wake you." She giggled. "I almost fell out of bed!"

"I thought that might happen." Naomi lay back and yawned and stretched. "There is not enough room for both of us on this narrow ledge."

"I agree."

"I will ask Elizabeth if they have a spare bed, but it will mean one of us sleeps on the floor."

"I do not mind. Anything is better than oxhide on the rocky ground!"

Standing, Ruth felt the cool dirt floor on her bare feet. She crossed her arms as a shiver ran through her.

"Come back to bed, Daughter. It is still early." Naomi rubbed her eyes.

Ruth looked at the shutters. There was just enough space between the slats to observe silhouettes of the townspeople moving about the street.

"The sun will rise soon." She knelt beside Naomi and took her hand:

235

"Please let me go to the field, and glean heads of grain after him in whose sight I may find favor."

And she said to her, "Go, my daughter." (Ruth 2:2).

"Thank you, sweet Mother!"

Ruth kissed her forehead and then scurried to retrieve one of the packs lying on the floor. Pulling the strap free, she removed her harvest clothing and shook it firmly. She stepped behind a woolen curtain secured to the wall with iron rings and pegs and removed her nightgown.

"My robes seem to have gotten larger," Ruth said as she pulled them about her body.

"No, my daughter, you have lost weight. I did not want to mention it, but I have been a bit worried."

"I tried to eat on our journey, but the food was rather bland."

Ruth evaluated her rash. It would heal now that she was out of her robes of mourning. The linen felt soft against her skin. She would do her best to make these robes last, as they would not likely have the luxury of new ones. Stepping from the curtain, she saw Naomi placing several bowls on the table.

"Apples and a pomegranate!"

"Yes. Elizabeth slipped them in with the bread and honey she left by the door."

Naomi sliced a piece of bread and cut the pomegranate in half. Removing a large handful of the bright red arils, she placed them on a plate and then added an apple.

"Come," Naomi said.

Ruth sat at the table as they bowed their heads.

"Thank you, Adonai, for this meal and Your great mercy. Amen."

"Amen. Now, please eat, Ruth. You will need all the strength you can muster for a day in the field."

Ruth drizzled honey over her bread and then took several arils of pomegranate and popped them in her mouth.

"How I have missed the sweet taste of fruit!" she said.

"Yes, as have I." Naomi bit into an apple as the succulent juices spewed across the table and down her chin.

"Haran and Gardish will certainly be surprised when they arrive back at Father's field."

"Why?"

"Father told me he plans to hand over supervision of the field to them upon their return."

"Your father is a generous man."

"Yes, but the men have also shown themselves to be hardworking and trustworthy."

"They certainly have. I am thankful they were willing to accompany us to Bethlehem."

Ruth watched her mother-in-law in silence as she finished her meal. *Is that joy I see in her countenance, Adonai? It is a miracle! Thank you!* She shook her head in relief as she stood to leave.

"I will not be home until evening."

Naomi approached, embracing her. "I will miss you while you are away. I pray Adonai keeps you safe." She kissed her hands and then lifted the latch.

As Ruth stepped onto the street, she heard Naomi close the door behind her. The first rays of sunlight appeared over the horizon as the townspeople moved about. Some stared at her; others smiled and nodded their heads in greeting. Did they know who she was? It was probably wise to hold her tongue and get to the fields as quickly as possible.

She straightened her shoulders and held her head high. *Please continue to heal Naomi's heart, Adonai, . . . and mine.*

Reaching the outskirts of town, she started back down the same road they had arrived on the previous day.

She could see the barley fields in the distance with various workers scattered throughout them. Taking a deep breath, she delighted in the familiar smells of ripening grain and dewy earth.

Where would You have me glean on this day, Adonai?

As she finished her prayer, she noticed a servant standing in a field nearby. Stopping, she watched him for a moment. He appeared to be in his early twenties with long dark hair tied at the base of his neck. His robes fell to his feet and he wore a roughly woven tunic over them. She made her way through the barley to where he stood:

And she said, 'Please let me glean and gather after the reapers among the sheaves.' (Ruth 2:7).

"Who are you and where are you from?" the servant asked.

"My name is Ruth. I am a Moabite and I have journeyed to Bethlehem with Naomi, the widow of Elimelech."

He hesitated a moment as he seemed to consider her. "Yes," he said. "You may glean in this field."

"May I ask who owns it?"

"Of course you may. Boaz is his name. He is a mighty man of wealth and stature."

"Please thank the master for his kindness." Ruth bowed her head as she took several steps away from the servant and then turned and began making her way through the stalks to where the reapers were harvesting.

As she neared the spot where she would begin gleaning, she knelt and dug her fingers into the rich brown soil and then bowed her head. *Thank you, Adonai, for preparing me for this day by teaching me Your mitzvah of gleaning when Elimelech and Naomi first arrived in the land of Moab.*

Removing her shawl, she positioned it over her shoulder, tying it at her waist. Strands of her long, wavy hair fell about her arms as she secured a cord across her brow. Leaning forward, her hand touched the first head of grain. She examined the slender tuft of hair-like bristles extending from the kernels and then laid it in her shawl.

Her heart raced with excitement as she worked steadily through the morning. The sun's rays were hot and perspiration trickled down her face and back. Pausing, she wiped beads of moisture from her lips, tasting the salt. Her body began to ache as she lowered her head.

Help me to be strong, Adonai. And thank you for watching over me and giving me favor.

When the sun was directly overhead, Ruth noticed the reapers walking toward a large stone house. A long thatched roof extended from its western side and was supported by multiple poles running its full length. Sheets of canvas were draped here and there from the roof and likely used to block the sun's rays.

Turning, she saw the servant who first greeted her. He waved and pointed toward the house. She smiled and waved and then hurried after the reapers.

Arriving, she walked under the thatched roof. A gentle breeze meandered through the canvas openings, cooling her skin. As she retreated to a corner away from the others, she noticed several maidservants moving about, filling goblets with water.

Sitting, she licked her parched lips and then closed her eyes as she leaned against a pole. Several minutes passed when she felt someone touch her shoulder. Her eyes flew open.

A very young maiden stood before her. She handed Ruth a goblet of water.

"Thank you!" Ruth said.

Taking the goblet she gulped. The water trickled down the sides of her mouth. *Ruth! It is unbecoming a maiden—*

She stopped mid-thought and chuckled. The girl tilted her head, questioning.

"Please do not mind me," Ruth said, wiping her chin and then handing her the goblet. "I was just reminiscing about my mother."

"Where is she?" the girl asked.

"In a land many days' travel from Bethlehem."

"Do you miss her?"

"Oh, yes, very much."

Taking the goblet, the girl dipped it in a pail that was slung over her shoulder with a thick leather strap. She looked to be between eight and ten years old and was a bit on the skinny side with long, dark hair. Filling the goblet to the rim, the maiden handed it to Ruth as drops splashed over the edges and onto Ruth's tunic.

"Forgive me," the girl said.

"Please do not ask my forgiveness, it is I who should be serving you."

The girl grinned. Her crooked smile warmed Ruth's heart as her thoughts wandered to Lior.

"My name is Anna," she said.

"I am Ruth."

She held out her hand, waiting for the goblet and then walked away.

Ruth closed her eyes again, settling against the pole as she wondered at the young girl's kindness. She continued resting until the reapers began making their way back to the field. Ruth followed along behind, thankful to feel refreshed again.

As she knelt to retrieve a head of grain, she noticed the servant waving at her from nearby. She waved in return. There was an older man standing beside him looking intently at her.

"How are you doing, Ruth?" the servant called.

"I am well, thank you," she said, keeping her eyes fixed on the older man.

There was something oddly familiar about him. His thick, brown hair was tied and pulled back at his neck. It held an occasional curl with strands of gray here and there. His brows were strong. Her heart pounded. *He must surely be Boaz!*

She bowed her head as she reached for another head of grain. Would he ask her to leave his field? Suddenly the man called in a loud voice to the reapers:

"The LORD be with you!"

And they answered him, "The LORD bless you!"

Then Boaz said to his servant who was in charge of the reapers, "Whose young woman is this?"

So the servant who was in charge of the reapers answered and said, "It is the young Moabite woman who came back with Naomi from the country of Moab. And she said, 'Please let me glean and gather after the reapers among the sheaves.' So she came and has continued from morning until now, though she rested a little in the house." (Ruth 2:4-7).

Ruth kept her eyes focused on the ground as she heard Boaz approaching. As he stood over her, she admired his large sandaled feet and held her breath. He stood motionless until Ruth lifted her head. Shyly she held his gaze. His eyes seemed kind and gentle, but his face was square and chiseled. He was undeniably a *very* handsome man. Her face flushed and she bowed her head:

Then Boaz said to Ruth, "You will listen, my daughter, will you not? Do not go to glean in another field, nor go from here, but stay close by my young women. Let your eyes be on the field which they reap, and go after them. Have I not commanded the young men not to touch you? And when you are thirsty, go to the vessels and drink from what the young men have drawn." (Ruth 2:8-9).

Ruth's body trembled at the comforting authority of his voice and the generosity of his spirit toward her:

So she fell on her face, bowed down to the ground, and said to him, "Why have I found favor in your eyes, that you should take notice of me, since I am a foreigner?"

And Boaz answered and said to her, "It has been fully reported to me, all that you have done for your mother-in-law since the death of your husband, and how you have left your father and your mother and the land of your birth, and have come to a people whom you did not know before.

"The LORD repay your work, and a full reward be given you by the LORD God of Israel, under whose wings you have come for refuge."

Then she said, "Let me find favor in your sight, my lord; for you have comforted me, and have spoken kindly to your maidservant, though I am not like one of your maidservants." (Ruth 2:10-13).

Ruth felt his hand on her head. Lifting her gaze, she searched his deep brown eyes, intrigued by the flecks of gold scattered here and there. He extended his hand. She hesitated and then laid her trembling hand in his. It felt strong and calloused to the touch. He tightened his grip as he slowly pulled her to her feet. He held her gaze a moment more, and then turning he walked away.

As he left, Ruth regarded his masculine frame with curiosity. His shoulders were broad and his robes fell at his knees revealing his muscled calves. His movement was as one with great power, yet his speech had been full of mercy. She wondered how old he could be and who he reminded her of.

Suddenly, he turned back and smiled. Her face turned crimson. Did he know she was studying him? She looked away, focusing her eyes on the grain that lay before her.

When it was time for the mid-afternoon meal, Ruth observed the reapers and maidens as they began making their way to the house. She followed behind, anxious to rest. As she entered, she saw Boaz look her way. He motioned and said:

"Come here, and eat of the bread, and dip your piece of bread in the vinegar." So she sat beside the reapers, and he passed parched grain to her; and she ate and was satisfied, and kept some back.

And when she rose up to glean, Boaz commanded his young men, saying, "Let her glean even among the sheaves, and do not reproach her.

Also let grain from the bundles fall purposely for her; leave it that she may glean, and do not rebuke her." (Ruth 2:14-16).

Ruth bowed and then lifted her head, smiling. The corners of Boaz's mouth turned upward, revealing a full, uninhibited grin. Her heart was suddenly full of joy. *Thank you, Adonai, for Your favor!* Turning, she walked out into the field.

✿   ✿   ✿

Ruth continued to glean until sunset. As she stood beneath the starry heavens, she finished beating out her gleanings. They equaled about an ephah of barley. Scooping the grain in her shawl, she tied it around her shoulders and began her journey back to Bethlehem.

The street was dark as she approached their room. Looking in the window, she saw Naomi sitting in a chair. As Ruth entered, Naomi kept her eyes on Ruth's bulging shawl tied safely about her shoulders:

"Where have you gleaned today? And where did you work? Blessed be the one who took notice of you."

So she told her mother-in-law with whom she had worked, and said, "The man's name with whom I worked today is Boaz."

Then Naomi said to her daughter-in-law, "Blessed be he of the LORD, who has not forsaken His kindness to the living and the dead! And Naomi said to her, "This man is a relation of ours, one of our close relatives."' (Ruth 2:19-20).

"I knew he looked familiar!"

"He should." Naomi laughed as she began pacing about the room.

"How old is he?" Ruth asked, amused at the sight of her. She was acting like a child, relishing the taste of apples roasted in honey!

Naomi paused. "Elimelech was about ten years old when Boaz was born, so he probably looks very near the same age as Elimelech was when he died."

Ruth removed her grain-laden shawl and placed it on the table:

"He also said to me, 'You shall stay close by my young men until they have finished all my harvest.'"

And Naomi said to her daughter-in-law, "It is good, my daughter, that you go out with his young women, and that people do not meet you in any other field." (Ruth 2:21-22).

"What do you know of Boaz?"

Naomi sat in a chair and folded her hands in her lap. "Oh, I know many things about Boaz, but what you will probably find most interesting is who his mother was."

"Why would that be interesting?" Ruth asked, sitting at the table.

"Because Elimelech shared a story with you about her."

"What story? He told me many. I do not recall one in particular."

Naomi laughed. "It was the story of Rahab."

"The Canaanite woman who hid the spies from Israel, in the town of Jericho?"

Naomi laughed again. Her voice rang merrily about the room and Ruth delighted at the carefree sound.

"What, Naomi? What is it?"

"Rahab was Boaz's mother."

"Rahab! Oh, Naomi! How miraculous that the man who showed us such mercy and kindness had a mother who was also a foreigner! No wonder Adonai led me to his field!"

"It is true! Adonai has provided for us."

Ruth approached Naomi and knelt in front of her, pulling her into her arms. Her hair was clean and brushed and smelled of lavender.

"Now, it is time for you to wash the dust from your body," Naomi said, "and then you must rest. Tomorrow will come quickly and you must be tired from a full day of gleaning."

Ruth looked over at the ledge and saw a new bed filled with fresh hay lying on the floor beneath it. "Oh, Mother!"

"I know," she said humming as she filled a basin with water. "Elizabeth's husband brought it this afternoon."

Ruth sighed. "It is true, Naomi. I am exhausted, but I want to stay up with you and visit more."

"There will be plenty of days ahead for visiting. Now you must sleep," she said as she knelt by the bed and pulled the linens back.

Ruth hurried about the room, securing the shutters, bathing and then slipping into her nightgown.

Finally she lay on the bed, pulling the soft linens over her weary legs. As she closed her eyes, she felt Naomi weave her fingers through her hair as she hummed a melody. It was one Ruth had never heard before. She tried to focus on the sweet sounds of her voice as her body gave in to sleep.

Chapter 25

RAHAB

Ruth stirred from sleep as she felt Naomi's hand brush against her shoulder.

"Time to awaken," Naomi said.

Sitting up, Ruth rubbed her eyes and looked about the room.

"I overslept?"

"No, Daughter, you have plenty of time to get to the field, but first, come and eat. I prepared fresh fruit and bread."

"Thank you, Naomi," Ruth said as she stretched and yawned.

Standing, she hugged Naomi and then hurried behind the curtain. Tugging off her nightgown, she grabbed her harvest clothing, jerking them over her head and yanking them about her body. Retrieving her head covering, she positioned it near her brow and tied the cord in place.

"I am dressed!" she said, beaming as she emerged.

Naomi chuckled.

"Daughter! You cannot go to the field with your head covering askew." Approaching, she removed it; giving it a firm shake and then laid it over her shoulder. Retrieving a brush, she took her time, humming as she removed the tangles from Ruth's tresses and then carefully arranged her covering, securing it with the cord. "There," she said, patting Ruth's arm. "You are stunning, even in plain clothing."

"Thank you," Ruth said as she sat at the table.

Naomi joined her. Taking her hand, they bowed their heads.

"Adonai, thank you for leading Ruth to Boaz's field. Bless her as she goes to glean and continue to give her favor. Thank you for providing us fresh bread and fruit to eat on this beautiful morning. Amen."

"Amen!" Ruth said.

Selecting a slice of apple, Ruth dipped it in honey and then shoved it in her mouth. She chewed and swallowed within a few moments and then did the same with the next slice, and the next. Finally, she finished the last of the apples and reached for the bread.

"Slow down, Ruth! You will upset your stomach."

"But I am late!"

"I do not believe I have ever known anyone so excited to glean in the field." Naomi smiled. "But I will not keep you any longer." She laid the bread in a cloth and handed it to Ruth.

"What will you do with your day?" Ruth asked, walking to the door as Naomi followed behind.

"Elizabeth is coming over with some linen she has been saving for a special occasion. She wanted me to make myself new robes. But I have changed my mind. I will be making them for you instead."

"But Naomi, you need them more than I do."

Naomi hummed as she lifted the latch.

"Daughter, please allow me to bless you as you have blessed me."

"Then of course, I accept your blessing!"

Ruth squeezed her hand and stepped outside, squinting as she viewed the horizon. The sun had already risen and the streets were bustling. She would be late to the field! What would the reapers think of her?

She greeted those around her as she walked. A few pulled her aside to welcome her. She attempted to keep her gait at a leisurely pace until at last she reached the outskirts of town. Taking a deep breath, she lifted her robes above her ankles and ran.

Within a few steps, she stopped and listened. Had someone called her name?

Turning, she saw Boaz standing in the road. He was holding the reins of the most beautiful mare Ruth had ever seen.

"My lord!" she said.

The golden mare flicked her tail and bobbed her head as Ruth hurried to him.

"Good morning, Ruth."

"Good morning," she said, inspecting his eyes. There was something about their shape that intrigued her. Perhaps it was the way they crinkled at the corners.

He smiled. She blushed.

"How is Naomi?"

"She is doing well," Ruth said. "She told me something wonderful about your family last night when I arrived home."

"And what would that be?"

"It has to do with your mother."

"Yes, what of my mother?"

"She was Rahab—the harlot from Jericho!"

Boaz crossed his arms, and laughed.

Ruth grimaced. "Please forgive me!" She covered her eyes for a moment. *Ruth! What must he think of you?* "I did not intend for it to come out that way. I meant to say she was a foreigner—like me."

He chuckled. "What you say is true. My mother at the time she lived in Jericho was a Canaanite and known to be a harlot. Although I have never heard it put in such a blunt fashion."

Boaz tugged the mare's reins and they continued down the road together.

"Are you on your way to my field?"

"Yes."

"It is good that you are. As it so happens, I am on my way there also. I will accompany you."

"Thank you, my lord," Ruth said, pondering her dilemma. Would it be unbecoming of her to ask a personal question? If she attempted to do so, she must be more careful with her wording or risk lowering his opinion of her. Gaining her courage, she glanced at him. He was eyeing her with a look of amusement. She sighed. "Do you mind if I ask about your mother?"

"No, please do."

"What happened after she survived the battle of Jericho?"

"They escorted her safely outside the fallen city. But as the children of Israel were leaving Jericho, my mother fell on her face and wept, begging them to allow her family to live with them."

"Did they mind?"

"No. She believed Adonai to be The One True God and that is why Adonai spared her. There was no other place for her to live but with the people of God."

"The same was true for me! I had been searching for The One True God and Adonai heard my cry. He sent Elimelech and his family to Moab to rescue me and they took me in as one of their own."

"He saw your heart, Ruth, just as He saw my mother's."

"Thank you for allowing me to glean in your field—and for accepting me. I hope your kinsmen will find it in their hearts to do the same."

"Do not worry, my daughter, they already have. I pray Adonai continues to bless you for all you have done for the living and the dead."

Boaz stopped and patted the mare's neck. Her long, braided mane bounced back and forth in response. "I am sorry Mahlon died," he said, looking at her intently. "I am sure you miss him greatly."

"Yes," she said, her voice trembling. Swallowing, she attempted to ease the tightness in her throat. She longed to speak of Mahlon, but did not want to burden Naomi with her sorrow. "It has been difficult to imagine my life without him. Some mornings when I awaken, I turn, expecting him to be there . . ."

Boaz shook his head in understanding, his eyes soft and filled with compassion. "I remember Mahlon well, Ruth."

"You do?" Ruth clasped her hands, attempting to control her excitement. "What was he like?"

"He was thoughtful," he said, continuing to rest his eyes on hers, "and hard working. He loved and served Adonai with all his heart, just as Elimelech. He was much like his father."

"He cared deeply for his parents. When his father died, he was still young, but willing and able to supervise my father's field."

"Your father allowed Mahlon to supervise his field?"

"Yes."

"You must have been proud of him."

"I was!"

"And your father is a man of wealth?"

"Yes, that is true."

"You have sacrificed much to come to this land."

"No, I have gained everything by coming here. I serve and love the God of your people."

Boaz smiled and it warmed her heart.

"Most young maidens, if faced with your circumstance, would return to their own people."

Ruth thought of Orpah and nodded. "Perhaps you are right."

Boaz motioned and they continued down the road.

"How did Rahab meet your father?"

"My father's name was Salmon. He was one of the tribal leaders of Israel. After my mother and her family came out of Jericho, my father was put in charge of seeing after her family."

"Do you believe that was part of God's plan for your mother?"

"Yes, and for my father, as well. They spent many days visiting as they traveled. In the evenings, when our people stopped for the night, my mother and her family ate and shared stories around the fire with the other Israelites. By the time Father's clan settled in Bethlehem, he knew he loved her and sought to marry her."

"And she was accepted by your people, even though she was a foreigner?"

"She was no longer a foreigner in the eyes of Israel. She trusted in Adonai, which was evident by her risking her own life to protect the spies."

Skipping ahead of him, she turned and walked backward as she spoke. "He rescued your mother, just as He rescued me! He is a kind and merciful God!"

"That He is."

His wide grin eased the loneliness she struggled to hide from Naomi. She waited for him to reach her and then walked at his side. He was old enough to be her father. She turned her head and eyed him for a moment. How was it he made her feel? She wondered for a time and then it struck her, like a stone hurled from a sling, hitting its mark! Being near him felt like being home—where all was familiar.

"I am thankful Adonai led you to my field."

Her cheeks flushed at his declaration and her mouth quivered as she considered the magnitude of his words.

He grinned and chuckled.

Turning her head in his direction, she frowned, perplexed by his response, and then sighed.

✡　✡　✡

As they arrived at the barley field, Ruth saw Anna running in their direction. She was holding her head covering and her long, stringy hair was flying about her slender frame. It bounced about her body as though having a life of its own. Ruth held her breath to keep from giggling at the sight of her.

"My lord!" Anna yelled as she neared.

Boaz smiled and extended the mare's reins.

"Good morning, Anna," he said.

She bowed. "May I take Bella to the house?" Anna asked, patting the mare's neck with her tiny hand.

"You may."

Anna grasped Bella's reins and then took several steps backward, smiling at Ruth.

"Greetings, Anna," Ruth said.

"You know Anna?" Boaz asked.

"We met yesterday. Anna filled my goblet with water as I rested at the house."

Boaz smiled and Anna lowered her eyes, staring at the ground as she shifted her feet.

"Thank you, Anna," he said.

She bowed and then turning, skipped toward the house as the mare pranced along at her side.

Boaz chuckled as they wove their way through the field.

As they neared the reapers, Boaz waved at a servant.

"Have a blessed day, Ruth, and please give Naomi greetings for me," he said, walking away.

"Thank you, my lord. I will."

As she knelt to glean, she heard him call to the reapers.

"The LORD be with you!"

She lifted her head and responded with the others, "The LORD bless you!"

Reaching for a head of grain, she paused and lowered her head in prayer. *Adonai, thank you for Boaz, and for his favor. Bless him, LORD as he has blessed us. I pray his harvest is plentiful with much bread in his house!"*

Chapter 26

HIS PROVISION

Thunder rumbled in the distance as Ruth poked her head out the window of their room, observing the massive gray clouds billowing along the late afternoon sky. The streets were empty. The shutters opposite theirs were closed in anticipation of the storm. A drop of rain landed on her brow and trickled down her nose. She took a slow, deep breath, relishing the cleansing smell of the wind as it whipped about her head. Moving her calloused fingers over her face, she wiped the moisture away. She was thankful it was Sabbath and a much needed day of rest for her weary body.

Turning, she observed Naomi sitting at the table with her head bowed and then surveyed the sacks of grain lining the walls. Almost two months had passed since their arrival in Bethlehem. Since that day, she had gleaned enough barley in Boaz's field to last well into the coming year. She placed a small basket of dates on the table and touched Naomi's shoulder. Naomi raised her head and smiled.

"I was just thanking Adonai for His provision," she said.

Ruth nodded as she handed Naomi a date. The thick, sticky juices clung to her fingers as she rubbed her hand on her tunic.

Taking a bite, Naomi fixed her inquisitive stare on Ruth. "Are you unhappy today, my daughter?"

"The day does seem oddly dreary."

"Perhaps it is because the barley harvest is near completion. I am sure you will miss the maidservants."

"Yes, I will miss them."

"Especially little Anna? You watch over her as a hen does her chicks."

"I do. Her father's health continues to decline, but thankfully Boaz is very generous to them."

Naomi laid her hand on Ruth's. "I was pleased to hear he employs Anna's mother to sew and allows Anna to serve the reapers when they recline at the house." Naomi paused a moment and then continued. "And what of Boaz? Will you miss him?"

"Will we not see him once the harvest is complete?" Ruth asked as her heart sank.

"Certainly not daily as you do now."

Of course Naomi is right! Oh, Adonai . . .

"You think highly of him, do you not?" Naomi asked.

Ruth remained silent for a time as she was deep in thought. Naomi nudged her. "There is much to admire about Boaz."

"Oh, yes, Mother," Ruth said, squeezing Naomi's hand. "He is a kind master and generous to his servants."

"Even in his youth, he was known for his charity to the poor and needy."

"I am not surprised," Ruth said, her heart still aching. "He comes to the field every day and greets the reapers."

"He greets them daily?"

"Yes, and the reapers respond in unison, asking the LORD's continued blessing toward him. He also takes time to walk through the field to acknowledge each reaper."

"And what about you, Ruth, does he speak to you as well?"

"Oh, yes, Naomi, he cares very much for us." She blushed, shifting nervously.

"I am sure he does." Naomi said as she patted Ruth's knee.

They sat silent for a time as Ruth reflected upon their conversation. Naomi seemed particularly interested in Boaz, and why should she not? He was, after all, a near kinsman.

Much had changed since the day they journeyed from Moab. Ruth had faced the possibility that Naomi might never be truly happy again. But now, as she sat beside her at the table, her countenance seemed full of peace.

"Does Boaz ask about me?" Naomi asked, interrupting Ruth's musings.

"Oh, yes! I am sorry I have not spoken more of him. Whenever he approaches me in the field, he always asks about you first—how you are; am I gleaning enough to provide for you; are we increasing our storage of grain. I have even invited him to stop by our room to see you."

"That is considerate of you, my daughter, but I have known I would not see Boaz during the harvest. I am sure he rises before the sun and does not return home until late in the evening."

"He reminds me of—" Ruth's voice trembled as a wave of sorrow swept over her.

Naomi's eyes filled with tears. "Please do not cry, my daughter."

Ruth buried her head in her arms. "I am sorry, Naomi," she said as her body shook. Naomi laid her head on Ruth's back and held her close.

"Being near him somehow lessens my longing for Mahlon."

"I am thankful to hear he brings you comfort. Knowing that gives me solace."

Ruth wiped her eyes. "He reminds me of Elimelech."

"I am truly grateful to hear it." She hummed as she walked to the basin and dipped her fingers in the water. "Now you must sleep."

Naomi closed the shutters and secured the door.

Ruth stepped behind the curtain and emerged a short time later in her nightgown.

"What will happen to us, now that the barley harvest is almost complete?"

"The LORD will provide." Naomi said, continuing to hum as she pulled the linens back and motioned for Ruth to come.

Ruth lay in bed, snuggling beneath the linens. Closing her eyes, she heard thunder rumble through the heavens as lightning illuminated the room. As she gave in to sleep, she smelled the sweetness of rain as drops beat against the shutters.

✧　✧　✧

Ruth arose and tiptoed about the dark room as Naomi slept soundly. She dressed in her harvest clothing and then tucked an apple, bread and roasted almonds in her shawl. Placing a basket of fruit on the table for Naomi to see, she crept to the door. Lifting the latch, she slipped from their room.

The street was wet and a cloudy mist hovered near the ground. She eyed the closed doors and shutters, realizing the townspeople were likely still sleeping. She hurried to the outskirts of town and then lifted her robes. Her sandals were wet and her feet slipped against the soles.

Looking about her, she noticed several wild flowers growing along the road's edge. Her thoughts wandered to home as she stooped and plucked one from the ground. Raising it to her nose she sniffed its delicate perfume, remembering the day she examined a flower petal in the land of Moab and considered its Designer.

Thank you, Adonai that Naomi is at peace and confident You will continue to provide for us. Perhaps now that the barley harvest is almost complete, Naomi and I can sew for the wealthy and barter our goods in the market.

Nearing the field, she saw Anna running in her direction.

"Good morning, Anna!" she called.

"Ruth!" she yelled.

"What is it, Anna, what is wrong?"

"I wanted to speak," she said, gasping, "—with you before I leave."

"Leave? Where are you going?" Ruth asked as Anna clung to her.

"My lord is sending Mother and me on to the wheat field today. I may not see you again." She lifted her tear-streaked face and stared at Ruth with her sorrowful eyes.

"Today? You are leaving today?"

"Now. A servant will arrive soon with camels." She pointed down the road. "But the wheat field is only a short distance away. Will you come and see me?"

"Oh, yes," Ruth said, wiping a tear from Anna's cheek.

Anna stepped back, locking her hands behind her as she scraped her sandal back and forth on the road.

"What is it, Anna?"

"Did you know my lord has never married?" She tilted her head with an inquisitive look and stared at Ruth.

"Never married?" Ruth asked.

"No," Anna said as she backed away and then took out running to the house.

Ruth stood motionless. Never married? She had wondered, but could not bring herself to ask. She shook her head in disbelief.

As she walked across the field, her sandals filled with mud. It squished between her toes, irritating the soles of her feet. She paused, watching the few remaining reapers. They were moving about the sheaves, securing them as the storm had thrown some to the ground.

Stooping to gather the few heads of grain that remained, she heard Boaz call to her. She turned to see him approaching.

"Greetings, Ruth," he said.

"My lord," she answered, standing.

"How is Naomi?"

"She is well."

She lowered her gaze to the ground.

"And how are you, my daughter?"

Absorbed in thought, Ruth looked in the direction of the house. *Would it be unbecoming to ask why he–*

"Ruth, is there something bothering you today?"

She drew her eyes to his.

"You never married, my lord?"

"No, Ruth, I never married." He chuckled.

She sighed, crossing her arms. "May I ask why? Is there some custom among your people that I do not know about?"

"No." He tossed his head back and laughed. "There is no custom that would have prevented me from marrying, if I had so chosen."

Ruth's heart beat erratically as she summoned the courage to continue. "You remind me of Elimelech."

He chuckled again. "In what way, my graying hair?"

She noted the shape his mouth. There was something about the way it curved upward–just before he smiled.

"I feel safe gleaning in your field." She avoided his eyes, keeping her gaze on the ground. "The other maidservants feel the same. You are a kind master."

"That is good to hear, Ruth."

She nodded and looked away. "I best get back to gleaning," she said, bowing.

"Yes, before the master finds you idle," he said, shaking his head in amusement.

Ruth took several steps and then turned back. "I forgot to tell you. Naomi inquired of you yesterday. She misses you greatly."

"Tell her I will come soon."

"I will!" Ruth bowed again and then turning, made her way through the field.

"Ruth!" he yelled.

She turned.

"See my supervising servant when you are done gleaning. He will direct you to my wheat field."

"Your wheat field?"

"Yes."

"Thank you, my lord!"

He nodded and then walked toward the supervising servant.

Ruth lowered her head.

LORD, do You set the order of our lives? As You determined when Sarah would conceive, did You also determine the number of Mahlon's days?

Her thoughts drifted to Boaz.

And if we marry . . .

A lump grew in her throat and she swallowed as she knelt and picked up a head of grain.

Teach me Your paths, LORD, and lead me in Your ways. Cause me to understand where I err and give me wisdom. For I long to live under the shadow of Your wings all the days You have determined for me.

Ruth continued to walk about the field. By midafternoon, she gleaned the last head of grain and headed back to town. Upon arriving, she found Naomi waiting by the open door.

"Daughter! I expected you home early today. Is the harvest complete?"

"It is, sweet Mother," Ruth said as she kissed her cheek. Approaching the table, Ruth dropped the grain, removed her shawl and slumped in the chair. Should she mention her conversation with Boaz? She thought for a moment. Perhaps it would not be wise.

"You seem deep in thought, Ruth."

"I am sorry, Naomi. Was there something you wanted to ask me?"

"I am curious if you saw Boaz today."

"Yes, I did," Ruth said as her heart raced.

"Did you tell him we are doing well?"

Ruth thought for a moment and then smiled. "Oh, Naomi, how could I forget!"

"Forget?"

"He invited me to glean in his wheat field."

"His wheat field!" Naomi said as a smile grew steadily across her face.

"He did!" Ruth giggled. "I knew you would be overjoyed by the news! Adonai continues to provide for us!"

Naomi began to saunter about the room. "Do you remember the day we left the land of Moab to journey here?"

"Yes, I do," Ruth said, recalling the heartbreak of that day. "Are you worried about something?"

"I am fine." Naomi strolled to the table and sat across from Ruth. "Did I ever share the story of Tamar?"

"No. Who was she?"

"She was the wife of Judah's eldest son."

"Judah was one of Jacob's twelve sons."

"Yes, and Elimelech is from his tribe. The tribe of Judah."

"What was the eldest son's name?"

"His name was Er, but he died, so Judah told his second oldest son, Onan, to marry Tamar, which he did, but he also died."

"Oh, Naomi. He lost two sons, just as you did. Please do not share this story if it causes you pain."

Naomi continued on without acknowledging Ruth's statement. "Judah had a third son, named Shelah."

"A third son? Did that son marry Tamar also?"

"Sadly, no."

"Why, did Tamar die?"

"No, Tamar did not die. Judah was afraid that Shelah might also die if he married Tamar. Because he was afraid, he wanted to protect his son."

"I can understand his fear. I might have been afraid, also. What did he do?"

"He deceived Tamar."

"Deceived her? How?"

Chapter 26 – HIS PROVISION

Naomi began reciting the story from memory:

Then Judah said to Tamar his daughter-in-law, "Remain a widow in your father's house till my son Shelah is grown." For he said, "Lest he also die like his brothers." And Tamar went and dwelt in her father's house. (Genesis 38:11).

"Tamar trusted Judah and went to live with her parents. But he had no intention of allowing his youngest son to marry her?"

"That is true."

"May I ask you a question?"

"Yes, always."

"It is one I have often pondered, but did not want to grieve you by asking."

"You will never grieve me, my daughter. On the contrary, you bring me great joy. Please ask your question."

"If Chilion had never married, would you have sought for me to marry him when Mahlon died?"

"Yes. Of course."

"Why?"

"It is the command of our LORD. It would have been Chilion's duty as a brother to provide an heir for Mahlon."

"That is why it was Shelah's duty to marry Tamar? He needed to provide an heir for his eldest brother?"

"Yes."

"So what happened to Tamar after she went back to live with her father?"

"It is a story with an ending much like the one of your ancestor, Lot."

"Lot? You mean to say that Tamar slept with her father-in-law, Judah, to produce an heir?"

"Yes, she did."

"Why would he agree to such a thing? Was it to spare his youngest son?"

"No! He would never do that. In truth, he did not know he slept with her."

Ruth laughed. "Naomi, how could he not know he slept with her?"

Naomi placed her hands on her rosy cheeks; her mouth twitching until finally she laughed. "Daughter, he did not know it was Tamar he slept with. He thought he slept with a harlot!"

Ruth raised her brows, questioning. "How did Tamar deceive her father-in-law into believing she was a harlot?"

"Judah's wife had, by that time, passed away. He had gone through a time of mourning and then went to visit a friend. Tamar heard of it, so she covered her face and sat at the entrance to the town where Judah was traveling. When Judah saw her, he thought she was a harlot because her face was covered."

"What did Judah say when he saw her?"

Naomi closed her eyes and continued the story:

Then he turned to her by the way, and said, "Please let me come in to you"; for he did not know that she was his daughter-in-law.

So she said, "What will you give me, that you may come in to me?"

And he said, "I will send a young goat from the flock."

So she said, "Will you give me a pledge till you send it?"

Then he said, "What pledge shall I give you?"

So she said, "Your signet and cord, and your staff that is in your hand." *Then he gave them to her, and went in to her, and she conceived by him. So she arose and went away, and laid aside her veil and put on the garments of her widowhood. (Genesis 38:16-19).*

"It does appear Elimelech had a few black sheep in his family," Ruth said with a mischievous grin.

Naomi chuckled.

"So what happened after she conceived? Did she give birth to a son?"

"She did. She produced an heir for the tribe of Judah."

"Did Judah find out it was his child?"

"Eventually he did," Naomi responded, continuing the story:

And it came to pass, about three months after, that Judah was told, saying, "Tamar your daughter-in-law has played the harlot; furthermore she is with child by harlotry."

So Judah said, "Bring her out and let her be burned!"

When she was brought out, she sent to her father-in-law, saying, "By the man to whom these belong, I am with child." And she said, "Please determine whose these are—the signet and cord, and staff."

So Judah acknowledged them and said, "She has been more righteous than I, because I did not give her to Shelah my son." And he never knew her again. (Genesis 38:24-26).

"So she bore a son?"

"She actually had twin sons. The firstborn was named Perez."

"Are Elimelech and Boaz from the line of Perez?"

"Yes," she said as someone rapped on the door.

Naomi approached and pulled it open.

"Boaz!" she exclaimed as she hurried past the servant standing just outside the doorway.

"Greetings, Naomi!" he responded as she nestled her head into his broad chest.

"It is so good to see you again, finally, after all these years." Naomi stepped back to look at him. "I see a little more gray hair but you look healthy enough."

Boaz laughed.

"It is good to see you, too, Naomi."

"Can you come in and visit?"

"No, not this evening. I am delivering fruits and vegetables to some of our reapers' families and have several more stops to make before the sun sets."

Ruth stood in the doorway, marveling at the cart. It was laden with baskets of dried dates, lentils, millet and fresh peas.

"Thank you for your continued kindness toward us," Naomi said.

"It is my pleasure," Boaz said as he retrieved several large baskets. As he approached the door, Ruth held her breath. His eyes rested on hers. Lowering her head, she stepped from the door.

Ruth continued to study his handsome frame as he placed the baskets on the table and then scanned the sacks of barley stacked neatly along the walls.

Turning to Ruth, he handed her two apples.

"I hope you and Naomi find these to your liking. They come from one of my best orchards."

"Thank you, my lord," she said.

He held her gaze and smiled. Her heart fluttered. *Ruth! What is wrong with you?* She glanced at Naomi—who appeared to be watching with great interest. Bowing, she stepped away as Boaz walked to the cart.

"Thank you again," Naomi said as she hugged him and then stood waving as Boaz and his servant continued down the street.

Upon entering the house, Naomi began to hum her favorite melody as she removed some of the lentils from the basket. Placing them in a basin, she covered them with water.

Ruth watched her for a time and then said, "It was kind of Boaz to visit us this evening."

"Yes, it certainly was," Naomi said, continuing to hum.

"Naomi?"

"Yes, my daughter."

"Will you finish telling me the story of Tamar?"

"It can wait," Naomi said, keeping her back to Ruth.

"Wait? But for how long?"

Turning, Naomi smiled. "Until the end of the wheat harvest."

"The wheat harvest? But why?" Naomi did not answer.

Ruth shook her head as she closed the shutters and prepared for bed.

Chapter 27

TAMAR'S STORY

Ruth leaned forward and grasped one of the few remaining stalks of wheat and then laid it on the ground as she examined her red, calloused hands. Turning them this way and that, she thought of her mother. *"Ruth!"* she could hear her say. *"A maiden's skin should remain soft with no hint of a freckle!"*

Sighing, she surveyed her harvest clothing. She had done her best to make them last. Nonetheless, months of gleaning in Boaz's fields had taken a toll on her robes. Inspecting her tunic, she noticed a small hole, touching the frayed edges. Thankfully, it could be easily mended.

Wiping moisture from her brow, she looked across the field. The wheat harvest was complete and few reapers remained. The late afternoon sky filled with clouds as gusts of wind ebbed and flowed, saturating the air with the smell of earth and grain.

She eyed the sheaves leaning neatly against each other, searching among them for the familiar form of Boaz. Where could he be? She had done her best to remain busy throughout the day as she continued to hope for his arrival, but as the sun crept along the late afternoon sky, she realized there was no more wheat to glean. Her throat felt tight and her head throbbed as she attempted to contain her sorrow.

Upon seeing Simeon, she stood, watching as he made his way toward her. He was the same servant she approached some months previous when she first asked to glean among the sheaves in Boaz's barley field. Since that meeting, he requested Ruth call him by his given name—to which she eventually acquiesced.

He appeared taller now. His robes were new and made from linen. They clung to his chest and rested just above his knees. He wore a brightly colored sash about his hips and thick leather sandal straps twined to the tops of his calves.

"Greetings, Ruth!" he called.

"Greetings, Simeon," she said, bowing.

He came near, eyeing her with his dark, olive eyes.

"It is good to see you today, Ruth," he said as he held her gaze. "You are looking well." He smiled.

"Thank you, Simeon, I am well." Turning, she scanned the field again. "I was hoping to see the master."

"Boaz?" he asked, dropping his shoulders. "I do not expect him at the field today."

"Do you know where he is?"

He sighed, pointing toward a hill in the distance. "He is at the threshing floor with the other masters. They are overseeing the winnowing of the barley harvest."

Her lip quivered and she lowered her head. *When will I see Boaz again, Adonai? Did he not know this would be my last day of gleaning?*

"Is something wrong, Ruth?"

Do not cry, Ruth!

"Ruth?" he asked again.

Her eyes burned as tears gathered along her lids. "Would you give him a message for me?"

"Of course, Ruth. But—"

"Please thank him—"

Turning, she ran, weaving her way through the sheaves as tears spilled down her cheeks. As she neared the road, she froze.

"Ruth!" Boaz called. "Come to me."

Her heart leapt at the sound of his deep, resonant voice. Dropping her gleanings, she grabbed the edge of her tunic and wiped her face. Feeling dirt smudged with tears, she cringed. *How can I go to him? He will question my sorrow.*

"Ruth!" he called again.

Stooping, she gathered her gleanings, arranging them quickly in her shawl and then turned to face him.

"Forgive me, my lord," she said, bowing.

"Why are you making such haste?"

She bit her lip, contemplating her dilemma. She wanted to go to him; tell him she would miss him, but how could she? *Why did you have to cry, Ruth?*

"I am sorry, but I must hurry home. Naomi is waiting to finish telling me a story."

"What story?"

Recalling the delicate nature of Tamar's life, she dropped her gaze. "One she started at the end of the barley harvest," she said, shrugging.

Boaz laughed. "Is that so? Why did she make you wait so long?"

The comforting sound of his voice made her body weak. "I have wondered—" Ruth said, her voice cracking as tears trickled down her cheeks. "I am sorry, my lord, I must go."

"What is wrong, Ruth? Is Naomi well?"

"Yes, my lord," she paused. "Thank you. We will always be grateful."

Boaz started toward her and then stopped and waved. "Please give Naomi my greetings."

"I will, my lord." Ruth bowed. Turning, she ran toward home.

Recalling a nearby stream, she left the road and hurried to its edge. Kneeling, she swirled her fingers through the water, eyeing her face as it rippled about.

I will miss him, Adonai.

She splashed her cheeks, gasping as the cool water took her breath away.

Surely Naomi is right. We will see him on occasion about the city, will we not, Adonai? Perhaps he will allow me to glean in his fields again next year. He is a kind and generous man. I am sure he will!

Oh, Adonai, what is wrong with me? And what a predicament I am in! I told Boaz I must hurry home, so hurry I must!

Rising, she tied her gleanings over her shoulders. As she made her way to the road, tears began to flow down her face. She had only taken a few steps when a whirlwind encircled her, covering her body in a gritty film of dirt. She threw her hands in the air, shook her head and laughed. *I will trust You, Adonai, no matter what our future holds!*

Grasping her tunic, she rubbed her face, smearing the dirt and then blew her nose.

As she reached the main street, she noticed several of the town's elders eyeing her with concern. "Such a beautiful day, would you agree?" she asked, waving. They nodded, their mouths dropping as though they wanted to speak, but thought the better of it. *Oh, Adonai, what a sight I must be!*

Arriving at their room, she shoved the door open and slammed it shut behind her.

Naomi stood as Ruth leaned against the door.

"What happened to you, my daughter?" Naomi asked as she scurried across the room, removing Ruth's shawl.

"I am so sorry! I do not know what has come over me."

"Was today the last day of the wheat harvest?"

"It was."

Naomi nodded and smiled. "I assumed it would be. Did you speak to Boaz today?"

"Only briefly," she said, sniffling. "He did not arrive at the field until I was already on my way home. He sends his greetings."

"Blessed be he of the LORD," Naomi said as she dipped a cloth in water and wiped Ruth's face and arms. "Come and sit at the table and eat while I finish the story of Tamar."

"Tamar? You remembered?" she asked, sitting. "I thought you would have forgotten, it has been so long ago."

"I have not forgotten. I have thought of it every day since the night I first shared it with you," Naomi said, placing a basket of freshly baked bread on the table.

Ruth pushed it away as her stomach knotted at the smell. "I am sorry, Naomi, I cannot eat."

"I understand. I knew this day would be difficult for you."

"Why?" Ruth asked as Naomi removed the basket and placed it on the hearth.

"Because Boaz and the reapers are like family. You will miss them."

Ruth held out her hands to Naomi. "Will you sit with me, sweet Mother?"

Naomi eyed her for a moment and then began walking back and forth across the room. Ruth watched her for a time and then stood.

"What is wrong, Naomi?"

"Nothing is wrong. I pray all will go well. Please, sit."

"What do you mean?" Ruth asked as she sat.

"Do you remember when Moses spoke of the Promised Land to the people of Israel."

"I think so. Adonai said the land was His."

Naomi stood motionless, closed her eyes and began to recite from memory, saying:

'The land shall not be sold permanently, for the land is Mine; for you are strangers and sojourners with Me. And in all the land of your possession you shall grant redemption of the land.

'If one of your brethren becomes poor, and has sold some of his possession, and if his redeeming relative comes to redeem it, then he may redeem what his brother sold.' (Leviticus 25:23-25).

"Do you refer to Elimelech's field which was sold?"

"Yes. Elimelech's, Mahlon's and Chilion's."

"Who is a 'redeeming relative'?"

"They are a very special person. They must be related."

"A near kinsman?"

"Yes, of course. But more importantly, they must be a person of wealth—in order that they have the means to purchase the field back in the name of the relative."

Ruth thought for a moment and then stood as her heart pounded wildly. "Boaz! He is your relative and a man of great wealth."

"Yes! Please sit, my daughter."

"Then he can redeem the field for you!"

"But there is more to being a kinsman redeemer than wealth alone."

"What else is required?"

"He must not only be a close relative, and a person of wealth, but he must also be willing to redeem."

"I know Boaz! He will be more than willing to redeem the field for Elimelech!" Ruth laughed. "Why have you not asked him?"

Naomi sat across from Ruth, taking Ruth's hands in hers. "Do you remember the details of Tamar's story?"

"Yes. She deceived her father-in-law to produce an heir for her deceased husband." Ruth lowered her head. "I am sorry, Naomi, but what does Tamar's story have to do with us and Elimelech's field? You have no more sons for me to marry, and you are beyond the age to bear children."

Naomi lifted Ruth's chin. "That is true, my sweet daughter," she said, tucking a lock of hair behind Ruth's ear. "But there is a way to provide an heir for Mahlon as Tamar did for her husband Er."

"Mahlon? I do not understand. He has no other living brother and even if Elimelech were still living, I would never do as Tamar did!"

Naomi chuckled. "Of course not!" She smiled, reaching across the table to pat Ruth's cheek.

"If Boaz agrees to become our kinsman redeemer, he will redeem the land *and* you."

"Redeem me?"

"He will take you to be his wife in order to raise up an heir for Mahlon!"

"Wife?" Ruth gasped. Attempting to stand, she caught her foot on the edge of the table and tumbled backward.

"My daughter!" Naomi shrieked as she ran to her side.

Ruth sat on the floor, looking at her wide-eyed.

Naomi pulled her to her feet.

Ruth began pacing about the room.

"How can that be?" She paused and then continued pacing. "I thought only you could provide a son for me to marry."

"I never thought it possible," Naomi said, following her. "But another close relative from Elimelech's clan can be a redeemer!"

Ruth laid her hands over her eyes, shaking her head in disbelief. Naomi remained silent until Ruth looked at her. "Boaz is a close relative from Elimelech's clan, Ruth, and I believe he is also willing."

"My lord might choose to take me as his wife? Does he know of this possibility?"

Naomi stepped away and began pacing. "Of course he knows," she said, turning toward Ruth. "But he will not speak of it. It is you who must ask him!"

"Me? What if he does not want to marry me?"

Naomi chuckled and said:

"*My daughter, shall I not seek security for you, that it may be well with you?*

"*Therefore wash yourself and anoint yourself, put on your best garment* and go down to the threshing floor; but do not make yourself known to the man until he has finished eating and drinking.

"Then it shall be, when he lies down, that you shall notice the place where he lies; and you shall go in, uncover his feet, and lie down; and he will tell you what you should do."

. . . "All that you say to me I will do." (Ruth 3:1; 3-5).

"Oh, Naomi!"

"I know, my daughter! Now we must go to Elizabeth. She is waiting for us."

"Elizabeth?"

"Yes, your robes are at her house. We must hurry."

Ruth walked to the bed and sat, lowering her head.

"What is wrong, my daughter?"

Lifting her eyes to meet Naomi's, she said, "Could it be the LORD has kept Boaz's heart for such a time as this?"

"Perhaps!"

"But what of Mahlon? Would he want me to marry another?"

"Of course he would!" Naomi said as she knelt at Ruth's feet, grasping her hands. "Of that I am certain!"

Naomi rose and sat next to Ruth, laying her arm on Ruth's shoulder.

"Have you been planning for this day for these past months?" Ruth asked, tilting her head as she studied her.

"I began planning the first day you arrived home with your gleanings and told me of Boaz."

"But how could you know he might be willing?"

"Simply because of the magnitude of your gleanings! You could never have amassed that amount of grain unless someone was purposefully dropping it for you!"

"Why did you wait so long to tell me?"

"There is a time for everything, my daughter. I wanted to wait to see if you were also willing."

"Oh, Naomi, what made you suspect?"

"When you avoided my efforts to discuss him, I knew you must care deeply for him. I supposed in my heart that you did not want me to know you could care for another as you did my son."

Ruth knelt at Naomi's feet and rested her head in her lap. "The day I first saw Boaz, he comforted me. I was overwhelmed by his generosity toward us. Since that day, my feelings for him have confused me. But today, I realized how deeply I care for him."

"I know, my daughter. I have watched you struggle. But know this, if Boaz chooses to redeem you, all will be restored."

"Thank you, Adonai!" Ruth said as she stood and lifted her hands in praise.

"Now come! We must hurry!" Naomi said, retrieving a small pouch.

Hand in hand, they rushed from the room, closing the door behind them.

Chapter 28

THE THRESHING FLOOR

Naomi tucked her arm around Ruth's waist as they hurried along the winding street. Various townspeople greeted them as they went. They nodded and smiled, but kept their pace steady as the sun crept along the western sky.

Rounding a corner, Naomi pointed to Elizabeth's home sitting at the road's edge. They entered her spacious courtyard. It was surrounded on three sides with towering walls of hewn stone. Massive doors of acacia wood were fashioned near the corner of each wall. Steps, resting along the base of its foundation, led to the second floor, which was similar in design to the first.

Ruth hesitated, eyeing the three doors.

"This one, my daughter," Naomi said, approaching the door on the left.

As Naomi rapped her fist against the dense wood, it responded in dull, muffled tones. Within moments, the door flung open and Elizabeth stood before them. Her hands were covered in flour and a fine white dust rested on her hair and brows. She lifted her finger to her lips.

"Shhh! My grandson is sleeping," she said.

Grasping Ruth's arm, she led her across the courtyard to the opposite door as Naomi followed. Lifting the heavy latch, Elizabeth swung the door open, guiding Ruth inside.

"Did I not tell you it would be today?" Elizabeth chortled.

"You did, my friend!" Naomi said.

Ruth's attention was drawn to several narrow windows towering above them. They emitted small streams of natural light, which bounced along the cedar beams spanning the length of the ceiling. Feeling Elizabeth's touch, she turned.

"Welcome to my home, Ruth."

"You are a dear friend to us," Ruth said, hugging her and kissing her floured hand. "Thank you for your kindness."

Elizabeth raised her brows, focusing her eyes on Ruth's mouth. Chuckling she brushed her tunic against Ruth's lips.

"It is the least I can do for you and Naomi." She pointed to the corner. "Ruth, the servants filled a cistern with water. When you are done bathing, Naomi and I will help you dress and arrange your hair."

"Thank you," Ruth said as Elizabeth grasped Naomi's arm and pulled her out the door.

The stillness of the room settled about her as she retrieved a small pitcher. Dipping it into the cistern, she poured cool water into a shallow basin of bronze lying on the floor. She continued adding water until it rippled against the sides. Removing her garments, she knelt in the basin. Her hands trembled as she moved a bar of soap along her skin.

She bowed her head. *Calm my heart, Adonai.* And then she heard a familiar voice as He whispered into the recesses of her soul.

Be strong, Ruth, and have courage. Do not be afraid, for I am with you, wherever you may go.

When she was done bathing, she dried her body with a loosely woven cloth. Taking a bowl of olive oil and myrrh, she dipped her hands in the mixture and rubbed it into her parched skin, savoring the fragrant smell.

Scanning the room, she saw new undergarments draped on a chair.

Hurrying, she slipped them on as the cool air sent shivers through her.

Pouring water into a basin on the table, she washed her hair until it squeaked between her fingers. At last, she was clean. She had not had a proper bath since arriving in Bethlehem and missed the days when bathing was a weekly event.

Twisting her locks over her shoulder, she approached the door and lifted the latch, peeking into the courtyard. Naomi and Elizabeth were standing nearby, visiting in hushed voices.

Looking in her direction, they hurried to the door.

"Prettiest maiden I have ever seen!" Elizabeth said, slapping Naomi's shoulder as she pushed the door open. "And what a figure! I do not believe my waist was ever so tiny as hers!"

Ruth blushed as she looked at Naomi.

Naomi shook her head and laughed.

"I told Hosea those windows would not be large enough." Elizabeth walked across the room and raised a lamp's flame. "We are going to need more light to arrange Ruth's hair properly."

"Knowing your husband, I am sure he thought they were sufficient at the time."

"I am sure he did," Elizabeth said, dipping her hands in a basin of water and drying them on her tunic. "And now you are ready for your new gown." Elizabeth scurried across the room and retrieved the garment hidden behind a curtain.

Running her eyes along the delicate fabric, Ruth smiled. The linen was snow white and flowed about as Elizabeth approached.

"It is beautiful, sweet Mother," Ruth said.

"No time for dawdling, Ruth!" Elizabeth said, chuckling.

"True, my daughter."

Ruth raised her arms as Elizabeth and Naomi lifted the exquisite gown over her head. Releasing their hold, it flowed over her breasts; clinging to her waist and resting on her hips in one fluid motion.

"My, my, but it fits well in all the right places," Elizabeth said, winking at Naomi. "Boaz will be pleased, I am sure."

Ruth felt her face fill with color as Elizabeth motioned for her to come. "Sit," she said, retrieving a small pouch Naomi brought from home.

Opening it, Ruth saw her pearls and thin gold bracelets.

"Naomi! I thought I left these with my mother!"

"You did, but your father entrusted their safe keeping with Gardish and Haran. They brought them to me on the morning they were to return to Moab and said your mother insisted you have them." Naomi's eyes glistened. "I hoped for the day you would wear them again, but never imagined it would be on your wedding day."

Elizabeth rubbed a cloth along Ruth's hair, drying it to the touch. Drizzling olive oil and myrrh in her palms, she anointed Ruth's head.

Taking long strands of the tiny pearls, Naomi wove them throughout her long, wavy locks. Lifting sections of hair, she arranged them about her head and secured them with a comb. Finally, she pulled several strands free to fall about her face.

Taking a small flask of sweet smelling fragrances, Elizabeth dripped the oils in her hands, and then massaged them over Ruth's face, arms, legs and feet.

Slipping the bracelets on her wrist, Elizabeth stood and smiled. "Fairest maiden in all the land, of that I am certain!"

Returning to the curtain, Elizabeth emerged with a long, purple shawl made from the finest linen. Fringe hung along the edges and Ruth gasped, delighted at the sight of it.

"It is beautiful!"

"My gift to you, Ruth!" Elizabeth said as she laid it across her shoulders. "Now you must hurry. The sun will be setting soon."

Ruth nodded as she knelt to retrieve her sandals.

"Oh, my, no!" Elizabeth said, pointing to a canvas pouch.

Ruth approached the table and unrolled the canvas, smiling as she smelled the fresh aroma of newly crafted sandals.

"Thank you," she said.

Slipping them on, she tied the delicate cords about her ankles and then wiggled her oiled toes against the soft, supple leather.

"You are welcome!" Elizabeth said. "Now pay close attention, Ruth. When you leave the house, go east along the street just outside our door and through the narrow gate. It connects to the road which leads to the threshing floor, but is seldom traveled."

Naomi pulled Ruth into her arms.

"Remember, my daughter, do not make yourself known to him. When he is finished drinking and eating, he will lie down. Notice the place where he lies. Wait until the threshing floor is still and then you may go to him. Uncover his feet and lie down at them until he awakens. He will let you know what you should do next."

Ruth kissed Naomi's forehead and squeezed Elizabeth's hand. "Thank you," she said as she lifted the latch and stepped outside.

Her heart raced with anticipation as she looked about the courtyard, observing the street leading from the city. It did appear deserted, as Elizabeth had said.

Closing her eyes, she bowed her head and prayed. *Adonai, I choose to trust You, no matter what lies ahead for Naomi and me.*

Lifting the delicate fabric of her gown, she hurried along the way, looking about her, but saw no one. When she reached the outskirts of town, she moved some distance from the road, so as not to be seen.

Upon passing a grove of trees, she looked to the hill where the threshing floor lay. The sun was now moving just below the horizon and the sky was awash in hues of pink, yellow, orange and blue. Stopping for a moment, she marveled at its beauty and then quickened her pace. A gentle breeze moved through her hair as she brushed a lock from her eyes.

At last, she reached the summit of the hill. She stood for a moment, catching her breath as she studied the dusky sky. The cool evening breeze lifted her robes and swirled about her body.

She searched the flat parcel of land where the threshing floor lay. A low wall of stone encircled the floor with massive mounds of barley scattered across it.

Approaching a small grove of tamarisk trees, Ruth knelt, hidden from view. As she listened to the music rising sweetly from the threshing floor, she searched for Boaz. At last she spotted him sitting among a large group of men:

And after Boaz had eaten and drunk, and his heart was cheerful, he went to lie down at the end of the heap of grain; and she came softly, uncovered his feet, and lay down.

Now it happened at midnight that the man was startled, and turned himself; and there, a woman was lying at his feet. And he said, "Who are you?"

So she answered, "I am Ruth, your maidservant. Take your maidservant under your wing, for you are a close relative."

Then he said, "Blessed are you of the LORD, my daughter! For you have shown more kindness at the end than at the beginning, in that you did not go after young men, whether poor or rich. And now, my daughter, do not fear. I will do for you all that you request, for all the people of my town know that you are a virtuous woman. Now it is true that I am a close relative; however, there is a relative closer than I. Stay this night, and in the morning it shall be that if he will perform the duty of a close relative for you—good; let him do it. But if he does not want to perform the duty for you, then I will perform the duty for you, as the LORD lives! Lie down until morning."

So she lay at his feet until morning, and she arose before one could recognize another. Then he said, "Do not let it be known that the woman came to the threshing floor." Also he said, "Bring the shawl that is on you and hold it." And when she held it, he measured six ephahs of barley, and laid it on her. Then she went into the city. (Ruth 3:7-15).

Chapter 29

KINSMAN REDEEMER

The road glistened beneath the starry sky as Ruth strained under the weight of her grain-laden shawl. Entering the city, she hurried down the deserted street as the townspeople slumbered unaware. Approaching the door of their room, she carefully lifted the latch and stepped inside. Scanning the darkened room, she recognized Naomi's silhouette as she sat in the corner.

"Is that you, my daughter?" (Ruth 3:16).

"Yes, sweet Mother!" Ruth answered as she felt her way along the wall and knelt at Naomi's feet.

Naomi moved her hand down Ruth's back, feeling the grain in her shawl.

And Ruth said:

"These six ephahs of barley he gave me; for he said to me, 'Do not go empty-handed to your mother-in-law.'" (Ruth 3:17).

"That is good, my daughter!"

"Oh, but Naomi! There is another kinsman who is closer than he."

"Yes, my daughter, I know," Naomi said, raising the lamp's flame.

"Why did you not tell me?"

"Because I trust that when all is said and done, Boaz will be our redeemer."

Then she said, "Sit still, my daughter, until you know how the matter will turn out; for the man will not rest until he has concluded the matter this day." (Ruth 3:18).

Naomi removed the shawl from Ruth and laid it on the table.

"Come, my daughter," she said, motioning for Ruth to join her.

As Ruth sat, Naomi took her hand.

"Boaz is a man of wealth and honor. He loves you, Ruth."

"Yes, I believe he does." Ruth smiled. "You are at peace, are you not, Naomi?"

"Yes. I assumed Adonai afflicted me, but I was wrong. Although I do not understand His plans or ways, I now know He led us back to Bethlehem and He cares deeply for us."

Pulling Naomi's hand to her lips, Ruth kissed it and then lay it against her cheek. "Elimelech trusted in Adonai as did Mahlon and Chilion."

"Yes. And Adonai has not forgotten them. Will you lie down and rest, my daughter?"

"I cannot," Ruth said as she stood and walked about the room. Naomi followed her. They stopped and laughed and then began moving about the room again.

They busied themselves for a time, removing the grain from the shawl and storing it in the sacks stacked along the wall. When they completed the task, Naomi gave the beautiful purple shawl a brisk shaking and then hung it on an iron hook.

They sat and waited as the sun rose, keeping their door and shutters closed. But he did not come.

"You must sit," Naomi said as she pulled Ruth to the table. Letting Ruth's hair down, she brushed it and then rearranged the pearls and locks as they were before.

Several hours passed and the sun shone directly overhead.

Finally, exhausted from waiting, Ruth sat on the bed and closed her eyes as she leaned against the wall.

Suddenly she felt Naomi's hand on hers. "Listen! Do you hear it?"

Ruth jerked her head toward the door.

"Hear what?"

Ruth held her hands over her mouth and listened. What was it she heard? A trumpet blast? She leapt to her feet and began to dance about the room.

"Oh, Naomi, is someone coming for me?"

"Yes, my daughter!"

"But is it Boaz?" Ruth asked as she heard tambourines and flutes in the distance.

"Have faith, my daughter!"

Ruth hurried to the door.

"Wait!" Naomi said, handing her the linen shawl.

She draped it about her shoulders and then pulled the door open, peering down the street. Townspeople were rushing about and speaking loudly.

"What is all the commotion?" asked an old man.

A young maiden yanked her mother's tunic. "Is there to be a wedding today?" she asked.

Suddenly a crowd appeared in the distance. Ruth moved her eyes back and forth among the mass, searching for Boaz.

Where is he, Adonai?

Young maidens began dancing about and a group of men moved here and there as they played their various instruments.

"Do you see him?" Naomi asked, her voice quivering.

Ruth spotted an arm lifted above the heads that were bobbing up and down in her direction. "No! But someone is waving something."

"What is it?" Naomi yelled as she ran to her side.

"It is a—" She strained her eyes until the object came into focus. "A sandal! What does it mean?"

"It means you have been bought with a price. Go, my daughter, meet your redeemer!"

Ruth hurried down the street.

"Please, Adonai, have mercy on me!" she yelled as she went.

Suddenly the crowd stopped moving and the townspeople began stepping to the side.

As she saw him, she froze.

"It is Boaz! Naomi," she said, turning to her mother-in-law.

Naomi stood by the door, weeping.

"Go to him, Daughter," she yelled.

Ruth turned to face him. He waved the sandal again as the corners of his mouth turned upward into a broad captivating smile.

His gaze was soft and fixed on hers as he approached—until at last he stood before her.

Tears streamed down her face as she smiled. Lowering her head, she knelt before him.

"My lord," she said, covering her eyes.

He knelt beside her and lifted her chin, holding her gaze. Slowly he brought his mouth near hers.

"I love you, Ruth," he said as he covered her lips with his.

She kissed him with all the joy and longing in her. And then she buried her head in his broad chest and clung to him.

The crowd cheered. Boaz stood, pulling Ruth into his arms as Naomi rushed to him.

"Tell me what happened!" Naomi cried, wiping tears from her face.

Boaz laughed.

"Naomi!" he said, lifting and swinging her about.

Simeon stepped from the crowd. "May I tell her?"

"Yes, by all means, Simeon," Boaz said, weaving his arms around Ruth's waist and tugging her against his chest.

Simeon looked about the townspeople and began speaking loudly enough for all to hear:

Now Boaz went up to the gate and sat down there; and behold, the close relative of whom Boaz had spoken came by. So Boaz said, "Come aside, friend, sit down here." So he came aside and sat down. And he took ten men of the elders of the city, and said, "Sit down here." So they sat down. (Ruth 4:1-2).

"What happened next?" an old man yelled.

"Tell them, Boaz!" one of the elders responded, emerging from the mass.

The townspeople began cheering and Boaz lifted his hand, waiting until they grew quiet and then he continued, saying:

"Naomi, who has come back from the country of Moab, sold the piece of land which belonged to our brother Elimelech. And I thought to inform you, saying, 'Buy it back in the presence of the inhabitants and the elders of my people. If you will redeem it, redeem it; but if you will not redeem it, then tell me, that I may know; for there is no one but you to redeem it, and I am next after you.'"

And he said, "I will redeem it." (Ruth 4:3-4).

"Then I informed him, saying:

"On the day you buy the field from the hand of Naomi, you must also buy it from Ruth the Moabitess, the wife of the dead, to perpetuate the name of the dead through his inheritance."

And the close relative said, "I cannot redeem it for myself, lest I ruin my own inheritance. You redeem my right of redemption for yourself, for I cannot redeem it." (Ruth 4:5-6).

"But why did my lord come for me, waving a sandal?" Ruth asked Naomi.

"It is the custom in all the land of Israel concerning redeeming and exchanging," Naomi said. "To confirm a transaction, one man takes off his sandal and gives it to the other."

"That is how you knew I had been redeemed?"

"Yes!" Naomi chuckled.

Simeon took the sandal from Boaz and held it over his head:

Therefore the close relative said to Boaz, "Buy it for yourself." So he took off his sandal. (Ruth 4:8).

And Boaz said:

"You are witnesses this day that I have bought all that was Elimelech's, and all that was Chilion's and Mahlon's, from the hand of Naomi. Moreover, Ruth the Moabitess, the widow of Mahlon, I have acquired as my wife, to perpetuate the name of the dead through his inheritance, that the name of the dead may not be cut off from among his brethren and from his position at the gate. You are witnesses this day."

And all the people who were at the gate, and the elders, said, "We are witnesses. The LORD make the woman who is coming to your house like Rachel and Leah, the two who built the house of Israel; and may you prosper in Ephrathah and be famous in Bethlehem. May your house be like the house of Perez, whom Tamar bore to Judah, because of the offspring which the LORD will give you from this young woman." (Ruth 4:9-12).

The familiar sound of Elizabeth's merry chortle caused Ruth and Naomi to turn in her direction.

"Adonai has redeemed you!" Elizabeth called as she came near.

"Yes, He has, my friend!" Naomi said.

"Quickly!" Elizabeth motioned toward several servants who were following behind. "Bring the cart; gather their belongings and take them to Boaz's home."

Boaz took Ruth's hand in his as they walked back down the road toward his home. The townspeople scurried about, gathering food and spreading the word of their marriage.

By the time they arrived, the field was alive with festive music and the smell of roasting lamb.

Anna ran from the house to greet them.

"My lord," she said, bowing.

"Anna," he said. "You know my wife, Ruth."

She giggled. "Yes, my lord." She wrapped her arms around Ruth's waist and lifted her big brown eyes and smiled up at her.

Laying her hand on Anna's head, Ruth said, "The LORD bless you, Anna."

"And the LORD bless you!"

Anna bowed, took several steps backward and then ran toward the house.

Boaz turned to Ruth, keeping his eyes fixed on her until finally, she smiled. "What is it, my lord?"

"You may call me Boaz," he said as he kissed her.

She felt safe in his arms and her heart fluttered at his touch.

"How long have you loved me, my lord?"

He shook his head and laughed. "When I heard of your arrival and all you had done for Naomi, I was drawn to you. But the moment I saw you gleaning in my field, I knew I loved you and prayed you would seek me as your redeemer. It has been a long wait."

"And Adonai has kept your heart for such a time as this?"

Lifting her lips to his, she asked for a kiss . . . and he complied.

As Boaz and Ruth walked toward the house, she turned to face him.

"There is something I must confess." Her voice trembled.

"What is it, my love?"

"I have been confused by my feelings for you until yesterday as I left the wheat field. It was then I knew I loved you, my lord."

Boaz tossed his head back and laughed. "It seems you were the last to know, but I am indeed thankful to hear it."

"You knew I cared for you?"

"I was not certain, but felt reason to hope the day you asked why I had never married." He touched her cheek and smiled.

Naomi approached. Boaz looked from Ruth to Naomi. "Naomi never told you of her plan?"

"Not until last night."

"Did her plan involve the story she made you wait to hear?" he asked, grinning at Naomi.

"You know me well, Boaz."

"You are a patient woman, Naomi."

"Truly I am!"

"Was it the story of Tamar?"

"Yes!" Naomi laughed.

Boaz shook his head as the three continued walking to the house.

Ruth observed the townspeople lighting lamps and filling tables with food under the same thatched roof she had rested under on her first day of gleaning in Boaz's field.

As they entered, Naomi pulled Ruth to the floor and they danced as they had the day she married Mahlon. Her heart was full of joy.

Thank you, Adonai, for bringing us to Your Promised Land and for redeeming us. You are my kind and loving LORD and I will live my life to honor and serve You.

Boaz watched, smiling as the townspeople and servants danced, ate and visited until the moon shone brightly and the night was lit with stars.

Finally, Ruth came to him and sat by his side. He grasped her hand as she rested her head on his shoulder and yawned.

Boaz stood, drawing the crowd's attention.

"The LORD be with you!" he said.

"The LORD bless you!" the townspeople responded.

Turning, he addressed Anna's mother. "Please show Naomi to her room."

She bowed. "Yes, my lord."

Boaz lifted Ruth in his arms and walked into the house, closing the door behind them.

Epilogue

FIELDS OF BLESSING

Boaz entered the room and sat beside Ruth as their newborn son suckled at her breast.

"The townspeople will be here soon," he said, pulling her into his arms.

The baby stretched and cooed as Ruth moved her fingers over his tiny face. "At last I understand one of Adonai's greatest truths."

"And what would that be?"

"Though we may plan our way, Adonai directs our steps. I began my search for The One True God as a young maiden in the land of my birth. Adonai saw my heart and directed Elimelech to my father's field in order to reveal His Word to me."

Boaz brushed her hair aside and kissed her neck. "And when Naomi thought all was lost, He brought you safely back to Bethlehem."

"Yes, and to your field. Thank you, Boaz. I never imagined Adonai would draw your heart to mine."

"He was faithful to sustain you in His fields of blessing."

"Yes, He did! In my father's field I learned of His love for me and in your field I experienced His grace and provision."

"And He did not forget Elimelech and Mahlon, for they will be forever remembered among our kinsmen." Boaz touched their baby's tiny hand. "I love you, Ruth."

The sweet sounds of music echoed in the distance as Boaz stood and lifted his son into his arms. "They are almost here. Come, Naomi," Boaz called. "It is time."

As Ruth walked from the room, her thoughts wandered to her homeland. She still longed to hear the sound of her father's voice and feel the touch of her mother's embrace. But most of all, she hoped her parents and Lior had discovered the truth of The One True God.

The smell of ripening grain wafted across the field as Ruth and Naomi followed Boaz from the house. The distant sounds of the music and conversation continued to grow until at last the townspeople came into view and began hurrying across the field.

As the crowd gathered around them, Anna emerged, running into Ruth's arms.

"You have borne a son!" she shouted.

"I have, sweet Anna," Ruth said as Boaz lowered the baby. Anna peered beneath the blanket and giggled.

"He is lovely, my lord."

"Thank you, Anna." Boaz patted her cheek and then lifted the baby for all to see. "The LORD be with you!"

"The LORD bless you!" The townspeople cheered in unison:

Then the women said to Naomi, "Blessed be the LORD, who has not left you this day without a close relative; and may his name be famous in Israel! And may he be to you a restorer of life and a nourisher of your old age; for your daughter-in-law, who loves you, who is better to you than seven sons, has borne him." Then Naomi took the child and laid him on her bosom, and became a nurse to him. Also the neighbor women gave him a name, saying, "There is a son born to Naomi." And they called his name Obed. He is the father of Jesse, the father of David. (Ruth 4:14-17).

David the king begot Solomon by her who had been the wife of Uriah.

Solomon begot Rehoboam, Rehoboam begot Abijah, and Abijah begot Asa. Asa begot Jehoshaphat, Jehoshaphat begot Joram, and Joram begot Uzziah. Uzziah begot Jotham, Jotham begot Ahaz, and Ahaz begot Hezekiah. Hezekiah begot Manasseh, Manasseh begot Amon, and Amon begot Josiah. Josiah begot Jeconiah and his brothers about the time they were carried away to Babylon.

And after they were brought to Babylon, Jeconiah begot Shealtiel, and Shealtiel begot Zerubbabel. Zerubbabel begot Abiud, Abiud begot Eliakim, and Eliakim begot Azor. Azor begot Zadok, Zadok begot Achim, and Achim begot Eliud. Eliud begot Eleazar, Eleazar begot Matthan, and Matthan begot Jacob. And Jacob begot Joseph the husband of Mary, of whom was born Jesus who is called Christ. (Matthew 1:6-16).

Family Tree

Abraham (Sarah)

Isaac (Rebekah)

Jacob—i.e., Israel (Leah & Rachel)

Judah—Fourth son of twelve sons born to Jacob (His mother was
Leah) (Tamar, his daughter-in-law, bore his son—Perez)

Perez (His mother was Tamar)

Hezron

Ram

Amminadab

Nahshon

Salmon (Rahab)

Boaz (Ruth)

Obed

Jesse

King David (Bathsheba)

. . . (Mathew 1:6-16) . . .

Joseph—the husband of Mary of whom was born

JESUS CHRIST

Glossary

- **Abraham** — father of a great multitude; husband to Sarah, father of Isaac
- **Abram** — exalted father; Abraham's name before God changed it
- **Adonai** — LORD, Master; Hebrew name for God (Genesis 15:2)
- **Ammonite** — son of my relative (incest); descendant of Lot's son, Ben-Ammi, by his younger daughter
- **Anna** — gracious, one who gives; (fictional character, young servant girl in Boaz's field)
- **Arnon River** — rushing stream; the northern boundary of Moab
- **Balaam** — not of the people, a foreigner; a false prophet, son of Beor
- **Bethlehem** — house of bread; home of Elimelech and his family in the land of Judah
- **Boaz** — in strength, swiftness, fleetness; close relative of Elimelech, kinsman redeemer
- **Chemosh** — the destroyer, subduer; god of the Moabites
- **Chilion** — pining, wasting away; younger son of Elimelech and Naomi
- **Dahlia** — slender branch, grapevine; (fictional character, wife of Goad, mother of Ruth)
- **David** — beloved; son of Jesse, grandson of Obed, great-grandson of Boaz and Ruth, second king of Israel
- **El Shaddai** — LORD God Almighty, The All Sufficient One (Genesis 17:1)
- **Elimelech** — My God is King; husband of Naomi, father of Mahlon and Chilion
- **Elizabeth** — the oath, fullness of God; (fictional character, close friend of Naomi in Bethlehem)
- **Elohim** — God, The One True God (Genesis 1:1)
- **Ephrathah** — place of fruitfulness; another name for Bethlehem

Glossary

- **Er** — watchman, awake; elder son of Judah
- **Gardish** — protector; (fictional character, servant in Goad's prize field)
- **Goad** — to prod or urge; (fictional character, husband of Dahlia, father of Ruth)
- **God Most High** — El Elyon (Genesis 14:19-20)
- **Gomorrah** — submersion, of iniquity, rebellious people; one of two cities God destroyed with fire from heaven
- **Haran** — mountainous country; (fictional character, servant in Goad's prize field)
- **Harrash** — tormenter; (fictional character, responsible for attempt on Orpah's life)
- **I Am** *or* **I Am That I Am** — God's reference to Himself (Exodus 3:14)
- **Isaac** — laughter; God's promised son to Abraham and Sarah
- **Ishmael** — God will hear; son of Abraham by Sarah's Egyptian maidservant (Hagar)
- **Israel** — God prevails, contender, having power with God; Jacob's new name after God changed it (Genesis 32:28), father of the Twelve Tribes of Israel
- **Jacob** — holder of the heel, he who supplants; son of Isaac, grandson of Abraham, father of the Twelve Tribes of Israel; God changed Jacob's name to Israel (Genesis 32:28)
- **Jehova** — The Existing One (Exodus 6:3)
- **Jehova Rapha** — The LORD that Heals (Exodus 15:26)
- **Jericho** — of the moon, fragrant; city in the Promised Land of Canaan; Rahab and her family dwelt in Jericho at the time it was conquered by the children of Israel
- **Jerusalem** — teaching of peace; home of King David, capital of current day Israel
- **Jesse** — God's gift, I possess; son of Obed, grandson of Boaz and Ruth, father of David (the second king of Israel)
- **Jordan River** — descender, flowing down; formed the eastern border

of Judah and flowed into the Salt Sea

- **Joshua** – Jehovah is Salvation, a deliverer; succeeded Moses as leader of the children of Israel
- **Judah** – the praise of the LORD; Naomi's homeland (Bethlehem, Judah), name given to one of Jacob's twelve sons, one of The Twelve Tribes of Israel
- **Kinsman Redeemer** – a male relative who had the responsibility or authority to restore property or rights for a close relative; Boaz became the kinsman redeemer in the Book of Ruth
- **Leah** – weary; first wife of Jacob, mother of seven sons (including Judah)
- **Lilia** – lily; (fictional character, aged woman servant to Dahlia, friend to Ruth)
- **Lior** – my light; (fictional character, son of Goad and Dahlia, brother of Ruth)
- **Lot** – wrapped up, hidden, covering; nephew of Abraham, father of Moab and Ben-Ammi by his daughters (incest), father of the Moabites and Ammonites, ancestor of Ruth
- **Mahlon** – sick, infirmity, wasting; son of Elimelech and Naomi, first husband of Ruth
- Melchizedek – king of righteousness, king of peace; priest of God Most High (Genesis 14:19-20; Hebrews 7)
- **Mitzvah** – any of over 600 commandments or precepts in the Bible (plural; mitzvot)
- **Moab** – of his father (incest); son of Lot by his eldest daughter; an ancient kingdom east of the Dead Sea
- **Moabite** – progeny of a father; descendant of Moab (Lot's son by his elder daughter)
- **Mount of the LORD** – the mountain (thought by some to be Mount Moriah) where Abraham offered his son Isaac as a sacrifice to God (Genesis 22:14)

- **Naomi** — my delight, pleasant, beautiful, agreeable; wife of Elimelech, mother of Mahlon and Chilion, mother-in-law of Ruth and Orpah, grandmother of Obed
- **Nun** — heir, posterity, fish (i.e., prolific); father of Joshua
- **Obed** — a servant, workman; son of Boaz and Ruth, grandson of Naomi, father of Jesse, the grandfather of King David
- **Orpah** — gazelle, the neck or skull; Moabite maiden, wife of Chilion (son of Elimelech and Naomi), daughter-in-law to Naomi
- **Passover** — to spare, pass over without penalty; commemorates the freedom and exodus of the Jews from slavery in Egypt
- **Perez** — divided, breach; elder twin son born to Tamar by her father-in-law (Judah)
- **Promised Land** — the land of Canaan promised by God to Abraham and his descendants
- **Rachel** — a female sheep; second wife of Jacob
- **Rahab** — spacious, wide; harlot of Jericho who married Salmon; mother of Boaz
- **Redeemer** — one who purchases or buys back, paying a price; the nearest relative who is charged with restoring the rights and avenging the wrongs of another; 'Goel' is the Hebrew name for redeemer
- **Ruth** — friend, companion; Moabite maiden, wife of Mahlon, daughter-in-law of Elimelech and Naomi, wife of Boaz, mother of Obed, grandmother of Jesse, great-grandmother of King David
- **Sabbath** — holy day of rest to the LORD (Exodus 20:10–11); 'Shabbat' is the Hebrew name for the Sabbath
- **Salmon** — garment, peaceable, he that rewards; husband of Rahab, father of Boaz
- **Shalom** — peace; a common Jewish greeting or salutation
- **Sarah** — noblewoman, princess, princess of the multitude; wife of Abraham, mother of Isaac
- **Sarai** — princess; name before God changed it to Sarah

- **Shelah** – a petition, that unties, that breaks; youngest son of Judah
- **Signet and Cord** – a cylinder shaped seal worn around the neck with a cord; used to stamp a signature, validating and guaranteeing a transaction
- **Simeon** – he has heard; (fictional name given to "the servant who was in charge of the reapers" in Ruth 2:5)
- **Sodom** – burning, their secret, their cement; one of two cities God destroyed with fire, home to Lot and his family at the time God determined to destroy the city
- **Sojourn** – to stay for a time in a place, live temporarily
- **Tamar** – palm, palm tree; widow of Er (Judah's oldest son); promised to youngest son, Shelah; bore heir (Perez) by Judah (her father-in-law)
- **The King's Highway** – an ancient trade route referred to in the Bible (Numbers 20:17, 19; 21:22)
- **The-LORD-Will-Provide** – Jehovah Jireh (Genesis 22:14)
- **Torah** – The law on which Judaism is founded; contained in the first five books of the Bible (Genesis, Exodus, Leviticus, Numbers and Deuteronomy)
- **Twelve Sons of Jacob** – Reuben, Simeon, Levi, Judah, Dan, Naphtali, Gad, Asher, Issachar, Zebulun, Joseph and Benjamin
- **Twelve Tribes of Israel** – Reuben, Simeon, Judah, Dan, Naphtali, Gad, Asher, Issachar, Zebulun, Benjamin, Ephraim and Manasseh; Ephraim and Manasseh were Joseph's sons; Jacob gave Joseph an extra portion by adopting his sons as his own; Levi was not a tribe because the Levites were not to own land as they were the LORD's priests

Reflections and Deeper Study

CONTRIBUTED BY BONNIE SLACK

TRUST:

1. How did Elimelech, Naomi, Mahlon, Ruth and Boaz trust Adonai?
2. Compare and contrast the way Ruth trusted God and the way you trust God.
3. How did Mahlon and Ruth respond to their inability to conceive?
4. Why does God require us to trust Him?
5. How have you trusted Him in the past?
6. How is Jesus asking you to trust Him now?
7. How has trusting God given you peace?
8. Is it easy or hard for you to trust God when you have enough or perhaps too much?
9. From the example of Ruth, can you trust that God has a good future for you? Elaborate.
10. Write your favorite Scripture on trust.

PROVISION:

1. How did God provide for Elimelech, Naomi, Mahlon, Ruth and Boaz?
2. How does God provide for you?
3. What spurs God's provision?
4. How did God specifically provide for Boaz?
5. How did God provide for Himself? (Refer to *Fields of Blessing, Chapter 11*; Genesis 22:8)
6. Ruth gave up her family, home, country and a secure financial future (fiction in this instance) for an uncertain future in Bethlehem. Since you have uncertainty in your future, how can you live in peace?
7. How are you blessed through Ruth?
8. Why do you think God chose Ruth to be in Jesus' line?
9. Write your favorite Scripture on God's provision.

JOURNEY:

1. Why do you think Ruth's journey to "The One True God" was filled with so much adversity and loss?
2. What adversity and loss have you faced on your journey?
3. Look back at a hard time in your life and recount how God brought you through it.
4. Do you view your life as a journey, or as circumstances that happen to you?
5. What is your response while on your journey when you do not hear from God?
6. Why should you enjoy your journey? Give Scriptures.
7. How did Ruth overcome adversity?
8. What are the rewards of the overcomer in Revelation Chapters 2 through 4? List all of them.
9. Why do you think Boaz did not marry before Ruth?
10. Write your favorite Scripture on enjoying life and the journey.

LETTING GO:

1. What did you let go of when you started following Jesus?
2. Do you miss it?
3. What blessing(s) did you receive from letting go of the past?
4. How did Ruth respond to losing Mahlon?
5. Have you lost someone close to you? What was your response?
6. Write your favorite Scripture on letting go.

HUMILITY:

1. How did Ruth humble herself?
2. What characteristics do you see in common in the people in The Book of Ruth?
3. What cultural norms in The Book of Ruth do you think we should return to?
4. Boaz was a humble, God-fearing man. How hard is it for a rich man in our culture to have the humility of Boaz?
5. Write your favorite Scripture on being humble.

Reflections and Deeper Study

OBEDIENCE:

1. How did Ruth obey God?
2. What keeps you from obeying God?
3. Why is it hard for you to obey God?
4. Why is it important to obey God?
5. What benefits have you received from obeying God?
6. In the story Elimelech and his family encouraged Ruth to obey her parents. How does this encourage you to obey God?
7. Why do you think obedience is not stressed in our culture?
8. Read Genesis 22:18. How does Abraham's obedience affect you? How does your obedience to Christ affect those around you?
9. Write your favorite Scripture on obedience.

DEEPER STUDY:

1. Many of the people in The Book of Ruth centered their lives around Adonai and spoke of Him often as they went about their lives. Read Malachi 3:16,17. What is your reaction to these verses?
2. God accepted foreigners into the nation of Israel when He grafted in Rahab and Ruth into Jesus' genealogy. Read Romans 11:24, Isaiah 56:8 and John 10:16. What do you learn from these verses?
3. Read Matthew 8:23-9:1. What do you learn from this, and how does it compare to The Book of Ruth?
4. Boaz is a type and shadow of Jesus because he redeemed Ruth just as Christ has redeemed The Church. Read Matthew 25:1-13. Compare and contrast The Book of Ruth and the parable of the Ten Virgins.
5. Read 1 Peter 1:24,25 and James 1:10,11. Since you are only here for a season, how are you living your life for Christ? How should you live?

Hope of Israel

BY DECEMBER TIDE

If you purchased *Fields of Blessing* as a book/eBook, *December Tide* band is offering you (for a limited time) a free recording of their original song, *Hope of Israel* (sung by the author's daughter, Emily Grace Blassingame). (Up to five hundred recordings given away; one per customer of a book/ eBook purchase.)

To receive your free recording, please contact Amy Blassingame at fieldsofblessing@gmail.com.

The song can also be purchased on iTunes.

CPSIA information can be obtained
at www.ICGtesting.com
Printed in the USA
FFOW04n0703231113
2452FF